The Optimist's Guide to Letting Go

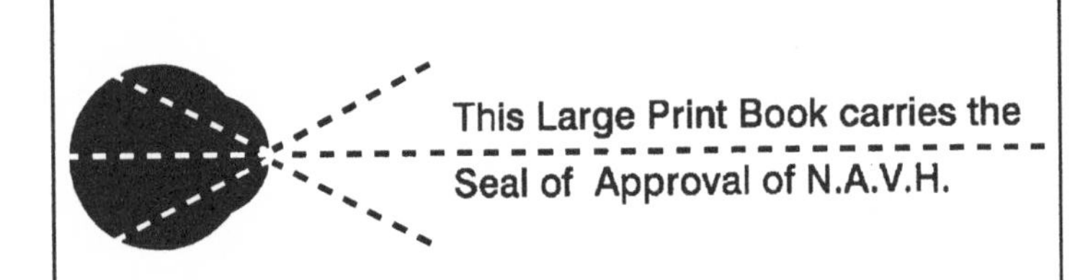
This Large Print Book carries the
Seal of Approval of N.A.V.H.

The Optimist's Guide to Letting Go

Amy E. Reichert

THORNDIKE PRESS
A part of Gale, a Cengage Company

Farmington Hills, Mich • San Francisco • New York • Waterville, Maine
Meriden, Conn • Mason, Ohio • Chicago

Thorndike Press, a part of Gale, a Cengage Company.

Thorndike Press® Large Print Women's Fiction.
The text of this Large Print edition is unabridged.
Other aspects of the book may vary from the original edition.
Set in 16 pt. Plantin.

LIBRARY OF CONGRESS CIP DATA ON FILE.
CATALOGUING IN PUBLICATION FOR THIS BOOK
IS AVAILABLE FROM THE LIBRARY OF CONGRESS

ISBN-13: 978-1-4328-5272-6 (hardcover)

Published in 2018 by arrangement with Gallery Books, an imprint of Simon & Schuster, Inc.

Printed in Mexico
1 2 3 4 5 6 7 22 21 20 19 18

To Ainsley, you are the best of us.
To Unc, we miss you every day.

The more a daughter knows about the details of her mother's life — without flinching or whining — the stronger the daughter.

— Anita Diamant, *The Red Tent*

■ ■ ■ ■

What Is One Fact You Know to Be True?

■ ■ ■ ■

Chapter One

1. ~~Throw away Xmas cards.~~
2. ~~Shower~~.
3. ~~Put May's clean clothes outside her door.~~
4. ~~Shred extra cheese.~~
5. Lunch prep.
6. Call Mom.

Gina Zoberski crossed out number five, then turned to her first customer, muscle memory curving her lips into a smile. In minutes, her griddle sizzled with grilled cheese sandwiches as she lined up waxed paper and cardboard boats, cold air fluttering the paper as it mingled with the warm air inside Grilled G's, her gourmet grilled cheese food truck. She checked the sandwiches as they browned, pausing long enough to look at the text message from her food truck neighbor Monica, who ran On a Roll — serving an ever-changing menu of food on rolls, from sausages to grilled veggies.

C'S MAKING THE ROUNDS.

Gina smiled as she looked out her own truck's window, above the heads of her waiting customers. Sure enough, Charlotte was headed her way, shuffling carefully across the icy sidewalk as she pulled her hand from the aged red plastic Sendik's bag looped on her arm. She wore an oversize black coat with large bulging pockets that fell past her knees. A spotted knit scarf hid half her face, and a dark hat with ear flaps covered her normally wild pale reddish curls. Though she wasn't old, she looked drawn thin from the lack of sleep, the skin hanging from her bones, as if lacking the substance to fill her out properly.

Gina finished up the sandwiches, handed them off to people who'd been waiting, and immediately started three of her Classic grilled cheeses, a combination of Colby-Jack, American, and provolone on fresh Italian bread with a lot of butter, crisp and golden. She'd learned long ago to grill both slices of bread for each sandwich at the same time, topping them with shredded cheese, and bringing them together at the end to complete it. It took half the time and was just as delicious.

"Hi, Charlotte. That's a pretty scarf. Staying warm?" Charlotte said nothing in response. "The usual?"

"Yes. I'm in a rush." The words were muffled by her scarf. She slid three crumpled and torn dollar bills and six quarters across the counter — the cost of one grilled cheese with chips.

"Be ready in a moment."

Gina slid the money into her cash drawer as Charlotte peered over her shoulder and clutched her bag closer. It looked heavy. She must have already visited most of the stands today. She finished the Classic, making sure to singe one corner. Gina then wrapped it carefully in aluminum foil and handed it to her with a bag of potato chips. As Charlotte stepped to the side of the line and greedily unwrapped the food, Gina took three more orders and finished grilling the other two sandwiches she had started, wrapping them like the first. Charlotte's "ahem" sounded like clockwork.

An ear-flapped head poked around the window.

"Yes, Charlotte?" Gina knew what was coming.

"You burned the bread. I'm not paying

for this." She held the slightly darkened corner up to the window.

"Of course not." Seamlessly, she handed Charlotte the waiting sandwiches. "Here's a replacement and an extra to make up for the inconvenience. I'm so sorry for the trouble."

Charlotte humphed and stuffed the new sandwiches into her bag and scuttled off toward the edge of the park, where she handed one of the aluminum foil packets to the bedraggled man sitting on the bench before heading down the street out of sight. Gina smiled in her direction before returning her focus to the growing line, settling into the lunch rush routine.

She was grateful for the familiar bustle. Being busy kept her mind focused — off the past, the present, and — most worrisome — the future. Once the lunch crowd swarmed, she couldn't think about the reason she could afford her shiny, custom-built food truck, or why she needn't worry about giving extra grilled cheese sandwiches to Charlotte on a regular basis. When her financial adviser had told her how much money she would receive, she had gasped, but the sum hadn't made her any less angry.

Take the order, butter the bread, add the cheese, grill, assemble the sandwich, cut, wrap. Repeat. One to-do list she had completed so often, she no longer needed to write it down.

Her little sister Vicky regularly suggested a therapist might be a healthier route, but Grilled G's had gotten her through just fine. In Gina's experience, cheese made everything better — Parmesan on popcorn, crispy fried goat cheese in a salad, a swipe of cream cheese on a toasted bagel, or melted gouda on an egg sandwich. She even liked a dollop of sweetened mascarpone on a slice of warm cherry pie instead of ice cream. But grilled cheese, gooey from the griddle, crisp on the outside, melty on the inside, that was the pinnacle of dairy possibility.

No matter how it was dressed up, with balsamic reductions or micro greens, a grilled cheese was still luscious goodness between carbs. Simple, wholesome comfort food at its finest. Handheld happiness everyone could enjoy. And Gina loved to make people happy, especially on a cold day like today. Her vibrant orange and yellow food truck gleamed in her regular spot at Red Arrow Park in downtown Milwaukee, a colorful beacon in gray, late December, drawing office workers and city employees like bees to a flower. She'd been running her truck for a little over a year, and she already had a loyal following. The other trucks, a homogenous line of white and silver, offered tacos, soup, and even fresh doughnuts. But no one could walk past Grilled G's without smiling.

In the small, stainless steel room, everything had a use, every item an assigned home, and it could all be scrubbed clean with bleach and a hose when a day became extra messy. Black cushioned rubber mats covered the floor so her footing was always sure, and a large window allowed her to stay in the warm portable kitchen and take orders from the customers lined up outside. One end led to the cab containing the driver's seat, a second seat that folded down for a passenger, and a few steps to get out the door, like a school bus. The other end held an emergency exit that doubled as shelving space. Lining the sides of her galley kitchen were the griddle, burners, a refrigerator, ample workspace, and the requisite number of sinks to pass a health inspection. Every inch had a purpose and had been custom designed just for her with love, including the slightly shorter-than-normal counter and movable shelves she could pull down rather than reaching up.

Clearheaded, Gina handed another sandwich to a waiting customer and looked up to take another order but was greeted with an empty window. Next door, Monica pulled down her awning, sending a wave before climbing back into On a Roll.

Gina's heart clenched and the blood thundered through her body. Another lunch rush over. Everything she'd been ignoring rushed in, like a wave filling a sandcastle's moat, pulling at the castle walls as it swirled. As she braced for the next wave, her phone rang. The tide receded.

Seeing it was Vicky, she pulled out the earbuds from her pocket, plugged them into her phone, and took the call.

Before she could even say "Hey," Vicky started into her tirade.

"Did you read the e-mail yet?" her sister began. While starting to clean up the counters, Gina mumbled something noncommittal, her body on autopilot.

Vicky must have interpreted her grunt as a negative response because she kept talking. "I need to read it to you so you get the full impact: 'Gifts this year were not good.' Can you believe her? I gave her perfume that cost more than my last epidural. You'd think that would count for something. Our mother actually put her judgment into writing and e-mailed it to us. It hasn't even been two days since Christmas. She couldn't even wait a week. I'm going to print this out and frame it. When she dies, it's going in her coffin."

Gina could hear the clank of silverware against a dish in the background. She pictured her sister, earbuds also connected to the phone that was tucked into her back jeans pocket, scrubbing the breakfast dishes while her two three-year-old twins, Maggie and Nathan, smashed Play-Doh together, noshing on freshly cut fruit while the eldest two, Greta and Jake, rolled snow across the backyard to build a snowman. She'd be wearing subtle makeup with her long shiny (faux) blond hair in a sleek ponytail precisely perched on the back of her head, just in case someone stopped by. She worked hard to insulate her kids from the expectations and pretensions of other families from the private school they attended on her husband's insistence. It was different from their own childhood of tennis lessons at the club and afternoons at the pool while their mom gossiped with the other country club women, who were content to let their children run free as they sipped their chilled white wine under striped umbrellas.

With her sister still talking, Gina closed up her truck, slid into the driver's seat, and eased her large truck into west-bound traffic, waiting for a break in the conversation. Her sister paused to take a breath.

"I'm sure she wasn't referring to your Christmas gift, the perfume is gorgeous. But you know Mom, she has very specific tastes," Gina said. They both knew well enough that their mother's criticism was directed at Gina, not at Vicky. Gina was the problem daughter and always had been, even though Vicky was the one who never edited her thoughts before speaking them. It was Gina who hadn't married well. Gina who ate too much bread. Gina who didn't wear the right clothes, or makeup, or dye her grays regularly enough. She'd been hearing the same criticisms her entire life — the worst being "why can't you be more like Victoria?" A disappointing Christmas gift didn't even register on the insult scale anymore.

"Don't try to spin her royal bitchiness — she knows what she's doing. Is that how we're going to be at her age? Crazy and bitter? I'm rooting for a fast-acting cancer or a falling meteor rather than waiting for menopause to do its worst."

Gina stilled, shoving the uncomfortable cloud of fear away, focusing on the silver lining. "Don't think like that. We're going to live long lives full of grandbabies to spoil.

And we'll always have each other." She pulled into her own driveway, the drapes still shut tight, no sign that anyone was home. She set her forehead on the wheel, hoping to keep the panic from spreading. It wasn't working.

The dead air stretched.

"You know what I mean," Vicky said at last, the sound of running water starting and stopping through the phone. She must be done with the dishes. "Where are you? Are you in the food truck?"

Gina leaned her head back against the steel wall, drawing from its reliable sturdiness the strength to stand and step outside. It didn't come.

Reaching over to the glove compartment, she pulled a plastic bag containing a T-shirt she usually kept hidden in her closet but she occasionally brought with her like a security blanket. She pulled open the bag, her hands twisting the worn jersey fabric between her fingers. She held it to her nose. After two years, most of the scent came from her memory rather than the ragged material, and even that was fading. The thought seized in her chest, kicking her heart into a frantic pace and trapping the air in her lungs. She couldn't get a breath. The slushy sounds of neighborhood traffic pulled away, and she could only hear her struggling body trying to cope. The cold stainless steel walls poked at Gina with memories.

Drew's smile.

Drew's laugh.

Drew's kiss.

Ignoring her sister's questions, she breathed in the fabric, drawing on all the good things around her to get her through this moment.

Her bright orange and yellow truck stood out in the cold, white Wauwatosa neighborhood made of brick and tan bungalows, the bare trees waiting for spring. She ran her left hand along the wall, the double-stacked wedding bands on her ring finger clinking against the metal — Drew's had been resized to fit her much smaller finger. Grilled G's was her husband's last gift to her before he left. He created it to stand out in a line of food trucks, drawing customers to the popular menu of gourmet grilled cheeses — ranging from a classic American cheese on crisp, buttery Italian bread to a rustic combo of creamy Brie, arugula, and prosciutto on a seed-studded multigrain. She even served a grilled peanut butter and jelly (made with coconut oil instead of butter) for dairy-intolerant customers.

Grilled G's was comfort on four wheels, not just for the patrons, but for her as well. Being in it was the closest sensation she had to still being in his arms.

"Gina, are you there?" Vicky said.

"I like the way the truck smells like him." She finally answered Vicky's question. She could hear her sister's sigh.

"Like melted cheese and butter?"

"Like leather and motor oil." She held the smudged T-shirt to her nose one more time before tucking it back into the plastic bag and into her purse.

"Should I come up?" She couldn't miss her sister's resigned tone — clear that she hoped Gina would turn her down, not really wanting to talk her through another panic attack, especially with the two-hour drive north from Illinois it would take to get there and the scrambling to find someone to watch her children. Stepping out, Gina gave the truck a little pat and slid the door closed behind her. She didn't want to burden her sister anymore. Vicky had enough to deal with, raising her four littles while her husband worked insane hours in downtown Chicago. She had no time for a sister who should be moving on.

Focus on what's next. Just on what's next.

1. Put the T-shirt back in the closet.
2. Talk to May.
3. Call Mom.

"Of course not. I was just pulling up, I'm going inside now."

The icy wind cut through her thin fleece. Up and down her street, neighbors walked dogs on the salt-speckled sidewalks. Snow-covered yards hosted deflated Santas and reindeer and one plastic nativity scene that had been used for so many years all the figures were faded to a sad, smudged beige. Her own house looked no different than it had two years ago, or how it would look in another month. For the past two Christmases, she hadn't had the energy to decorate — save for one wreath she would hang on the door. It was simply too much effort and pain to decorate, when it only reminded her of the good years she and Drew had together. Now she and May went to Illinois to spend the holiday at her sister's with their mom. They'd drive down early in the morning and leave after Christmas dinner, dropping her mom off at her apartment. It was a long fourteen-hour day, but then it was over and they could spend the rest of the holiday season without having to put on a brave face.

Patty, the new mom from across the street, power-walked past with her baby bundled into a jogging stroller. She waved and paused, as if to chat with Gina. Gina pointed at the earbuds in her ears and waved at her. Patty nodded and moved along. Gina closed her eyes, relieved to have delayed Patty's blow-by-blow recap of her first Christmas with a baby.

"If you're sure. I could be there in two hours. The kids would love to see May again." Vicky clearly felt comfortable offering the second time, now that she knew Gina wouldn't take her up on it.

"No. And I'll check in on Mom, too. If she doesn't answer her phone, I'll stop by before dinner. She won't hold back on how much she hated my present. It'll make her feel better to get it off her chest, and then you don't have to hear it, too."

"You don't need to be her whipping post, Gina."

"It makes her feel better. I don't mind. I know she doesn't really mean it."

"Do you? What has Mother ever done to make you believe that?"

Gina shrugged, watching Patty disappear around the corner.

"I gotta go. I'll let you know how it goes."

She hung up and stared at her house. May

would still be in her room, listening to music or watching videos on YouTube. She inhaled, steeling herself for today's battle, and climbed the porch steps to open the old wooden door with a creak. She scowled at the hinges — she'd known the coconut oil her mom had put on them wouldn't work. There should be some WD-40 in the garage that would do the trick. WD-40, another domain that used to be Drew's, but now was added to Gina's list.

She wiped her feet on the thick blue rug protecting the battered wood floors inside the front door. Dust dulled the surfaces, but Gina couldn't be bothered to remedy the problem. They never used the family room anymore, so why clean it? Straight through the hallway in front of her was the kitchen — small and functional, with a table where she and May ate their meals, usually at different times to keep the peace.

She wanted to go about her day, but that's not what a good mother would do, and she wanted more than anything to be a good mother. She wanted to be a mommy, or a ma, or a mama. Not the cold "Regina" May had taken to using the last year . . . when she deigned to address her at all.

After a quick trip upstairs to her room to change clothes and return Drew's shirt to its hiding spot, Gina backtracked to May's door. The door was dark, six-paneled oak, only two inches thick, yet it seemed like an impenetrable wall. Friends had warned her about the teen years since the day May had been born. "Just wait until the teens, it's like a monster takes over your perfect child for seven years, then miraculously gives her back when she turns twenty." If Drew were here, he could talk to May, make her see the logical side. Without him around every day, Gina was on her own.

She knocked on the door, waited five seconds for a response she wouldn't get, and then opened it. It took her eyes a few seconds to find May among the scattered clothes — including the clean clothes she'd set outside the door that morning — schoolwork, and books, like a Where's Waldo? puzzle of her sulky child. May lay on her bed, blue headphones covering her ears with her iPad propped on her bent legs. She didn't even look up to acknowledge Gina's arrival.

"May, can you take off your headphones, please?"

Gina waited ten seconds, then carefully stepped through the piles and plucked the headphones off May's head, revealing an orangey-yellow streak in her brown hair that hadn't been there yesterday. Should she yell at her? Compliment her? Ignore it completely?

"Hey!" May reached for the headphones, but Gina lifted them higher. She'd go with ignoring the hair streak for now. She hated that parenting had come to a game of keep-away and constantly second-guessing herself.

"I need to talk to you and I want to know you can hear me." May glared as only a disgruntled teen can, so Gina took that as a sign that she could continue. "I'm heading over to Grandma's. Did you want to join me? I'll make your favorite bacon and cheddar grilled cheese."

"I don't eat meat anymore, Regina." She moved her eyes to look at Gina, then returned to staring at her paused YouTube channel. Ah, the dreaded "Regina."

"Since when do you not . . . actually, never mind. I'll make you a bacon-free one."

"No."

"You can bring your iPad."

"No."

"I don't like the idea of you being home all on your own for all of break. Do you want me to drop you off at one of your friends' houses? What's Olivia up to?"

"No." She held her hand out for the

headphones. Knowing she had lost, Gina handed them back and leaned in to kiss May's forehead. May blocked it with her arm as she reinstalled her Beats. Gina wanted to yank them off her ungrateful ears again — after all, Gina had purchased those headphones — but counted to ten instead.

"Call me if you need me. I love you," Gina said, knowing that May had not heard her. She exited the room, leaving the door open behind her. If May wanted it closed, she'd at least have to get off her bed to do it. All the parenting books Gina had read told her that May's emotions and behaviors were normal, but she missed the little girl she laughed with, and snuggled and tickled, and made smile with her grilled cheese sandwiches.

With another parental failure under her belt, she shut the front door behind her and started toward her golden Mini Cooper, which was barely visible in the shadow of the truck.

"Gina! I was hoping I'd catch you on my way back."

Gina cringed, immediately twisting her lips into a smile and turning to face the woman attached to the cheerful voice. Patty and her husband were new to the neighborhood, new enough to not have been among the many who had dropped off casseroles and coffee cakes by the ton at Gina's house, as though noodles and ground beef could fill up the space a husband left behind. Drew had been the rock that kept their family strong. Without him, she and May tumbled through each day, flailing in the rushing waters, occasionally bumping into each other. Alone, they didn't pretend. But out in her driveway, she had to pretend to float, to swim, to glide on the pristine waters of life, when she was just barely keeping herself out of the turbulent undertow pulling at her legs.

"Hi, Patty. Good walk?" She looked down at the baby, soundly asleep in the cozy blankets, a blue elephant hat sliding over one closed eye. Such peace and innocence. Gina missed the unconditional love of a baby. Her eyes lifted to Patty's, whose normal smiling face was crunched into sad eyes, like she had to tell a third grade class they'd lost the school spirit competition and wouldn't get a pizza party. What had Gina done to warrant that look? And then it hit her, even before the words were out of Patty's mouth. She had seen that expression on the faces of everyone who'd known Drew.

"I am so sorry. The Greebles told me at

the Christmas Round Robin about your husband. I'd just assumed you were divorced. You're too young to be a widow. I can't imagine how hard that loss has been for you and May."

There it was. Two years later, and the sting was as fresh as yesterday. Patty reached for her hand, and Gina let her grab it. The gesture wasn't meant to bring her comfort. The handgrab was to make Patty feel better, so she could walk away believing she'd reached out and done the neighborly thing. So she could return to her perfect baby and loving, alive husband, comforted by her own sensitivity and the belief that she would never be on the receiving end of a horribly sympathetic hand grab.

Gina silently counted to three, then squeezed Patty's hand back. She'd learned through way too much practice that this made the squeezer feel more comfortable, the pause let them think their gesture was successful. Gina took a step toward her car — something she'd also learned was important. Insert some distance, so they knew it was okay to leave.

"Thank you for saying so," Gina said, the often-used phrase coming to her lips naturally, even though she hadn't needed to use it recently. It was rare anymore to meet someone who didn't already know her history. All her earlier determination felt like rapidly cracking ice beneath her feet. "It's been a little under two years." She slid on her sunglasses to hide the welling water and grabbed the door handle to the car for support — and to hint that she really needed to get going. "And we're all okay."

Chapter Two

May just wanted everything to go back to the way it was. She knew that wasn't possible, but it didn't make her stop wanting her dad to come back.

The video had ended, so she could hear her mom scuffling out the front door. Why did she keep pretending like nothing had changed, like nothing was different? Everything was different. She didn't even notice May's hair. How could anyone miss a giant stripe of yellow? Was she really that determined to ignore her?

She pulled off her headphones and rubbed her ears where they were sore from being crushed by the padded speakers — she really only wore them when her mom was home so she could pretend not to hear her. The car rumbled to life outside, and May waited until it faded, enjoying the solitude and knowing she'd have the entire empty house to herself for the rest of the day. She kicked some clothes out of the way to make a path from her bed to the door, keeping the clean clothes on the left and dirty on the right.

She could have gone to Olivia's today to get her mom out of her hair, but she didn't want to be around anyone, not even her best friend. She rarely did. None of her friends even got why she was so angry at her mom. She didn't really get it either, but she knew she was mad.

Pulling out the ingredients for brownies from the cupboard and fridge, May grabbed the bacon on a whim. Mom's face when she said she didn't eat meat anymore was classic. Would she become a vegetarian to try and "connect" with her? Would she forget, like she forgot most things on most days? If her mom didn't put it on one of her stupid lists, her mom didn't remember it. Bacon, chocolate, and caramel — those were all things May liked. Maybe after she fried the bacon, she could crumble it into caramel and drizzle that on top of her favorite brownie recipe. She set to baking.

Once the brownies were done and glazed with the bacon caramel, she cut a huge slab out of the corner and slid it onto a plate, burning herself on the gooey, piping-hot concoction. The plate in one hand, she took the stairs two at a time to her mom's bedroom. She set the plate on the nightstand and beelined for the closet, going to the farthest corner, where her mom always hid the bag. She found the Ziploc and pulled it out, opening the sealed edge and inhaling. Inside was her dead dad's favorite T-shirt, soft gray material smudged with motor oil stains. On the front it said BIKER DAD. LIKE A NORMAL DAD, BUT COOLER. On the back was the Harley-Davidson logo. She crawled onto the middle of her parents' bed with the bag in hand, balancing the plate on one knee and the Ziploc on the other. She took a bite of her brownie and chewed, using her free hand to clutch the soft fabric, not removing it from the bag. The salty bacon and sweet caramel gave her gooey brownie a nice salty/sweet kick, and she wished she could bake them for her dad. He would have loved how she'd improved on her brownie recipe. When she finished the treat, she returned the plate to the nightstand next to the jar of coconut oil Grandma'd given her mom, careful to lick all the sticky sauce from her fingers.

Pulling the comforter over her and rubbing the soft T-shirt material between her fingers, she curled into a ball and pretended her dad was just downstairs. She could only do this when her mom was gone. Regina never wanted to discuss her dad or his death. It was like May was the only one who wanted to keep him alive.

She had only seen her mom cry once, at her dad's funeral. The cemetery had been gray and dull green and flat brown. Clumps of dirty melted snow lined the curving roads. She and her mom wore black dresses under their colorful parkas — it was confusing to be somewhere so sad and wearing purple and pink. May couldn't wait to take her jacket off. The large crowd of people still hovered around the open grave where her dad's ashes had been lowered, all except his biker friends, the group of twenty that would cruise together before her dad stopped riding, and used to come over for cookouts. They were mounted on their bikes, lined up two by two near the crowd with a single rider at the start and a single rider at the end.

The lead rider started his bike, revving the engine three times, then the rest of the riders joined in. The rumble of all the engines revving together shook the ground. Her mom clutched May to her side as she closed her eyes. May worried the sound would break them apart, sending their shattered pieces to join her dad. A baby across from her started to cry, but she couldn't hear the wails. All she could hear was the bike thunder, like a special kind of deafness that only allowed engine thunder in. Would she ever hear another sound again?

On the leader's signal, they all stopped at once, then the last bike revved three more times. With barely a sound, especially for Harleys, the riders drove out of the cemetery. Her body still vibrated from the noise as her mom pulled her in tight, her face scrunching as she wept into May's hair. They clung to each other in the overwhelming silence as the crowd dispersed to the church hall for a lunch of cold cuts, potato salad, and lemon bars.

Life had returned to normal after that. Or as normal as it could, May guessed. Her mom stopped talking about Dad, and May's friends sort of faded away. They had all listened to her as she cried, which was nice, until they stopped asking her over. They had comforted her and didn't want to do it anymore, which was okay, except that May wasn't done. They only wanted to talk about cute boys and which girls in their class were bitches, and which teacher was the most unfair. The only one who had wanted to talk to May about her dad was the school counselor, and who wanted to share their personal life with Mr. Matycheck? Everyone knew he put what you said in your file.

May smelled the T-shirt one last time, detecting a lingering motor oil scent, reminding her of all the times he'd brought her to his motorcycle shop. Saturdays when she was little were always "family days," all of them doing chores, watching a movie or playing board games, and Mom always made delicious snacks. May's favorite part of those days, though, was when they'd pack a lunch and spend the afternoon at her dad's motorcycle shop. The first time he'd shown her how to take apart an engine, she was hooked.

He'd spread a quilted blue blanket onto the shiny cement floor. Her mom sat in the front office entering information on the computer, leaving the two of them alone. As he took each part off the engine, he lined it up in a straight line on the blanket.

"It's important to keep the parts in order so you don't lose any. It will also help you when you put it back together." Her dad handed her a rag. "I'm going to hand each part to you, and you need to clean all the grime off. Can you do that?"

She nodded and took the job very seriously, using her fingernails to get into the crevices, wiping until she'd gotten it as clean as possible, then moving on to the next part. They worked in silence. As she got older, he started explaining each part, showing her how to make each part like new or the tricks needed to remove stubborn parts.

When she was ten, he had surprised her with a rusty, battered v-twin engine, hers to take apart and put back together until she could do it without any help. He said that if she was going to drive one day, she had to learn how to take an engine apart and rebuild it herself. It had taken her six months to get it apart and another year to rebuild it, only needing his help twice — and he hadn't butted in like her mom did, he waited until she asked him to help her. Then she took it apart again and put it back together, even faster. Then he died. The engine now sat in the back of their garage collecting dead spiders and dust under a dirty bedsheet.

Now every time she saw it, she thought of him. And cried. So she didn't look.

May wiped her eyes and carefully sealed the bag, extracting as much air as possible. She returned it to Regina's hiding place in the closet, then carefully straightened out the bedding, fluffing up the material to remove her body's imprint. She tugged at each corner, making sure the wrinkles were gone and that it looked exactly like it had when she came upstairs. She picked up the plate and gave the room one last look to make sure Regina wouldn't know she had been there.

She didn't know what it meant or anything, that she snuck into her own mom's room to feel better. All she knew was that they were definitely not okay.

Chapter Three

The phone kept ringing, but Lorraine refused to answer it. She knew Regina and Victoria wanted to tell her what they thought of her e-mail, but they simply didn't have the right. She was their mother, and it was her job to coach them through life so they wouldn't make fools of themselves. So far her job was 50 percent complete — Victoria had always been the better child. The *idea* of perfume for Christmas wasn't awful, but Lorraine didn't care for gardenias, and her own daughter ought to know that.

She sat in her spacious condo overlooking a small flower garden in the courtyard. Right now it was layered in small, white lumps marking where existing plants hid. In the summer it was quite lovely with roses, day lilies, and no gardenias — not that they would grow this far north. She rocked in her chair and rubbed her hands. Dry skin caught her up short. She held them up to her face, giving her eyes time to focus. The skin looked rough, like she'd been carrying stone. Lorraine Price didn't labor. She'd already complained to the property manager twice this winter about the dry air. She opened a tub of coconut oil, one of the many she had tucked around her apartment. Taking a fingerful, she rolled it between her hands until it started to melt, then rubbed it into her dry hands, using the excess on her elbows and smoothing the rest onto her ash-blond bob. She didn't look her nearly seventy years, and she attributed it to frequent coconut oil use. She enjoyed the envious compliments she often received from the other residents when they discovered her age. One gentleman had even asked who she was visiting when she'd gone to get her mail last week.

The phone started ringing again. The sound made her light-headed. She stood, pausing a moment before taking her first step to make sure her balance was sound, then walked to where the phone hung on the wall between the kitchen and living room, her right foot tingling with each step like it had fallen asleep. She reached for the phone cord with her right hand, but for some reason she couldn't get a good grip on the cable leading from the wall to the cordless phone's charging station. Odd. No matter, she simply used her left hand instead and yanked the cord out of the wall.

Silence.

Lorraine shifted her weight to her left foot to give her right a little shake, trying to return the feeling back into it. She hadn't been sitting any differently than usual — it must be a sign she should be moving more. Perhaps she'd join one of the walking clubs whose flyers she'd seen posted in the condo building's lobby. She shifted her weight back and forth, but the feeling did not return. She shuffled to the bathroom, expecting the pinpricks of regaining feeling to start any moment, but the numbness continued to spread up her leg. Finally reaching the bathroom, she looked in the mirror above the sink to check her hair and saw that her right eye sagged a bit. That wasn't how it should look. She opened her eyes wide, the left opening much wider than the right. She opened and closed each eye, alternating the winks. When she shut her left eye, everything became blurry. But when she switched, her vision cleared. This wouldn't do. She had never needed glasses before — she didn't want to start now.

Her right hand tingled. She used it to

poke at her face, but couldn't really feel it — like when the dentist numbed to fill a cavity. She knew her skin was moving around, but she didn't feel it. Suddenly, a sharp spike of pain shot through her head, and she sucked in her breath. She'd felt that. Her heart skipped a few beats, then raced to make up for the missing ones. Something was happening. Something very bad. Lorraine didn't like circumstances she could not control.

I'll call Roza. She stumbled out of the bathroom, bumping against the wall as her right leg struggled to keep her upright. Lorraine took two more steps toward the phone, and her leg crumbled beneath her until her right hip, arm, and the side of her face collided with the hickory floors. At least she was numb so she couldn't feel the unsightly bruises she was sure were forming. A jar of coconut oil — that would help the bruises heal and ease the discomfort — sat next to the phone, but both were out of reach.

Pushing with her left hand, she tried to sit up, but half her body felt like wet sand, impossible for her age-weakened muscles to move — loath though she was to admit it. She focused on her target with her non-blurry eye and filled her lungs with air, ignoring the fear bubbling inside of her. She'd always found a way to survive. Whatever was happening now would be no different. She had done harder things in her life — she could get what she needed even if her body resisted. Using her left foot, she slid her body closer to the small table where the phone and coconut oil waited. The elastic on her pants was too loose and they slipped down her hips as she scooched, leaving her foundations-covered bottom exposed. Spanx, her girls referred to them, but at least they were full coverage to spare her the indignity of an uncovered behind. She would have expected slithering across the floor to hurt, but other than the throbbing still in her head, she surprisingly felt nothing. One more push and she reached the leg of the table. She grasped it, pulling it to her, shaking it until the phone and jar of oil toppled off — onto her head. Insult to injury.

Her hand reached and grabbed the phone, through sheer force of will. She pressed speed dial number one, the button to call Roza — Roza would help her. In the forty years they'd known each other, her old friend had never let her down. But this time there was no dial tone. She tried again, then remembered she had yanked it from the wall just a few moments ago. Can that have only been minutes? Or was it hours?

Her muscles refused to cooperate further. She really wished she had relieved herself before falling, before losing control of her muscles. She regretted that decision now as warmth — along with her remaining dignity — spread down her legs. She lay in her own urine, realizing her greatest fear had come true. She was going to die alone, mortified, without even a cat to curl next to her.

While she lay there, her husband improbably appeared from her bedroom, looking as handsome as ever. Where had he been this whole time? He wore his army uniform, crisp and freshly pressed. She could smell the lavender starch she had used on his collars, the polish he'd used to shine his boots. His brown hair was clipped short to his scalp, but she remembered how soft it felt when he grew it out, like a rabbit's fur. His large, soft eyes took her in. Her fear and self-consciousness evaporated.

"Oh, lovely Lorraine, what are you doing down there?" he said. His shiny shoes flashed in front of her before he tucked them under his legs as he sat crisscross next to her. She tried to say something, anything, to tell him how glad she was to see him after all this time, but he touched her lips. She couldn't feel anything through the numbness. "Now, I'm here. Don't you worry how. I'll keep you company until someone arrives. It won't be long."

He brushed her out-of-place locks off her forehead and ran a finger down her cheek that must look so old to his young eyes. She wanted to lean into his touch.

"It's been so long, and you look exactly the same," he said.

Flatterer. He'd always had a way with words. How she missed this, his flirtation that never felt insincere. A tear trickled over the bridge of her nose and fell to the floor. He was so beautiful and young. Was it finally time to be with him? Finally their time?

"Not yet, my lovely. You have some things to sort out before that. Our girls need to know."

She tried to shake her head, but couldn't. She didn't care if anyone came, and she had no plans to tell anyone anything. She wanted to go with him, be with him. But if she couldn't go with him now, then she was going to memorize everything about this moment. His hands rested on hers, the nails perfectly square and neat, his skin tanned from working in the sun. Dark hairs dotted his knuckles, hints at the dark hair dusting his covered chest. His lips were the exact shade of pink champagne she remembered. He must have just shaved, because his ordinary stubble was absent.

A key slid in the lock, and he looked toward the door at the sound, a smile on his face.

"She's here."

Faced away from the door as she was, she couldn't see who entered — she could only watch his smile spread wider as he saw who had come. Lorraine blinked at the tears, trying to clear them up before whoever had arrived could see them. When she finished blinking, he was gone. And her heart broke again, just like it had so long ago.

"Mom," Regina said. Her feet clomped across the floor. She hadn't taken off her shoes, forgetful girl. "Mom. Mom!"

Regina slid a hand under her, moving her body so they could see each other. "Why aren't you saying anything?" Her voice rose in panic. "Mom?"

Finally she was catching on. Why couldn't Victoria have been the one to find her? Regina always was the slow one. At last, Regina pulled out her cellular and called 911.

"Hi. My name is G-Gina. My . . . my mom is on the floor."

Tsk. Hardly any relevant information at

all. Her daughter's chest expanded and deflated.

"Sh-she's not talking." Regina looked her in the face. "Her eyes are open, but she's not talking. Help me."

This verbal stumbling was hard to watch. Lorraine shut her eyes.

"Now her eyes are closed. Please, please come quickly." Regina's hand, warm and surprisingly comforting, held her own. Her voice dulled to a buzz, and Lorraine let the darkness come. Maybe when she woke, he would be back. And then they'd both be okay.

■ ■ ■ ■

Have I Lived Up to Your Expectations?

■ ■ ■ ■

Chapter Four

Her mom was warm, that was something.

"Mom. Mom." Gina gently slapped her face. No response. Gina's breath quickened. She couldn't panic. She could help her mom. She started making a list.

1. Call 911.

She didn't know what to do after that. But it was a start. Something she could do to improve the situation. Gina had worried about finding her mother on the floor more than once. She was always curious what her reaction would be. Would she fall to pieces? Would she respond like a good daughter should and call for help? Or would she close the door, go to Starbucks, get a latte, then come back in a half hour? She was reassured, at least, that leaving for Starbucks had never crossed her mind.

While she waited for the EMTs to arrive,

she assessed her mom, talking to her as she checked her body, even though she seemed to be unconscious. Maybe it was like a coma, and she could still hear her and be reassured by her presence — though Lorraine being reassured by Gina would be a first.

"Okay, Mom. Let's see how you're doing here."

She put a hand on Lorraine's wrist and watched her chest rise and fall.

"You're alive. You have a pulse and you're breathing. That's all good."

Somehow her mother's pants had come down her hips, and she was in a puddle of water. Maybe she'd fallen in the spill and hit her head. Gina got a paper towel to wipe it up.

"Did you slip in some water? Is that what happened? I'll get this tidied up right away."

But when she set the paper towel on the liquid and watched it turn yellow, her nose finally picked up the distinctive scent.

Not water.

"Oh, Mom. Okay, don't worry. I'll get you cleaned up. You're going to be fine."

Gina couldn't leave her like this for the ambulance. Her mom would never forgive her. Reluctant to leave her side, she rushed to the closet and grabbed the first skirt she saw — a long, floral print one she usually wore on hot summer days. Not ideal for the time of year, but her mom could reprimand her later about it. She grabbed the scissors from the desktop pen holder where her mother kept them and went to work.

"I know this is a summer skirt, but I think it'll be easier than pants. This will only take a minute, and no one will ever know what happened."

She slid the pants completely off and used them to dry up the rest of the puddle. Then she slid the skirt over the slender legs and hips, leaving it bunched around her waist and above the damp Spanx, which would make it easier to cover her again once the undergarments were cut free. Using the scissors, she cut each side of the elastic shorts from top to bottom, her heart racing that the paramedics would arrive while her mom was so exposed. Lorraine would never forgive her for that faux pas. With a snap, the material gave. Averting her eyes, she slid the damp fabric away, dried her mother with a clean towel, and pulled the skirt quickly down over her legs. She added a blanket to keep her warm and a pillow under her head so she looked more comfortable.

"There. Now it looks like you're napping."

Oh fudge, that's what people said at funerals. Her mom wasn't going to die, was she? Gina violently shook her head and rearranged her thoughts to be more positive.

Busying herself, she threw away the ruined undergarments and tossed the towels into the laundry so all the evidence was gone before any other witnesses arrived. Where were they?

"See, we've got you all cleaned up for the paramedics. They'll be here any minute, and you'll be back to your normal self in no time."

Gina kept rambling to fill the silence, more for herself than her unconscious mother. Alone and waiting, she opened the condominium's door wide to the hallway, not wanting to leave her mom's side but keen to know the second the EMTs arrived. Her mom must have been so frightened, not being able to move or talk. Lorraine's voice was her weapon of choice in life, and without it, she was less fearsome — like a defanged cobra. She returned to her mother's side, holding her hand and watching the nearly invisible rise and fall of her chest — counting the seconds between breaths to make sure they stayed consistent.

Tears still lingered on her mother's face. She must have started to cry before she lost consciousness.

"I bet it hurt when you fell."

Gina dabbed the tears off with a wadded-up tissue she had in her pocket. In her forty years, she had never seen her mother cry, or even have a moment of helplessness. Maybe the tears were a symptom. She glanced around for something else to comfort her mother and her eyes landed on the jar of coconut oil. She scooped out a small dab and gently took her mom's hand in her own, rubbing the oil into her already soft skin like she'd seen her do all her life, moving her thumbs in circles on her palm, then down each finger. She repeated it with the other hand, relieved that her mother's skin stayed warm and her breathing steady.

A whoosh of air from down the hall moved the door a few inches, followed by bustling feet. Gina stepped out the apartment door to see the EMTs hustling in her direction. A few neighbors poked their heads out of their nearby doors like prairie dogs watching an approaching predator. As the paramedics arrived, Gina waved them in. Giving them space to do their work, she stood against the wall, answering any questions they asked.

Did her mother have a history of fainting? No.

Does she have any allergies? No.

Does she live alone? Yes.

What medications does she take? Gina read the line of pill bottles on the kitchen counter. Blood pressure medication, yes, but nothing serious for a woman in her late sixties.

What hospital should we take her to? St. Al's.

Gina watched as they strapped her mother to a gurney and covered her with a thin blanket. *What came next? Would she be okay?* Gina had questions, too, but had to force herself to speak up, for fear of being inconvenient.

"What do I do? Do I come with you? Follow? She's going to be all right, right?"

"Follow when you can. Go to the ER entrance. If you have her insurance and end-of-life instructions, it's a good idea to bring those along. And she's stable for now," the paramedic said.

Before Gina could form any follow-up questions, they were out the door.

End-of-life instructions?

End-of-life. Instructions.

End of life.

End.

It couldn't be. Her mom was too tough. She was going to outlast them all, right?

Gina clung to that thought and used it to rally, to get moving. She would find the insurance information. She would get to the hospital. She would call Vicky. She would text May.

Gina scanned her mother's home. She'd never been alone in it before. Her mother had moved only a few years ago, tired of maintaining the property where Gina and Vicky had grown up. Finding her a suitable place to live had been a nightmare. Most senior apartments were "no better than hovels," according to Lorraine. She had wanted granite countertops, real wood floors — no parquet and, heaven forbid, no laminate — and beautiful grounds, and she'd paid accordingly. Thank goodness Gina's father had left her a small fortune.

She pulled out her mother's monogrammed overnight bag from the hall closet. If only Gina had time to make a proper list of items to pack, but she'd have to wing it. She started with the desk, finding bills, take-out menus, and programs for events held in the complex's main building. She also found two unopened jars of coconut oil. She set these on the kitchen table, adding any more she found as she went. As she searched she set aside things her mom might need at the hospital — a toothbrush, fresh pajamas and underwear, deodorant, and a new jar of coconut oil — shoving it all into the bag.

She searched the closet for slippers and a robe, peeking in the corners for anything that could be important. Under a stack of neatly folded towels, she found a safe with the keys dangling in the lock. Inside was an expired passport and a battered brown accordion file, held together with clear packing tape. This must be it. She scanned the first compartment's documents, which made reference to who she wanted to make decisions for her and what kind of medical care she wanted to receive. The phrase "do not resuscitate" stood out, but Gina chose to ignore what that meant. This must be it, though the folder was stuffed with a lot of other papers. She didn't have time to go through it now, so she tucked the entire file under her arm, zipped up the overnight bag, and locked the door behind her. After racing across the icy parking lot, she slid into her car, and the folder's elastic closure gave under the pressure as it hit the cement. Before Gina even realized what had happened, she heard a tear and papers fluttered onto the ground, scattering immediately. *Mother fudge.*

She stomped on the papers that flew the farthest away, while reaching for the largest clump next to the car, not wanting any to blow in the winter breeze or tumble into one of the slushy puddles dotting the parking lot. She scurried to collect them all, finding a brown paper grocery sack in her backseat to hold the ruined accordion file and stray papers. She didn't want to, but she'd have to stop and replace it — her mother's lecture about not taking immediate steps to fix her clumsiness practically echoed in her ears already. But, then again, she'd need to stop for flowers anyway.

When her mother had had her appendix removed ten years ago, Gina had arrived without a bouquet. Her mom lay on the hospital bed waiting for the surgery prep to begin. Vicky already sat at her side in the only visitor's chair.

"Hi, Mom. How are you?" Gina had leaned in to kiss her cheek.

Her mom rolled her eyes.

"Why did you even bother to come if you weren't going to bring flowers? I taught you better than that." Gina met Vicky's eyes over her mother's horizontal body, conveying all she needed to know. She had screwed up royally. "Victoria brought me some, even if they are carnations."

Sure enough, a cheerful arrangement of

lilies, fern fronds, and carnations sat in the window nook.

"They're not all carnations, Mother," Vicky said.

"I suppose it's too late to say they're from the both of us," Gina joked, hoping to gloss over her mom's ire with humor.

"That would be even worse. If anything, you should bring extra to fill up this drab room."

And that was the core of her mother's life philosophy — always make sure you present your best side at all times.

Which was why Gina purchased a ridiculously overpriced gift box decorated with a colorful Noah's Ark scene. It was the only container they had in the hospital gift shop that would hold all the papers. She didn't want to make additional stops, and she had also bought two bouquets of stargazer lilies and combined them in one opaque green vase. One bouquet had seemed too scant.

Carrying the overstuffed vase, the crammed overnight bag, the brown paper bag stuffed with papers, the Noah's Ark box, and her purse, she arrived at the emergency desk out of breath and sweaty, even though the temperature outside was well below freezing. As she joined the short line of worried faces and grumpy children,

Gina fretted she was being too optimistic to think that her mom would even need any of this stuff. She probably shouldn't have even stopped at the gift shop. She should have come straight to the emergency room and not worried about disappointing her mother with flowers or a torn folder. Besides, she had been a disappointment all her life, she was used to it. What if her mother had died while she debated over roses or lilies? Surely missing your own mother's death while shopping was the greater sin.

At last she was at the front of the line. She felt ridiculous, like the camel from the ark had shown up at the reception desk.

"Hi, I'm Gina Zoberski. My mom was brought in by an ambulance. Her name is Lorraine Price."

The woman hunt-and-pecked the information into her computer. Gina hadn't typed that slowly even when she'd learned in high school, but she stuffed her irritation down.

"A nurse will be out to get you as soon as there is any information."

"Right. Thank you. I'm sure she's fine, so sorry to bother you, but do you know if she's all right?"

"I'm sorry, ma'am. I can't disclose that information, even if I did know — which I don't. A nurse will be out when there is any information to share."

Gina nodded and forced a smile. The woman was just doing her job. Surely the nurse would be right out.

"Thank you."

She nestled into a chair as far as possible from the other waiting people. With each passing minute, she became more and more convinced she should have come straight over. How long would she have to wait? Would Vicky be waiting around, or would she demand to be let in?

Vicky.

She hadn't called Vicky. In the rush to pack her mom's bag, dash to the hospital, and, of course, buy flowers, she had completely forgotten to call her sister. Gina dug her phone from her purse and gathered her thoughts as she waited for Vicky to answer.

"What did Mom do now?" she answered followed by a sigh.

"Vic, she's in the hospital." Gina took a deep breath, gave the news time to sink in. "I don't . . . I don't really know what happened."

"Start at the beginning." Vicky's voice became all-business, acknowledging this was not the typical bitch-about-Mom call. Thank God for Vicky.

"She didn't answer my calls, or the door, so I used my key. I found her on the floor trying to reach the phone — or the coconut oil, it's hard to be sure. She couldn't move or talk. Vic" — Gina dropped her voice to a whisper — "she'd peed herself."

"Did the EMTs see her like that?"

"No, I was able to clean her up and put her in a skirt." The seriousness of the situation started to pull at Gina. Her voice shook. "Our mother is in the emergency room, and I don't know what's wrong with her. No one's told me anything yet."

"Do you at least have flowers?"

"Of course." They paused in their conversation. "I had to find her end-of-life documents. What if this is her end of life?"

"Gina — don't be dramatic." Vicky's voice was so no-nonsense, she could have been explaining to her daughter why she couldn't wear her princess dress to school. "Mom will outlive us all. I'll find a sitter and get up there as soon as I can. Jeff can be in charge for a few days. Which hospital?"

"St. Al's."

"I'll text when I'm on my way."

"Thanks, Vic. Love you."

Gina ended the call and held the silent phone in her hands. She should let May know. Knowing she wouldn't answer a call, she sent a text.

Grandma in hospital. Not sure when I can leave. Aunt V is on her way. She can pick you up if you want to come.

Gina didn't expect a response, and she didn't get one. Seconds, then minutes, ticked by. Maybe she should insist she come to the hospital — not give her a choice.

"Ms. Zoberski?" A businesslike nurse stood by the entrance to the ER, her tone the same as the ladies behind the deli counter calling out the next-to-be-served number, but she lacked the solemnness of someone about to give bad news. That had to be a good sign, right? "Gina Zoberski?"

"Me. That's me. Coming." Gina gathered the assorted items, shoving her phone back in her purse. Truthfully, she didn't have the energy to think about both her mother and her daughter. One thing at a time. Tomorrow, she'd deal with it. She started a mental list.

1. Bring May to hospital to visit.

The nurse waited patiently as she juggled the flowers and bags and led her to a room where her mom lay on a hospital bed, wires leading to several different machines. Her clothes had been replaced with a worn hospital gown, and a skimpy blanket covered her. Everything about her seemed thin, from her hair to her skin to her lips pressed together even in unconsciousness, as if Lorraine had sensed the poor quality of the hospital linens. She passed judgments even in a coma.

"Thank you, so much. Is she asleep?" Gina stared at her mother, her arms already aching from keeping the flowers in the crook of her arm.

"I'll let Dr. Patel update you." A tiny part of Gina eased. She knew Dr. Patel — they would be in good hands. "If you have any insurance papers, or power of health care forms, we'll need them. Someone will be in to help you get all the admission paperwork filled out."

Gina dumped the bags on the floor and set the flowers on a small counter, making sure the bouquet's best side was facing the bed. Questions popped into her head, but she didn't want to bother the nurse as she flitted about the room checking the machines. By the time she found the courage to speak up, the nurse had left her alone with her mom. She expected some beeps, maybe a whir, but all the machines were eerily silent, working their magic without a sound. There were two hand sanitizer dispensers stuck to the walls — a not-so-subtle hint to de-germ. She released a blob into her palm and rubbed the foam between her hands until it evaporated. A ghost of a smile twitched at her lips as she remembered the days when May referred to it as hanitizer. Little May would have loved the never-ending supply of hanitizer. Gina marked it as her happy thought for the day, something she could use to cheer herself up if needed.

Lorraine appeared comfortable and content — maybe she was overreacting and by the time Vicky arrived her mom would be complaining about the lack of flowers and scolding her for snooping through her condo. Gina settled into the corner chair and pulled over the rolling table. She should make use of the time and at least do something that might be helpful. After setting the Noah's Ark box in front of her, she began to empty what hadn't fallen out of the accordion file, making one large pile she'd sort later.

The uncertainty of her mother's future threatened to pull her into the emotions she kept carefully tucked under her smiles and lists. She had to focus on what needed to be done, not on what she couldn't do. Gina pulled a notebook and pen from her purse and got to work.

1. Sort documents into new box.
2. Fill out admissions paperwork.
3. Change guest room bedding for Vicky.
4. Prep coffeemaker for a.m.
5. Update Grilled G's website.

There. Maybe she couldn't make her mother better. She couldn't wake her up right now. She couldn't make May answer her phone. But she could make a list.

Chapter Five

May didn't even glance when her phone choo-chooed. That was the sound it made when her mom texted — a train whistle. It made it easy to ignore messages from her mom and still read the ones she wanted, not that she got many.

May wrapped a blanket around herself and wandered from room to room in their home, walking in circles, dragging the blanket train behind her and leaving a trail on the dusty floors. She would never give her mom the satisfaction of knowing, but being home alone was super boring. She ate another brownie.

Her phone dinged. It didn't choo-choo. But it only ever choo-chooed. She raced to the kitchen table where it sat, sliding on her stocking feet to see who it was.

It was a text from Connor Patel.

A text from Connor.

Connor.

What r u doing?

Connor Patel wanted to know what she was doing. She couldn't tell him she was dusting the floor with her blanket cape, watching YouTube, and eating bacon caramel brownies. What would an interesting person do while home alone on winter break? Remixing songs or painting or practicing guitar, something effortless and not dorky. Those all sounded cooler. But, then again, she didn't know anything about guitars to fake a conversation if he asked. She thought about the engine in the garage, her last real project, but the memory was too sharp.

She should call Olivia. Olivia would know what to say. But they hadn't talked outside of school in months. She'd have to handle this on her own. Her thumbs twitched above the letters as she figured out her response. Okay.

Watching videos and making bacon brownies.

Ugh. That was such a dumb answer. She should have made up something, but his response was almost immediate.

I like brownies and web antics.

OhmyGod. Oh. My. God. Did he mean what she thought he meant? Did Connor Patel want to hang out? With her? A part of her, way down deep where she used to frantically anticipate a new Pixar movie or Santa Claus, stirred, slow at first but picking up momentum until actual butterflies took flight. In just a few seconds, her irritation with her mom seemed more like mild annoyance, the day was less boring, and she had no idea what would happen next. May was *excited.*

I can share.

Her chest thumped as she waited a few seconds for his response. The emptiness and loneliness from earlier was gone, replaced with Pop Rocks in her stomach.

Cool. Be over in 20.

May dropped the blanket and stared down at herself, taking in her rainbow leggings and old T-shirt. She couldn't face Connor in this. Racing to her room, she grabbed her best jeans and a blue sweater from the clean pile of clothes. She shook them out and sniffed quickly. These would do. Her body felt like a Katy Perry song come to life. She ran from room to room looking for what to do, but accomplished nothing. No time to shower, she managed to brush her teeth, wash her face, and pull her hair into a bun on top of her head, so it looked casually messy. She slathered on her favorite strawberry lotion and lip gloss just as a knock sounded at the back door.

As she opened it, a flash of worry burst in her conscience — her mom didn't like it when she had people over while she was home alone — not even friends like Olivia, let alone a boy. If Mom found out, May would definitely be in trouble. Maybe she should send a quick text, just letting her know what was happening. Then she thought about how her mom didn't even bother to make her get dressed that morning, or even get out of bed. If she really cared, she wouldn't have left May to fend for herself. She pushed the worry away and opened the door to the cutest boy at school.

Connor Patel played baseball in the spring and performed in the school play in the fall. He was athletic and artsy and smart. He was in all the advanced classes the school offered, and volunteered at the Humane Society on the weekends. Actually, she didn't really know about that last one, but he probably did — or maybe he spent time reading to the elderly at a local nursing home. He was literally perfect. His dark brown hair swooped above his forehead, his long lashes brushing his cheeks and framing his understanding eyes, one dark brown the other a warm blue. His family must have traveled somewhere tropical for winter break because his skin was more tan than usual. Both his parents were doctors at the nearby hospital, so when they had the time off to travel, they went big.

The collar of his navy-blue winter coat was pulled high around his ears against the cold wind with his hands shoved deep into the pockets. They usually had a bunch of the same classes together, ever since middle school started, so she'd seen him sprout from short and scrawny to taller than she was in just a few years. His lips were a rosy peach that matched the cold-sparked color on his cheeks, and they smiled wide when she opened the door.

They'd always been friendly, especially in elementary school, but ever since her dad died, she didn't really talk to many people, and now he was standing on her doorstep all of a sudden. "Come in. Did you walk here?" she asked, nervous in the best way.

He stomped his snowy feet on the rug and nodded. They both lived on the east side of Wauwatosa, not far apart, but far enough that it wasn't a fun walk in midwinter.

"I may have cut through a few yards to make it shorter."

"Do you want some hot chocolate or tea to go with your brownies?"

"Hot cocoa. Do you have marshmallows?"

He unzipped his coat. Underneath it he wore a sweatshirt for Tosa (short for Wauwatosa) East High School, where they would both be going next year. She could see a white T-shirt peeking out from underneath. She liked the way it looked against his smooth brown neck. Her cheeks warmed with the thought, and she hoped he didn't notice.

"Plenty of marshmallows." She looked at the floor, praying her blush would fade.

Taking his coat, she hung it in the front hall closet like her mom did when guests visited. When she returned to the kitchen, he stood in the middle, studying the pictures on the fridge.

"It smells amazing in here," Connor said.

"Bacon makes everything better."

He laughed a little and turned back to the picture. Why did she say something so dumb? He probably already regretted coming over. May warmed the milk and stirred in extra powdered chocolate mix from a large yellow tub, heaping the cup with marshmallows. Connor leaned in closer to study one of the pictures, the one from a few years ago when she, her mom, and her dad had gone to their church picnic. In the picture, she was ten and wearing a white sundress covered in mud, and her dad and mom were almost as dirty.

It had rained that day — no, poured. She could still feel the mud squishing between her toes. Her mom had been volunteering in the beer tent, and May and her dad had been playing the carnival games when the storm hit. It had been one of those summer rains that felt like a warm shower and drenched you before you had time to find shelter. Her dad had picked her up and run — not in the direction of a tent, but into the baseball field on the edge of the parking lot. He stopped on home plate and said, "Race you around the bases."

She was giggling even before they started running, and the laughter only made it harder. The mud was slippery, and as she turned the corner on third, her dad obviously letting her win, her heel hit a slick spot and she went down. Her eyes widened in worry because she was now absolutely covered in mud. Instead, her dad slid down right next to her, laughing.

"You missed a spot."

He smeared some mud on her nose.

"You missed a spot, too," she said, making a streak on his forehead. The falling rain washed some of the mud off, but they would only replace it, laughing so hard her sides hurt.

When the rain stopped, her mom came out from under the tent carrying a roll of paper towels and with a face as dark as the sky.

"Mom looks mad. I ruined my dress."

"Nah. Sometimes you have to get a little messy. Even Mom." He winked at her, then stood. When her mom finally reached them, he gave her a big hug, wriggling against her for maximum mud transfer. May jumped in the middle, squishing her mom in a hug against her halfhearted protests. The picture was taken a few moments later. Why couldn't Dad still be here instead of Mom? The thought pulled her back to the present, shocking herself with the horror of what she had just thought. She blinked, almost missing when Connor spoke again.

"That looks like fun," Connor said. "I don't think my parents have ever let me be that dirty. Let alone them, too."

"Yeah." Her voice croaked. She moved around him to open the fridge, careful not to touch him. With such an awful thought in her head, she didn't want it to rub off on him. "That was a good day."

She pulled out a can of whipped cream to top the cocoa, adding a towering swirl.

"You really know what you're doing, don't you?" He stood next to her as she added a drizzle of caramel she had left over from the brownies.

May wasn't prepared to be funny or clever, never having been alone in her kitchen with a cute boy before, or alone with one anywhere, really. Sure, they were always friendly in class or passing in the hall, or if they were at the same party with other friends, but they didn't really socialize. Or, to be more accurate, she didn't really socialize. She was sure he always had plans on the weekend or during school breaks, not like her, who'd become a fourteen-year-old hermit.

The concept of small talk eluded her, so she went for simply answering his question.

"I like to make stuff in the kitchen. Homemade is always better. Besides, it's sort of fun."

"My parents never let me eat this much sugar."

May shrugged. "The only perk of living here — all the sugar you want."

Connor chuckled, then took a sip of his

hot cocoa as she started to make a cup for herself.

The longer the silence stretched, the harder May thought to think of something to fill the silence. The more she tried, though, the blanker her mind became. Connor rocked on his feet and rubbed his hands together, then took another sip. The timer dinged on the microwave, letting May know her milk was warm.

"Oh, I forgot to get your brownie." She stopped mixing her hot chocolate and pulled a plate from the cupboard.

"While you're doing that, how about I finish the hot chocolate for you? Team effort."

"Add three spoons of the powder, then the marshmallows and whipped cream."

Each with their own task, the awkward silence between them evaporated, and soon they sat at the table with the snacks. Ghost-shaped marshmallows bobbed in their hot chocolate, left over from Halloween. Connor pulled his brownie apart, letting the gooey caramel string out.

"This looks amazing." He took a bite. "It tastes even better. You're a great cook."

May looked down at her food. She'd never thought of herself as great at anything. "Baker." Connor looked confused. Why did she correct him? He'd think she was bossy.

But now she had to finish the thought. "Baking is more precise, like science, my dad used to say."

She sipped her hot cocoa.

"You make great hot cocoa, too."

"You, too." She held up her mug. "I'm following you when the zombie apocalypse starts."

They finished their snacks and put their dishes by the sink. Now what? Why did he even text her? What if this was some joke? Like one of those movies where the cute boy makes a bet he can get the loser girl to fall for him? Her butterflies died just thinking about it, and now that the thought was there, she couldn't let it go.

"So . . . why are you here?" The words flew out before she could rethink them. She had to know.

Connor rubbed his hands on his jeans. "Besides the food?"

Was he avoiding the question? His joke made it seem like he wasn't taking her seriously.

"Yes. Besides the food. It doesn't make any sense. You have plenty of friends. Why did you text me? Are you making fun of me?"

He put his hands in his pockets and looked at the floor. Isn't looking down one of the signs of a liar? Oh God, was he going to lie? Then he looked right at her, his eyes so big, one blue and one brown, both honest.

"No. Do you really think I would do that to anyone, let alone you?"

"What does that mean?"

"I . . ." His voice squeaked and he cleared his throat. "Remember how we used to play Harry Potter in fourth grade?"

"Hannah always made me be Professor McGonagall, and you would volunteer for Professor Flitwick so I would have someone to hang out with." May smiled at the memory. "That was nice."

"Well, I was watching the last movie last night, where McGonagall enchants the castle to fight. It made me think of you." He shrugged. "I like you. I have for a long time. But you stopped hanging out with anyone after your . . ." His voice halted, and he pointed to the picture on the fridge. She understood why he didn't want to say it. People always thought not mentioning her dad's death would make it easier. But it didn't. It wasn't just an elephant in the room, it was an entire herd. Even a blind person can't ignore a herd of elephants, and she wasn't blind.

"After my dad died. Yeah, having fun

wasn't fun anymore."

He went back to rubbing his hands on his legs, like he was trying to tuck them in his pockets but kept missing. Could he really like her? Was he nervous? And why wasn't she nervous anymore? She felt like she was watching the scene from above, knowing exactly what she needed to say — not worrying if it made him uncomfortable. Like a for-serious out-of-body experience.

"Well, that sucks," he said.

"It really does." Her skepticism evaporated with his honesty. "Thanks for saying it."

"So do you still think having fun isn't fun anymore? Because maybe I could help with that?"

His mouth curved into a half smile, absurdly cute and charming. Did he even know how adorable he was? Her calm disappeared back into a wave of nerves, making her skin twitchy and electric.

"Sure?" Her voice went up in pitch as she spoke the word — turning it into a question. "We have an old Wii. It's kind of dorky, but . . ."

"Not dorky. I haven't crushed anyone at bowling in a long time."

"Dream on. I'm the reigning Zoberski champion — I think I can take you."

Chapter Six

When Lorraine woke up, her husband was still gone.

A light flashed in her eyes, blinding her for a moment. She swatted the light away from her face and blinked until she could see the room. Regina sat in the chair near the bed, sorting papers into neat stacks — so like her.

"Mrs. Price, ... awake?" Lorraine wasn't catching all the words coming toward her — they sounded garbled, like the adult voices in a Charlie Brown special. Now that the light was gone, she could see the doctor above her. The doctor was youngish — but, then, everyone was youngish to her — with smooth black hair, porcelain white skin, and smudged glasses. How could she see anything through them? Lorraine tried to respond, but nothing came out. She tried again, this time making sounds, but nothing resembling words.

"I see . . . Price. You . . . have . . . . . . speaking, but . . . start . . . on that. Let . . . finish my . . . exam and I'll tell you what we know."

The doctor went back to shining lights in her eyes and asking her to move different body parts. When she couldn't understand the instructions, the doctor would point to the body part she wanted to test. Her left hand moved all right, but her right arm barely flopped, despite the clear instructions she was sending it. After each request, the doctor would poke at her computer pad, then ask Lorraine to perform another action. Regina had stopped sorting and was watching with her ever-present notebook in her lap, a line dividing her forehead. As soon as she regained her speech, Lorraine would have to tell her to put some coconut oil on it or the line would become permanent.

The room looked to be a regular hospital room, rather than a bustling emergency room, so whatever happened must have been bad enough to get her admitted. On the wide windowsill, a beautiful bouquet of stargazer lilies basked in the sun. She could smell their distinct scent from her bed — which is why they were one of her favorite flowers. She was impressed Regina remembered to bring them. Perhaps Victoria had reminded her. Out of the very corner of her eye, she could see that her room even had a decent view of the snowy park next to the hospital.

While she waited for her doctor to start talking, Regina came to stand by her bed.

"Hey, Mom. You feeling okay?" Lorraine could only blink, but Regina seemed to think that meant yes because she kept talking. "Vic will be here any minute. She ran out to get some more flowers, since we know how much you like them."

How long had she been unconscious? She last remembered early afternoon and now the sun had set, so it must be well into the evening. Disconcerting, to say the least, this loss of time. She should be angry and frightened, but she was alive, and one daughter was here with the other on the way. At least they were being properly attentive. She smiled, then stopped. Was that a little drool escaping from her lip? Regina scrambled for a tissue to wipe it away, alarm on her face.

"There, I got it." Regina reached for Lorraine's hand and squeezed. "You scared me. Us. I'm getting you one of those alarms for your neck when you go home — you know, the 'Help, I've fallen and I can't get up' ones — because you are going home,

Mother." Regina smiled — always looking for the positive side, this one. When would she learn that optimism led only to disappointment?

"Okay, Gina, Mrs. Price, it's time to chat," the doctor said, her face pleasant and smooth. She must use sunscreen. The doctor directed all of her words at Lorraine, which she appreciated. She could think, after all, even if she couldn't talk. "You've had an ischemic stroke, which means that a clot blocked one of the blood vessels in your brain, cutting off the blood flow and affecting everything on the opposite side of the body. We'll keep running tests, but it's compromised your speech and all the movements on your right side — so it is most likely in the left hemisphere of your brain. Your eyes aren't exceptionally dilated, so I expect your vision is okay, at least in your left eye. The ER injected you with a drug that breaks up clots, and we've got you on blood thinners as well. They are being administered via your IV. We've scheduled you for a CT scan, and we're already running tests on your blood. We'll proceed from there once we know more."

"Could she have another stroke?" Regina asked, her pen poised over her notepad.

Good question, thought Lorraine.

"It's possible. Once an individual has had a stroke, they are more likely to have another." The doctor looked Lorraine in the eyes. "The blood thinners and tPA should reduce the risk, but it is still much higher than that of an average person. The CT scan will give us a better idea if you need surgery to open up some arteries. You arrived at the hospital quickly, so that's a plus. At your age, a mostly full recovery isn't impossible. We'll need to keep you for tests and discuss the best rehab strategy based on that."

"What about her speech? Will she get that back?"

Lorraine tried to nod, but it felt more like she'd become a bobblehead doll on a roller coaster.

"Stroke victims can recover most of their lost functionality with daily therapy. So the chances are good she'll be able to communicate again. The key is patience, because it's easy to become frustrated and depressed with slow progress and an inability to communicate. While she can't tell us, she can probably understand what is happening, so feel free to talk with her as much as you'd like."

The doctor checked her chart and then her watch.

"I need to get these orders in so the nurses

can deliver you to radiology on time, Mrs. Price. I'll be back to discuss the results when they are in. If you need anything, the nurses can help."

She slipped out of the room, leaving Lorraine alone with Regina. A nurse came into the room carrying a white Styrofoam cup of water and ice. In efficient movements, she held the cup to Lorraine's lips, tidied her table, adjusted her IV, and checked her vitals while keeping up a steady stream of reassuring chatter.

Regina moved her chair and table closer to the side of the bed as Victoria arrived, arms full of flowers. She looked lovely in slim dark jeans and a black cashmere turtleneck. If only Regina could pull herself together like Victoria, she would have found a new husband already. She was too young to be alone forever. Widows should be older and regal, like herself. Regina, Lorraine could see, wore much too baggy jeans, even though she was decidedly on the chunk. A slimmer cut would be much more flattering with her hips. And her hair tumbled out of a ponytail, leaving wispy strands that frizzed even in the winter. Would it be too much trouble to wear a splash of lipstick and mascara to come see your only mother in the hospital? Her doctor was a woman, yes, but there could be handsome doctors Regina's age somewhere around.

While Lorraine resolved to take her eldest jeans shopping as soon as she got out of the hospital, Regina updated Victoria on the doctor's news, reading diligently from the careful notes she had scribbled in her notebook. Victoria, nodding, arranged the flowers so that Lorraine's room suddenly resembled an overgrown flower shop, which she adored. As her daughters chattered about their children, and her, Lorraine caught only a handful of the words, but the familiar voices and faces eased her earlier fear of dying alone and lonely — like Floyd had.

It had been fall. Lorraine had just returned home after setting up at the club for the Harvest Gala. After ten years of lobbying and sucking up to the Ladies Club chairwoman, Maxine Fuller, she finally was assigned a meaningful event. It had taken that long to recover socially from Regina's outburst at the club's bar where everyone, including Maxine, had witnessed her humiliation. That day had stung, seeing her daughter make the same mistakes she had made so many years ago. She had tried to teach her that marriage was about security and compromise and comfort. Passion and love would get her nowhere. But overcome that setback she did, and now she was in charge of what was shaping up to be the best Harvest Gala in years.

She pulled off her Tory Burch flats, setting them on the bottom step. The house was quiet, but Floyd's car was in the garage, so he must be working in his office. She should make sure he picked up his tuxedo at the cleaners. He had been disappointed that she hadn't already retrieved it, but she was too busy making sure the florist didn't sneak any carnations into the centerpieces that'd cost a fortune. He hadn't been feeling well. Tired and achy. But he was old, what did he expect? He better not think that a couple of aches and pains would get him out of attending the gala — there is nothing that would stop her from attending.

She should check on him, make sure he had everything he needed. That's what a good wife would do. Lorraine tapped on his office door, then opened it. Odd. His desk chair was empty. She scanned the room. It was all dark wood and polished leather, exactly the portrait of a successful businessman's office. The large wood desk was in front of bookshelves full of pictures of Floyd with various political and business celebrities from the fund-raisers he attended. To Lorraine's annoyance, not one picture of her or the girls, let alone their grandchildren, decorated the room. A large window overlooked the backyard where a stream tumbled beneath huge oak and willow trees. Ah, there he was, in front of the window in the large squashy leather chair where Floyd would often read or enjoy his nightly scotch.

She could see his arms and feet dangling around the edges. He must have fallen asleep. He'd be cranky tonight if she let him sleep too long. She walked around the chair's back, ready to shake him awake, but his eyes were open and his body was . . . wrong. His head rested on his shoulder like he didn't have any muscles to hold it up, his lips dark, almost blue. She picked up a hand. Cold. She dropped it and it flopped down, the gravity shifting his whole body, causing his head to drop from where it had been perched to his chest.

Floyd was dead.

She was a widow.

Again.

And Floyd had found an excuse to get out of the gala. He could always find the loophole.

She called 911, efficiently gave them the

necessary information, then picked up one of the crystal glasses next to his scotch decanter. She poured herself four fingers and settled into the chair behind his desk where she could see his profile.

She took her first sip. The first was always the worst, burning up her taste buds, shooting fire down her throat, but the second sip always made it worth it. That's when the layers of peat and wood, maybe a little brown sugar came through. This was his best stuff — some small batch distillery in the Highlands. Mac-something or another.

She took another sip. It really was magnificent scotch. They had just had their thirty-fourth wedding anniversary, and while Floyd may not have been a great husband, he had impeccable taste in everything. He had never once questioned her spending three hundred dollars on a pair of shoes or picking up the latest purse she'd spotted in *Vogue.* He did his thing, she did her thing. It worked. She may have been a bit lonely, but that's what friends were for. She could always head to the club and find someone to chat with over white wine and a Cobb salad.

She took another sip and let the flavors melt into her senses as this new widowhood settled into her bones.

She didn't have to worry about security, Floyd would have left her the estate in his will. They had agreed she would sell the company if he died first. She'd have more than enough for the rest of her life, even if she lived to one hundred and twenty. Which meant she didn't need to hide the truth anymore.

The EMTs arrived, confirmed he was dead, and they waited together for the police. Once the police arrived and asked her some questions about when she'd found him, they called the coroner, who again confirmed he was dead and packaged him off to the morgue. She agreed that it would be all right to come by the station in the morning to finish any paperwork.

With the house completely empty, she finished her scotch, picked up her phone, and called Roza. But before her old friend could speak, Lorraine did.

"Floyd is dead."

She heard Roza gasp, then take a meaningful pause before forging ahead.

"I'm sorry. Do you want me to come over? Did you call the girls?"

The scotch had wrapped around her like a fuzzy blanket. This time was so different from the last.

"No. I just wanted to let you know right

away. I'll let them know in the morning. There is no reason for them to rush over. I have the gala tonight."

Lorraine filled her in on the rest of the details and assured Roza she would call her again tomorrow. Roza always did worry about her.

She pushed Floyd's chair to where she always thought it belonged, next to the bookshelf and farther away from the window. That was better. Word would be out. In their small community, where everyone made sure to know everyone else's business, the grapevine would already be buzzing. She walked upstairs, picking up the shoes she'd left on the bottom step, and went to her room. Holding up the dress she had planned to wear, a beautiful tan gown with lace and crystals — and the right amount of coverage for a woman her age — she hung it back in the closet and pulled out a black gown, embellished with rhinestones, a few at the top, then increasing to a heavily bejeweled hem.

She couldn't skip the event and sit home staring at the walls. She had spent months planning, and now she would be the stoic widow who honored her husband's work ethic by seeing her event through to the end. It was what he would have done. Work always came first, and her job was the social hierarchy. He would have approved, and she would play the role gloriously, cementing the club's collective memory of him.

The house already felt too big for one person. The girls and Roza would come in the morning, but for now, she was truly alone.

No, Lorraine thought now as she lay in the hospital bed. *I wasn't entirely alone like Floyd had been.* Her husband had come to her. That was reassuring. She smiled, content to just watch her daughters interact, recognizing their resemblances. Victoria had his strong chin and long, dark lashes. Regina had his eyes. And frown. That same line on her forehead had returned, just like his always had when he worried, though Regina worried more than her father ever did, despite how hard she tried to hide it.

"What's that? Is she having another stroke?" Regina directed her question to the nurse, who was still fussing with the computer.

The nurse studied Lorraine's face, looking into her eyes and checking her pulse, measuring her for any difference from a few moments ago. Lorraine could have told them nothing had changed — if only she could speak.

"I think she's just smiling."

Regina studied her face again. Then sat down in her chair, still watching her mother. Victoria paused her flower arranging and glanced over.

"That's new," she said.

Lorraine barked out a laugh — more of a wheeze. Victoria wasn't wrong. Her younger daughter always spoke her mind. It was one of her traits she was most proud of, even if she was often at the end of her barbed comments. Victoria had strength and was willing to make the tough decisions life demanded. Regina was the one who floundered, that let her heart choose her path.

Worry line still intact, Regina returned to her sorting and Lorraine watched, finally realizing what she was going through. It was the accordion file, the one she kept tucked in the safe in her closet, where all her secrets were locked away. She was always careful to keep it covered so a casual glance wouldn't discover it. She'd often take it out and look at the memories it contained, memories only she and Roza knew.

The brown cardboard and paper organizer was clearly torn after so many years, edges ragged from use. Regina was pulling each section out and sorting the papers into piles. From where Lorraine lay, one pile looked like it consisted of important documents like her passport. Another pile contained photos — photos the girls had never seen.

"Hey, Vic, do you know who this is?"

She held one of the pictures up to her sister, who had been looking out the window. Lorraine could tell which one it was. Joe. In the photo a much younger — though not much slimmer, she was proud to say — version of herself wore a pink fitted polo with elastic-waisted jeans and a white belt. The jeans were all that would fit over her barely growing belly. She hadn't wanted to start wearing pregnancy clothes yet when she'd just started to fit into her normal size. Standing next to her was a handsome man with short dark hair, a strong chin, and familiar eyes holding a chubby baby girl. He wore a uniform. Lorraine had hated that blasted uniform. The baby had both hands clasped to his face, as if pulling him down for a kiss or making sure she had all of his attention. And she did. He was entranced by her sweet cheeks — they both were.

"That's Mom, but I don't know who the man is."

Victoria looked at the picture closer.

"No idea. I'm pretty sure that's you. I've

seen that dress in other baby pictures of you."

Of course it was Regina, and Victoria was there, too, under that white belt set to its last hole. She had been so happy.

"Mom's really rocking the bell bottoms." Regina checked the back for a date, which was written in Lorraine's hand: 1974, NOV. "She must have been pregnant with you by then. You can kind of see a tiny bump. She looks so happy."

Regina held the picture up for Lorraine to see, and Lorraine lifted her left hand to touch it, not sure if she had the strength to grasp the photo. She only managed to point at the blanket on her lap.

"Who's this holding me?" Regina asked.

Lorraine could only blink. Even if she could speak, she wouldn't answer. She'd kept the secret for so long, it seemed like a long-cherished dream rather than truth. Telling the girls wouldn't change anything in their lives; it would only create an abyss where their perfect family once stood. They didn't need to know what they had lost when they had never even known it existed. You couldn't miss someone you'd never known.

Once Regina realized she wasn't getting an answer, she set the picture down and moved on to the next pile, and the document peeking out from the stack caused Lorraine's chest to clench. She may not be able to tell them anything verbally, but all the pieces were there, if they put them together. She had selfishly kept these mementos rather than store the memories where they belonged: in her head. Fear spread through her body like numbness had hours ago. What would they think of her? Would they forgive her? Could they forgive her? She should have burned that certificate years ago, but it was the last thing she owned that said his name. Everything else of his had been taken from her.

Lorraine leaned forward with all her might. Perhaps she could grab the page, keep her secret for a few moments longer. Concentrating on gaining forward momentum, she rocked a few inches, then fell back against the pillows. Neither of the girls noticed her movement. She tried again, this time gaining another inch. Her breath was ragged, but fear compelled her to try one more time, gaining a few more inches, then the beeping started. In rushed a nurse, grabbing her wrist then checking a nearby machine. Regina stood and stared, mouth agape. The beeping continued until another nurse followed a cord from one of the machines to where she had pulled it loose from her arm during her pathetic attempt to grab the papers. Exhausted, she let the nurse fix the slack line as Regina thankfully closed her mouth and returned back to her sorting.

Regina peeled back her marriage certificate to Floyd Price and Victoria's birth certificate — setting them aside. There'd be no reason she'd find those interesting, of course. Then she picked up her own birth certificate, running her finger over the tiny footprints pressed onto the paper minutes after she was born. Lorraine held her breath as she waited for Regina to see it when another nurse entered, disrupting Regina's sorting.

"Okay, Mrs. Price, it's time to scan that head of yours. Here we go." The nurse lowered her bed so she was lying flat and made the necessary adjustments so the bed was movable. "We'll be back in an hour or so. Now would be a good time to get some supper, ladies. Dr. Patel will be back in a few hours to go over the results and discuss her treatment."

"Thank you." Her girls echoed each other, as polite as she'd raised them.

Lorraine wasn't paying attention to what the nurse said; instead she watched Regina as she set the birth certificate down and pulled out her notebook, jotting down information. Her Regina, always so diligent. Maybe she'd forget what paper she had held and move on to the next piece of paper in the pile. Maybe she wouldn't notice the discrepancy. Maybe she wouldn't ask the questions Lorraine didn't want to answer.

The nurses maneuvered the bed toward the door, taking her daughters out of her line of sight. Lorraine threw one last thought out as she was wheeled into the hallway, hoping her eldest could do her this one favor.

Please stop looking through the file. You might not like what you find.

■ ■ ■ ■

How Did You Meet My Father?

■ ■ ■ ■

Chapter Seven

"What if Mom can't ever talk again?" Vicky said as Lorraine was wheeled out the hospital room door. "What will we do?"

"She'll talk again. She's already talking."

"That isn't talking, that's gibberish. Stop trying to sugarcoat it. Mom's probably not going to recover from this. I was googling it just now."

Gina set down the paper she was holding and placed her palms on the table in front of her, counting to ten, then twenty. Vicky always insisted the answer was on the web.

"Of course you googled. Now that makes you an expert on strokes. The doctor has said recovery is possible, even in these cases where it seems like there is far to go. She'll just need to practice. Knowing how stubborn Mom is, she'll be back to her usual self in no time. Think positively."

"I know you'd rather think it will all be sunshine and unicorns, but you need to accept she might not get better."

"I choose to have a different point of view."

"I don't like the idea either — the thought even has me wishing she could complain about how I don't visit enough, or that you need to dye your hair more."

Gina's hands flew to her hairline, covering the inch of gray she knew was there.

"Not all of us can get to the salon every six weeks, or have blond hair, no matter how fake, that hides the gray when it does come. I'm thinking about letting it go natural anyway."

Vicky gasped.

"Are you trying to kill our mother? Because that'll do it. Did you learn nothing from her? Lesson number two, after coconut oil cures everything, is to never let them see your natural hair color." She tapped her chin with her finger. "Actually, just make sure I'm here when you tell her. I don't want to miss it. If that doesn't motivate her to start speaking again, nothing will."

Gina rolled her eyes.

"Stop it. She's been through a lot since Dad died. Moving out of the house was hard on her, and the club is farther away, so she's not seeing her friends as much."

"She's better off without them. Trust me,

the club ladies are more interested in gossip. You know what they used to say about Dad, right? Mom spent years combating those rumors."

Gina chewed her lip. She'd heard the rumors, yes, but they'd never bothered her.

"It was just gossip." She shrugged it off. "Mom never even acted like it bugged her."

Victoria snorted, such an indelicate sound. Gina loved that for all her sister's polish, she would still snort.

"Maybe, but Mom likes to keep her secrets." She looked out the window, again. "I'm going to grab some coffee. Want some?"

"Yeah. A lot of cream."

"I remember. You like a little coffee with your half-and-half."

Vicky left, leaving Gina to return to her piles of documents. She'd found the end-of-life and insurance information and given it to the admitting department, but now she was entranced by the photos and documents that she'd never seen. They pulled at her. She returned to the last piece of paper she'd picked up: a hospital birth certificate — her birth certificate. Her fingers traced the tiny foot and handprints, remembering how small May had looked in Drew's arms when she'd been born. She'd never seen her own hand and footprints, though, on her copies from Milwaukee County. None of them had the prints, and she didn't recall ever seeing this version.

Her eyes scanned the expected information about her weight and height and paused on the lines that said her parents' names. It read "Regina Ann Sandowski was born to Joseph and Lorraine Sandowski." She'd never heard that last name before, but all the other information was correct. It was her birthday, July 7, 1973. All the other information seemed right. Except the names. There must have been a mistake by the nurse who filled it out — she was born Regina Ann Price. Her mom probably kept it as a grudge against the hospital after they fixed it. Besides, right below it in the pile was her official birth certificate with her name listed correctly, as well as her father's, Floyd Price.

Gina set the birth certificates to the side, picking up the picture of the strange man holding baby her again. The baby in the photo couldn't take her eyes off the man whose face she was holding between her tiny hands. She had clearly known and liked him, and the smile on his face proved it was reciprocated. He looked familiar, but Gina couldn't figure out why. His nose had a bump like hers and Vicky's did. Maybe he was a long-dead cousin who had visited her mom. She set the photo on the birth certificate and returned to sorting and transferring the rest of the documents into the Noah's Ark box, replacing the lid when she finished. But after seeing the photo and the birth certificate she had to wonder — what other stories had her mother not told her?

"One cup of cream for you." Vicky set the cup on the table.

Gina held up the certificate.

"Have you ever seen this? It lists someone else as my dad. Weird, huh?"

Vicky examined the paper and shook her head, her ponytail swaying with the effort.

"Do you think it was a joke? Or maybe Mom had an affair and this is your real dad?" Vicky waggled her eyebrows. "You're a love child from our mother's torrid affair."

"Can you see our mom doing anything torridly? Let alone an affair."

"I don't know. It was the seventies; lots of crazy stuff happened. Maybe Roza knows."

Gina pictured her father. They'd never been close. He was older than their friends' dads and definitely from the "children are to be seen but not heard" school of parenting. Growing up, they were allowed only in the kitchen, the playroom, their bedrooms, and their bathroom. On special occasions, they were allowed in the dining room to eat with their parents, but everyday meals were adults in the dining room and kids at the kitchen table with Roza, keeping the noise to a minimum.

Her dad always had short gray hair circling his head, creeping back from his forehead with each passing year, and tiny ears. Gina could never figure out if his ears were truly small, or if his head was just that large. He looked like every other dad to her, not particularly special; soft in the middle, glasses he wore for reading, and a loud laugh he saved for other adults. Her most vivid memories of him from childhood were few, but they had made an impression. She remembered standing in front of him with her report card. If he was satisfied, she got a pat on the shoulder and a dollar for each A. For a C grade or lower, she would owe him money. She was still proud that she had never owed him a dime.

Or the summer she had her first lemonade stand. She was eleven and it was screaming hot, the kind of hot where she couldn't eat a Popsicle fast enough while outside before it melted down her hand in cherry-red rivulets. She had been saving up for a Cabbage Patch Doll like Tracy Bernard, one with a tuft of blond hair and a tiny tooth. She had only collected $5.64 from spare change she found in the couch and vending machine coin returns.

On that hot summer day, genius struck. She would start a lemonade stand and sell it for the high price of fifty cents a glass. She would make a killing. She spent the morning making batches of lemonade, setting up a chair and table, and decorating a sign that read BEAT THE HEAT! ICE COLD LEMONADE FOR 50¢! She sat down and waited for the crowds, but the streets were empty, everyone either at a nearby pool or hiding in their air-conditioning, until her dad came out with a crisp one-dollar bill.

"I'll take two glasses, please."

Gina poured the cups and pushed them to the edge of the table.

"That will be one dollar, please."

Her father handed it to her.

"You know what you need to do with that, right?"

Gina shook her head. She had planned for it to go into her doll fund.

"That's your first sale. You need to save it." He pulled a black pen from his chest pocket and wrote a few words on it. "Here. This is the first dollar your business has earned. It's important to save it as a reminder that everyone starts with a single dollar."

He patted her head and took the lemonade into the house. Gina looked at the bill. He had written the day's date, July 1, 1984, and "Dad" on it. At the time, she was disappointed that she wouldn't be able to use it to buy the doll, but now it was one of her favorite Dad memories. She still had that dollar in a box somewhere.

Vicky was probably right about Roza. Growing up, she and Vicky had been the only kids she knew who had a nanny. Nannies were something from Mary Poppins, not Milwaukee. Their nanny, Roza Wisniewski, was an older Polish woman — she wasn't really from Poland, but she was born and raised in Milwaukee's Polish neighborhood, south of downtown, where you could stand between neighboring houses, stretch out your arms, and touch both buildings. In all of her childhood memories, Roza hovered on the edges with her short white hair, large nose, and gentle hands, making sure to remove the girls from their father's line of sight before they annoyed him.

Roza's children were grown when she had started watching them. She always looked much older than their mother, more like a grandmother. She still lived in the house where she had raised her own family, renting out the lower flat to young couples getting started. Gina and Lorraine had tried to convince her to move closer to them, but she insisted the old neighborhood was the best. On most days, she would arrive at their house with a red kerchief wrapped around her head and a covered plate of something delicious, often pierogi. Her husband had run a small store not far from downtown Milwaukee, and one of their sons helped him manage it. Roza had started working as their nanny when Gina was a baby to earn money on the side.

In the twenty years that Roza had worked for them, Gina had never once seen her speak to their father. On his part, though, he never spoke to her either, or even acknowledged she was there.

"I'll ask Mom first," Gina said. Vicky settled into a chair, picking at an invisible speck of dust on her sweater. "What are we going to do if Mom doesn't get better?"

"I'm sure she has instructions in that file of hers. We can find her a good facility."

"We can't put Mom in a home."

"I love Mom, too, but do you really think it's a good idea to have her live with either of us? She might require a lot of extra care, and we both have families that need us, too. I have four kids, remember? Besides, if I tried to bring her home with me, Jeff would leave me for sure." Vicky frowned at the thought.

"You say that like he's already contemplating it," Gina said with a smile, expecting her sister to come back with a quick retort.

Vicky shrugged.

"Wait, is something going on?" Gina's forehead wrinkled. "What happened?"

"Nothing, really. The usual I suppose. He's been working later than normal. Not as interested in me. Doesn't text me back as quickly as he used to. It's probably just the big project he's been working on, but this time feels different somehow." She nibbled her lip, a bad habit she and Gina shared. "Or maybe I'm the one who's different."

"What if you surprise him at the office for dinner sometime? Pull the ole' naked-under-a-trench-coat trick?"

"When would I have the time? Between ballet and soccer practice? After cutting up the orange slices but before doing the laundry? My entire life is keeping them out of his hair so he can work all the time. We're not a family, we're a corporate day care. I can't remember the last time we did anything just the two of us."

"The world wouldn't end if you skipped some obligations for a date night. I promise the kids won't require therapy — at least not because you missed a library hour or a second grade basketball game."

Vicky bounced her foot, ignoring Gina's suggestion. It was clear she didn't want to talk about it anymore — at least not while they were already worrying about their mother. "Well, I'm here for you. Whatever you need," Gina said.

Her sister nodded as the nurse wheeled their mom back into the room, finally returned from her CT scan. Her eyes were wide and found Gina's immediately.

"How did it go?" Gina asked.

"Dr. Patel will be in shortly to discuss the results, but your mom did great. She's a real trouper." The nurse smiled down, securing the bed and making sure all the tubes and wires were connected as they should be. "I'll get some fresh water for you, Mrs. Price."

Gina picked up the picture and birth certificate and held it out to her mother.

"Mom, I found these in the file, but I don't know who this man is or why this birth certificate is different. Was there a mistake at the hospital?"

She laid the papers on her mom's lap where she could reach them. Her mom patted them but didn't pick them up. Her eyes grew watery. *She must be frustrated because she can't grasp them,* Gina thought, scooching them closer.

"Can you tell me who this man is?"

Her mom worked her lips and a low hum came from her throat.

"Fa . . . Fabershim. Fabershim."

"Fabershim? That doesn't make sense." Gina looked at Victoria. "Does that sound like a name? A word? Maybe she's slurring. Fab he is? Favorite him?"

"Please don't ever go on game shows," Victoria said. "You're the worst guesser. Dr. Patel said she might only be able to speak gibberish. We'll need to be patient. Let's just ask Roza, she'll probably know."

Gina nodded and kissed her mom before picking up the papers. Tears dripped from her mother's cheeks, so Gina wiped them away with a tissue.

"I know, Mom, you're frustrated. I promise we'll get you the help you need so you can get back to normal as quickly as possible."

"Fabershim." Her mom's voice was much softer.

Dr. Patel breezed into the room, her dark

hair pulled into a bun at the nape of her neck, and displayed the images of Lorraine's scans on the large TV in the room. Even Gina could see something wasn't right, and a glance at Vicky's face told her that her sister saw it, too. On the screen was a brain shape with the exception of a large shaded blob on the left side, like someone had set a drippy coffee mug on the film. It didn't look good.

"Here, you can see, is the damage from the stroke." Dr. Patel directed her comments toward her mom, as if she could follow along. That must be a good sign. "This confirmed it was ischemic, and it's quite large, which explains why your motor functions and speech have diminished."

She kept talking and gesturing, but Gina's mind stared at the blob, absorbing its enormity. There was so much she didn't know about her own mother, and now she might not be able to ask her ever again. How could a brain sustain that much damage and ever recover? Each sister stood by their mom as Dr. Patel explained the upcoming rehab, tests, possible surgeries. Best- and worst-case scenarios. The worst case was bad — one out of four stroke victims would have another, usually fatal, one. Gina took notes and asked questions as the doctor spoke. Somehow a part of her brain was able to stay present even as another part adjusted to her new reality.

"But she spoke. She just did it before you came in. That has to be a good sign. She said 'Fabershim,' " Gina said.

"Yes. She is trying to communicate." Dr. Patel looked at Lorraine. "You know what's happening and understand, but your brain is blocking you from getting that information out. It's called apraxia of speech, and speech therapy will help you rebuild those connections. Your brain underwent a lot of damage, and older patients don't always bounce back fully. Now, I'd recommend all of you get some rest."

"One of us should stay with her," Gina said. "She shouldn't be alone. I can stay tonight."

Dr. Patel rubbed Gina's shoulder.

"Your heart is in the right place, but there will be some long days coming and a lot of decisions to make. We'll call if anything changes, but she's stable for now. You should both go home and get some sleep."

The sisters nodded.

"And Gina," Dr. Patel continued, almost visibly shifting gears from doctor mode to fellow-parent mode. "I'm glad our kids decided to hang out today. I worry about

Connor when he has to spend these long school-break days by himself. And Connor always says the nicest things about May. If he's still there when you get home, can you send him home for a late dinner, please?"

What was she talking about? May had never returned her text and certainly didn't say that she was having a guest over. Gina smiled and nodded, pretending she knew what was going on in her own house.

"Off to finish my rounds, then I'm home for dinner," Dr. Patel said with a smile. "See all three of you tomorrow."

Before Gina's mind could adjust to the topic change, Dr. Patel had left, moving on to her next patient. It must be a good sign that May was hanging out with someone, right? And Connor was a good kid, but it would have been nice to know before being blindsided by his mother. And May wasn't really supposed to have friends over without asking first — but Gina was too happy to find out her daughter was doing something normal instead of closeted up in her room.

Gina tucked the birth certificate and picture into her purse and gave her mom a kiss on the forehead.

"Vic, the key is in its usual spot. I'll get your room ready so you can slide under the covers when you come in. Take your time."

Vicky nodded absently, still looking over the scans hanging on the screen.

As Gina drove home along familiar dark streets, she reached for her phone, wanting to call Drew and tell him about everything going on with her mother and with May, but she paused. Right. He wasn't there to answer. Using her right hand, she rubbed the two wedding bands on her left hand, wishing she could just ask him a simple question again.

After she graduated college, Gina was hired by Harley-Davidson as a technical writer in their IT department. It wasn't glamorous, but it paid well enough for her to have an apartment far enough away from her parents' house that it was inconvenient to swing by or join them at the club — that had always been more Victoria's scene. She'd never cared enough about who was marrying whom, or who was vacationing in the Caribbean. More often than not, it seemed like a bad parody of *Dirty Dancing.* And not the fun dancing parts.

She had a small group of work friends who would go to movies or out to the bars on the weekends, but she would also host mini dinner parties, cooking wonderful meals on a budget, like lasagna or beef stew.

She'd supply the food and her friends would bring the wine.

Sure, she wished she had more dates, but she hadn't met someone worth spending more than an evening with until she was assigned to a project for a new engine. She walked into the first meeting with the mechanic who would be her resource. She didn't know what she'd expected — not much of anything, really — but it certainly wasn't the tall, blond man she met. At the time, his sun-kissed hair was long enough to tuck behind his ears. His gentle, blue eyes made her feel safe and welcome immediately. Never mind the stunning black-and-white tattoo that covered his very well-muscled arm. A winding road twisted up his forearm where a motorcycle, complete with waving flags, cruised. The winding road disappeared under his black T-shirt's sleeve, and she, from the first moment she saw it, longed to pull up the cotton and follow its trail.

Gina knew she was ogling. She also knew the ogling was not professional. Still, it took her a full minute to care and pull it together enough to speak.

"Hi, I'm Gina Price. I'll be writing the documentation for the new engine."

He wiped his hand on a rag from his back

jeans pocket before extending it toward her. "I'm Drew Zoberski."

His hand was rough and warm, and grasping it made her knees wobbly. Or maybe the wobble came from his smile. Or his fitted T-shirt. There were so many reasons to wobble, the urge to make a list of them coursed through her.

"I guess I'll give you a rundown of the engine, then you can let me know if you have questions."

Gina nodded and diligently took notes.

Then the next day she came back.

"Um, Drew, I have a few follow-up questions." Today his shirt was blue, and it made his eyes electric. How could eyes be that color without the help of Photoshop? They were like when there was no line between the water and sky on a clear summer day at the beach — just perfect blue for a perfect day. That's what seeing his eyes felt like — the perfect day. She realized he was waiting for her question, a smile in those eyes twinkling at her. "Could you explain what a piston does, again? So sorry to bother you, but my notes from yesterday don't make much sense."

He scrunched his forehead, and Gina knew why — you didn't work at the greatest motorcycle company in the world and not know what a piston did. Drew patiently explained, Gina thanked him, and returned to her desk, mortified and victorious at the same time.

The next day she asked about valves. The next day about spark plugs. The next day about bolts.

The next day he asked her out.

When he picked her up on his Harley, she heard him coming well before she saw him. He handed her a leather jacket and helmet, making sure she was well protected before they rode the rolling hills around Holy Hill, enjoying the fall foliage, and stopping for the best bar burgers she had ever had in one of the small towns that dotted the area. After dinner, he held up the jacket as she slid her arms into the stiff leather sleeves. He straightened her collar and slowly zipped the jacket closed, her heart racing as he finished. Standing so near to him, surrounded by the scent of leather, she swayed into him, her face turned up to his. His lips found hers, soft and eager. His arms wrapped around her, leather creaking on leather. She never wanted it to end. It was the perfect first kiss — all leather and sunshine.

After that, they spent time together every day. She loved how when he really smiled, his eyes almost squinted closed, and how his kind soul saw the best in her, and how he could fix anything with a motor, from the broken KitchenAid mixer she found at a rummage sale to an antique Indian motorcycle engine.

On a June evening, he came to her apartment after work and ended up under the Civic her parents bought her as a bribe to go to college. She had wanted to go to culinary school, or anywhere that didn't involve more essays and struggling for decent grades, but she had wanted a car more.

He slid out from beneath the car and stood, his fingers greasy, and wiped them on a towel already covered in dark streaks. She loved watching him wipe his hands, even if it was on one of her towels.

"I'm going to need to replace your muffler. I'll pick up the parts and do it this weekend. It'll be fine, just noisy until then."

She wrapped her arms around his neck, pulling him close so their bodies aligned, stretching up on her toes so she was closer to his face.

"You're too good to me. I think you'll need a reward."

"I'll take it, but let me get cleaned up or I'll get you covered in grease."

"You make that sound like a bad thing."

She reached for his lips and he bent to meet hers, careful to keep his hands off her grease-free clothes. Before she could completely distract him, he pulled back.

"I'm going to get cleaned up, then we can resume." She followed him into her apartment. This was the perfect life. Working all day, then spending every night with Drew. She'd let her eyes follow him down the hallway — man, did she like to watch him go — before pulling the ingredients for dinner out of the fridge. Her kitchen phone rang, and she answered it, on cloud nine.

"Regina, I want you to come to the club this Friday," her mom said.

"Hi, Mom."

"A new family from Connecticut just joined. They have a son who is already a partner at one of the big law firms. I want you to meet him before the Meier girls get their hooks into him."

"I have plans that night, Mom."

She hadn't told her parents about Drew. At first, she didn't know if the budding relationship would last, but now she didn't want to subject him to their scrutiny, at least not yet. She wanted to keep him to herself for a little while longer.

"Break them. This is more important. You

aren't getting any younger. Even if you meet someone tomorrow, it'll be two years to date, then at least eighteen months to plan a decent wedding, and another year before kids. You'll almost be thirty by then."

Her mother made thirty sound like her ovaries would shrivel and fall out of her uterus, rendering her useless for the rest of her life. With every conversation, Gina felt like she wasn't living up to her parents' dreams of perfection. That Gina's dreams were irrelevant — not that Gina had specific dreams for her future, but she knew she didn't want to be like her parents, shuttling endlessly between the house and the country club.

"Mom. No. I'm not interested in the Connecticut boy or anyone else from the club." Fresh from the shower, Drew stood at the kitchen sink, the fluorescent lights bouncing off the plywood cupboards and bland cream countertops, but his damp hair making her heart thump. She took a deep breath. It was time for him to meet her parents. She twisted the phone cord around her finger, then let it unwind. "I've actually been seeing someone."

Drew turned with his eyebrows raised, somehow becoming even more sexy.

"Oh, Regina. That's wonderful. What does he do?"

Of course.

"He works at Harley, too, but he's planning to start his own business." Let her parse that out.

"Why don't the both of you join us on Friday, then?"

"We really do have plans." They were spending the day at Polish Fest, then meeting some friends for dinner and games later that night. "How about we stop in for cocktails really quick so you can meet him?"

"I'll tell your father. And make sure to wear a color. All those neutrals wash you out. A skirt wouldn't kill you, either, Regina."

Gina hung the phone back up on the wall, the cord swinging for a few moments before going still.

"I guess I need to buy a sport coat, then?" Drew said.

"I should have asked you first." Gina scrunched her nose. "I can cancel."

She wrapped her arms all the way around his waist, and he threaded his fingers into her dark hair. He smelled like her shampoo — an ocean breeze, and his Drew-scent that no amount of soap could wash off. She loved when he showered at her apartment

— it was like a preview of their future together, even if that preview included a wet towel on her bathroom floor. It was totally worth it for the breathtaking man in front of her.

"Beautiful, these are the people that made you the brilliant woman I love. I want to meet them."

"I'm sorry in advance."

He smiled and kissed her nose.

"I've ridden to Sturgis with guys who can make a man cry by just looking at him. Your parents don't scare me."

"Would you be willing to sign a waiver? Or I could give you a reward for future bravery?"

Her fingers curled around his belt loops, and she tugged him closer.

"I'm all cleaned up, so I'll take that advanced reward, if you're offering."

Drew bent down to kiss her neck as she pulled him toward the bedroom.

"For you, I'm always offering."

Gina missed his fearless attitude. Nothing happened in their lives together that could upset him, and his calm always brought her back to reality. She should have given him ten rewards for future bravery that day.

Between her mom's stroke, the mysterious birth certificate, and May's rebellion, she needed to lean on some of Drew's strength now more than ever, as the questions kept bubbling up from her brain to hover before her eyes.

1. How do I get May to talk to me?
2. What if my mom never speaks again?
3. What if she dies?
4. Who is Joe Sandowski?
5. Dammit, Drew, why aren't you here when I need you?

"Dammit, Drew," Gina whispered.

His strength and patience weren't available now, so she turned to the only reserve she had: make more lists. But lists didn't feel like quite enough at the moment.

Chapter Eight

May and Connor collapsed on the couch, sweaty and laughing.

"Okay, I admit defeat. You are the Wii bowling master. I'll never doubt your Wii athletic skills again," Connor said.

"And don't forget it."

The couch in the basement was wide and squashy, the perfect place to get cozy with blankets and watch a movie, or sit close to a boy you liked. May couldn't help but lean into his shoulder, solid from training for baseball year-round. All that laughter had worked muscles she hadn't used in years. It felt good to be wobbly and tired. May flicked the TV back to a regular channel.

"You're both a bowling and brownie master — that's epic in my book."

He turned to look at her, and their faces were suddenly inches apart. She'd never been this close to a boy before — at least, not one that she liked. His deodorant or cologne, probably some weird scent name like Icy Chill or Rugged Rocks, smelled like boy and drew her closer — she never wanted to forget it. What if he kissed her? She'd never kissed anyone before, but she liked the idea of Connor kissing her, especially after the fun afternoon they shared. What if she kissed him? Her body tingled at the thought, not even caring about how cliché it was to kiss a boy on the basement couch. It would be something a million other people had experienced, something she could share with Olivia, something to make her feel normal.

That's it. She was going to do it. She was going to kiss Connor Patel.

In the time it took her to decide, Connor turned to face her, putting more room between them. His face looked serious.

Oh no, something was wrong.

Did she have bacon breath?

That would be a good thing, right?

He gently took her hands in his. They were shaking and a little clammy, but so were hers, so it was probably okay. Then he moved them up her arms, over the long sleeves and onto her shoulders.

"May." He paused and took a really deep breath. "Can I . . . can I kiss you?"

Now it was her turn to suck in her breath.

He wanted to kiss her, too? He wanted to kiss her. HE WANTED TO KISS HER! Wait, she hadn't responded yet and wasn't sure if she could speak. She managed a nod instead.

Connor smiled, one corner twitching up a little farther. He leaned in closer to her. This was really happening. Then he paused.

"But, like, more than just a peck. Okay?"

How did she know? She'd never kissed anyone. Had he? What if she was awful? More than a peck . . . ? Like with tongue? The pulse in her throat hammered, making her tongue feel thick and her mouth dry.

She nodded again.

Connor licked his lips, so she did, too. Maybe that made it better. Whatever, she'd follow his lead.

He closed his eyes, so May closed hers.

The distance between them narrowed, and he set his lips on hers. They were kissing! His mouth was soft and a little damp. He moved his lips like he was eating M&M's off a tabletop, so she mimicked him, eyes still shut. He switched the angle of his head so it was going the other way, so she adjusted hers. He slid his right hand into her hair like they did on all the CW shows. He pulled her head closer to his and opened his mouth wider. She did the same, their breath mingling in the space. Okay, she liked this. She really liked Connor. What would Olivia say? She didn't think Olivia had kissed anyone yet.

Connor made a sound and moved his left hand to her lower back, so she reached her arms around his neck, bringing them even closer together. She tried to envision all the places the people on TV put their hands when kissing because she didn't want to run out of ideas. Then Connor stuck his tongue in her mouth. It was hot and wet and eager. And weird, like he was trying to lick her tongue. This couldn't be right. Right? It seemed sort of unsanitary and kind of gross but also good. She opened her eyes to see if Connor was as surprised as she was at this new sensation, but his lids were closed. Because she was so close to him, he looked like the Cyclops they had learned about during the Greek unit in social studies. May burst out laughing. Connor pulled back, his forehead scrunching and his eyes becoming two again.

"Did I do something wrong?" he asked. His voice sounded deeper.

"No, no. I'm sorry. I just opened my eyes, and you had one eye. It seemed funny."

"You opened your eyes . . . while we were kissing?"

"Yeah."

"And then you laughed?"

"Yeah."

He ran his hand through his almost black hair, leaving some sections sticking out at odd angles. Had she offended him? Was this a major kissing foul? It was too late to lie, she'd already admitted it.

"Was it that bad?"

"No. Not at all." May chewed on her lip. "It was a little different than I expected."

"Me, too . . ." He rubbed his pinky finger against her hand. "Different like way better. If that's kissing, I want a lot more."

Wait . . . was that his first kiss, too? How did they even know if they did it right? What if they were both awful kissers, and they couldn't tell? Did she even like it? The first bit was nice. Totally nice. Having his tongue in her mouth seemed like overkill, but maybe she just needed to get used to it.

"Wanna try again?" she asked.

His yes came in the form of action and before she could blink, his lips were connected to hers again, bumping his teeth against hers in his eagerness, but he pulled back before either of them chipped a tooth. The second time was nicer. She knew what to expect and relaxed into it, enjoying the twirling sensation in her stomach. Connor moved his hand to her back, finding the small bit of skin between the top of her pants and the bottom of her shirt. With each kiss, their tongues twisted, and it seemed more normal. She leaned into him, sending him backward on the couch with her on top, their legs all tangled up.

Then a "Hello" from upstairs filtered through the kissing fog.

Her mom.

Was home.

She pushed herself off Connor, losing her balance because their legs were intertwined and all mixed up, and fell to the floor with a yelp. Shit. She hadn't told her mom that Connor was over. She wasn't even supposed to have guests without asking first. Let alone making out in the basement.

"May? Where are you?" Her mom's voice rang through the house.

"Basement," she shouted back, then wiped her face, ran her hands through her hair, and smoothed her clothes. Her lips thumped from all the kissing. She was certain her mom would be able to tell with one look. How horrifying! Connor sat up and pulled a fringed pillow onto his lap, looking cool and collected. And cute. May smiled at him, flopped back onto the couch, careful to leave a few feet between them, and tossed him a Wii controller.

They heard her mom's steps before she appeared in the doorframe at the top of the stairs.

"Hey, Connor." Mom didn't seem surprised to see him here. Wow, she was playing it cool. Either she didn't care that May had a boy over while she was gone, or she didn't want to yell at her in front of a guest. Probably the second option. "It's nice to see you. I saw your mom at the hospital."

The hospital? Her mom looked okay.

"Why were you at the hospital?"

"I texted you. Grandma had a stroke this afternoon."

Her mom said it so matter-of-factly — that must mean Grandma was okay. She was acting like this on purpose so May had to ask questions. She didn't want to fall for it, but she wanted to know about Grandma.

"Is she going to be okay?"

Regina's mouth twitched upward.

"So far. Connor's mom is her neurologist, so we have the best." She smiled at Connor.

May slouched into the couch cushions and crossed her arms. Her mom's eyes studied the room, taking in their very appropriate distance and viewing choice.

"What have you been up to all day?" Regina asked.

"Playing Wii and watching TV," May said.

"May made me the most incredible brownies with bacon and caramel. Regular brownies are ruined forever now," Connor said. May almost elbowed him.

"Bacon." Her mom's eyes narrowed. Busted. "Bacon does make everything better."

"That's what May said. She learned from the best, obviously."

May looked at Connor. Was he sweet-talking her mom? What a suck-up! Though it was kind of sweet — maybe he wanted to be on her mom's good side because he really liked her.

"Well, your mom said if you were still here to send you home. She'll be home soon for dinner. Do you want me to give you a ride? It's gotten chilly out."

"No." He set the pillow aside and stood. "The cold will feel good. I'll probably jog most of the way."

He followed May's mom up the stairs as she fussed about getting his coat. May clicked off the TV and followed after them then walked Connor to the door. She felt super weird again, now that her mom was here, like she didn't know what to say.

"Thanks for coming over. It was nice to have company."

"Maybe we could do it again."

May blushed and couldn't even look directly at him, staring at the edge of his coat collar instead.

"Yeah."

"I'll text you later."

"Okay."

He waved and disappeared into the already dark evening. May could hear her mom in the kitchen, loudly pounding out chicken breasts to make a point about catching her in her vegetarian lie. But for some reason, getting caught didn't feel so bad.

Chapter Nine

Lorraine wasn't one to dwell on the past, but now it was jumping up to find her. Seeing that picture and realizing everything she thought was safely buried was about to resurface filled her with fear, more fear than when she thought she was going to die alone. After Regina left, Victoria went to grab more coffee and something to read. Outside the hospital room door stood two older gentlemen, clearly together. Older, of course, being a relative term, as they were several years younger than she was. One of the men had his arms wrapped around the other, as he wept inconsolably, shoulders shaking. They were sad, yes, but they had each other. Whatever difficult moment they were experiencing, they were experiencing it together. She and Floyd had never had that, could never have had that. Alone again in her hospital room, Lorraine's hand found the gold cross still hanging on her neck as she let her mind drift to how her second marriage had all begun.

Lorraine's father welcomed Floyd Price for a small family dinner. Floyd owned a business in Illinois that her father worked with frequently, supplying him with the custom-cut metal that Floyd's company manufactured into parts used in the agriculture industry. It wasn't glamorous, but it was essential. He had never married or had a family of his own. Now approaching forty-five and looking to move to Milwaukee to expand his business, a wife and children seemed a natural way to slide into society and make new connections. Over brandy old-fashioneds and cigarettes, her parents made the introductions while Lorraine sipped tea, leaving her chocolate Bundt cake untouched. Regina sat on her ever-shrinking lap picking up the small cake pieces Lorraine had cut for her and stuffing them in her mouth. Floyd would get an insta-family, and Lorraine would get financial security for herself and her daughters. Lorraine numbly listened to her father list all the wonderful reasons this was an ideal situation — most had to do with selling parts for machines she knew nothing about.

"Is this what you want, Lorraine?" her

mother asked, leaning in close so she could whisper.

Lorraine brushed cake crumbs off of Regina's frilly pink dress, the baby's fingers damp from sticking them in her mouth. The one still in her belly squirmed, pressing a foot against a rib. She pressed on the spot, letting the little one know she had noticed. She was already exhausted from lack of sleep. What would it be like once she had two children? How would she work? Feed them? Clothe them? She'd finished high school, yes, but she'd never been on her own.

She nodded.

"If we are going to do this, it will have to be seamless. There will be no question of whose children they are."

Floyd was handsome in a full-lipped, boyish way, with gray speckles in his combed-back dark hair, exposing a high, smooth forehead. His pale skin was clean-shaven, a nice compliment to his custom-made suits and clearly expensive shoes. Neither of them suffered under the delusion that this was a love match.

"I'm sure Lorraine feels the same way," her father said. He puffed on his cigarette, blowing out smoke like a steam engine.

Lorraine sat up straighter. She wanted to

cry, to scream, to break things. But she wouldn't. She didn't have any way of supporting herself and her children the way they deserved, and this was the best way forward, now that Joe was gone. Lorraine had to believe she was doing the right thing. She couldn't do it on her own, not without support. This was the support offered, financial and social stability and the best chance for her girls. Regina started to fuss, and her father shot her a look.

"We'll be married within the week," she interrupted. "How will we explain why people haven't seen me at the club the last few years? Why I haven't spoken to anyone from school?"

"We've told people you were working out east for some life experience before you settled down," her mom said. "People stopped asking after a while."

Oh. Lorraine didn't know they had lied to people about her. They didn't like her decisions, so they had rewritten history, and now it would be her real life.

"All right." Taking control of the conversation eased some of the pain. She thought about what would make the arrangement as seamless as possible. "If anyone asks, we'll say we married quickly, and had our first child." The world *our* stuck on her tongue, making her want to gag. Floyd seemed nice enough, but nobody compared to Joe. And though raising her children as Floyd's wouldn't be easy, it would be possible. "We can sort out the exact details later. With our second child, I felt unwell and wanted to be closer to home, so we've moved back. By the time I'm back in public, people will be more interested in the children than the timeline."

"We'll start dropping hints this weekend that you're coming home with big news," her mom said. Her parents were clearly old pros at manipulation.

Lorraine stood, but before she left the room she had one more request.

"I would also like to hire a nanny to help care for the children, and a housekeeper to help keep up the house." If she was going to do this, she was going to do it in style, and with allies.

Regina wiggled in her arms and started to fuss. Lorraine could smell that she needed her diaper changed and soon the entire room would know, too, but she waited for his answer. She wasn't the only one getting something out of this arrangement. He was getting a turnkey family. Floyd met her gaze and gave her a measured smile.

"Of course. You can have whatever help

you require. I already have a housekeeper, but you should hire a nanny. I want all of us to feel . . . taken care of."

She nodded and left the room, carrying Regina upstairs. Yes, they would all be taken care of.

Lorraine pinned Regina's diaper and slipped her droopy arms and legs into her tiny pajamas. She'd fallen asleep mid-diaper change, her sweet cheeks still flecked with cake crumbs. Lorraine brushed them off, then scooped her up. She sniffed her head, smelling faintly of the Baby Magic lotion she always used on her after baths. Her tiny hand found the gold cross around her neck, and clutched it, pulling on the chain around Lorraine's neck in her sleep, those dear tiny feet nudging the top of her round belly. Lorraine swayed in the dim bedroom they had been sharing for a few days. Right now, holding her child, with another inside her, she almost felt whole again, like the nightmare of their loss had never happened. She let herself pretend, just for a moment.

"Lorraine, might I have a word, please?"

The peaceful moment was shattered by Floyd's smooth voice. She nodded and set Regina into the old crib her mother had pulled out of the attic. She closed the door and stood in front of her soon-to-be husband in the narrow hallway, smelling cigarettes and coffee and cologne. She stood in front of him patiently, waiting for him to speak first.

"I have a few more items I wish to discuss without your parents."

Lorraine's mouth dried. She hadn't given any thought to what marriage to Floyd might entail, beyond the solving of a problem. Panic swelled at the thought of being with someone other than Joe in that way, no matter how pleasant he was.

Lorraine propped her hands on her belly. Exhaustion was creeping up and she just wanted to go to bed, but she wasn't going to try to guess what he had to say. Floyd looked around the hallway, then spoke.

"I won't be expecting you to perform any marital duties." His mouth formed the words like they were uncomfortable to say aloud. "In fact, I have no interest in sharing a bed with you. Or any woman. Do you understand?" He looked at her directly.

What did he just say? Her mouth popped open. This wasn't something ever discussed in polite conversation.

"Lorraine?" His voice was edged with uncertainty and his eyes darted downstairs, where her parents were. He had taken a big risk revealing his secret. Could she keep it for him?

"I do." She said the words slowly. Floyd let his shoulders relax at her response.

"It's important we're honest — honest about everything — for this partnership to work. We need each other, and I really believe this . . . arrangement can benefit us both. Now you understand that our marriage will help keep people from asking questions I'd rather they didn't ask, for the sake of my business and my personal life and now your personal life as well. I want you to know, though, that I will have . . ." He paused to look over his shoulder again. "I will have friends. Very discreet friends, of course. I understand if you feel the need to do the same, as long as you are equally discreet."

Lorraine didn't think she could have been any more shocked than she already was, but she was wrong. Not only did he just tell her he would be taking lovers — men — but that she could do the same. She had been worried he would expect to make love to her, but the truth was quite the opposite. The new information settled into her brain. Her soon-to-be husband was a homosexual. Their marriage would be . . . well, a working one.

Other than caring for her children, her entire life would be an act, a lie. She would have to wake up each day and pretend their marriage was real, that their family was real. She and Floyd would protect each other with very few expectations beyond what was best for the whole. Was she trading her chance at another love for this stability Floyd was offering?

But no. She'd already had her one true love. There would be no others. But there would also be no room for mourning Joe. She had a choice. She could live this life, give her children the future they deserved in a stable home, the knowledge they would never experience the heartbreak of growing up fatherless. Or she could be honest about Joe and struggle every day and every moment to survive on only happy, but brief memories. She wasn't naive, her memories, she knew, would not be enough to sustain them.

The reality of the situation, of what Floyd was asking of her and of what she was asking of him, hardened around her, a mask she could use. She would be the supportive wife and encouraging mother, always putting her children first.

Lorraine let her hands fall off her belly and stood up taller. She wanted to be as tall as he was when she spoke, when she decided her own path instead of letting fate take over.

With each moment of resolution, her protective armor grew more and more firm, her practicality rising to the surface.

"I understand and agree to your terms, Floyd. We'll be good for each other. Hopefully, good to each other, as well. Now, if you'll excuse me, I need rest." She patted her stomach. "I'm sure my father would enjoy speaking with you more in his study."

She about-faced, opened the bedroom door where Regina already lay, and left Floyd in the hallway, closing the door behind her on a sigh. It was done. She crawled into bed still wearing her black dress, clinging to the belief that a hard decision was still better than being flung about by love.

Lorraine hadn't remembered those early days with Floyd in many years. Looking out into the hallway, she was sad for both herself and Floyd that they'd never had the same intimacy as the couple in the hallway. Their marriage had been friendly, yes, if not affectionate, and she would always be grateful for the security the marriage had given her. She had been single-minded in her separation of her past and future, thinking the latter could not exist without abandoning the former. At her age, she was starting to realize her foolishness, and it stung.

From behind closed lids, Lorraine heard Victoria return, sipping a cup of coffee and flipping through a magazine from the gift shop. Lorraine didn't open her eyes. She had more choices to make, hopefully better choices than the ones she'd made in the past, and she wasn't sure how long she had to make them.

How Are We Alike? Different?

Chapter Ten

Gina couldn't believe it had been less than twenty-four hours since she had found her mom. Her eyes struggled to open, still heavy with the rest that hadn't come after a sleepless night sorting out what she knew and what she didn't know. She'd heard Vicky creep into the guest room sometime after midnight, and her sister was still sleeping when Gina left to go to Roza's. Having solved nothing during the night, she left a note for May and Vic by the coffeemaker and headed out. She had so many questions that needed answering, and they needed answering before she took Grilled G's out for the day.

She stopped her car in front of Roza's duplex, or a "Polish flat" as they were called in Milwaukee. It was tidy and white, with a base of painted cinder blocks and cheerful red trim. White painted stairs led to her porch on the second story. The first floor had a separate entrance in the back for her tenants who lived there. As long as Gina could remember, Roza had lived in this neighborhood of Polish flats and small yards. Neighbors had come and gone, but Roza remained. Her ancient blue VW Beetle sat on the street out front. She'd been driving it so long that it had evolved from rust bucket to restored vintage machine. Every part on it had probably been replaced over the years, many of them by Drew. Happy thought.

Gina knocked on the front door, holding the mystery papers in one hand and a bag of Roza's favorite candy, a Polish caramel in a white and yellow wrapper, in the other. When Roza had been their nanny, she used to sneak the caramels to her and Vicky to keep their mouths busy during errands or when they needed to be silent.

Roza's familiar smiling face answered the door in her housedress, pulling Gina into a hug before she could say anything, her wrinkled pale hands cool but strong from years of kneading dough and wrangling small children. As cool as her hands were, she was always warm, like her enormous heart could heat the entire world. Her house always smelled like something delicious — even at this early hour. Right now, it smelled like chocolate chip cookies. She must have grandkids coming.

"Gina, what a perfect surprise! I was just thinking about you and your mom. How is she?" Roza guided her to the kitchen table where they sat down across from each other.

Gina blinked. With all that had happened in the last day, she and Victoria had completely forgotten to tell Roza about the stroke. Guilt welled up inside her. How could she have forgotten to tell one of the most important people in her and her mom's lives about what had happened to Lorraine? "Mom . . . Mom had a stroke yesterday." Gina blurted it out, probably best to get the confession over as soon as possible.

Roza brought her hands to her mouth. "Is she . . . ?"

"She's good. She can't talk or move well. Yet. But the doctor says she can fully recover. She'll start rehab soon. Vicky came up, too." Roza still looked shocked. Gina set her candy offering on the table, sliding it across to Roza. "I'm so sorry I didn't call you sooner. I should have."

Roza patted her hand and slid the candy over to the side.

"These things happen. I don't expect your first thought in a time of crisis to be me.

Now my own kids." She rolled her eyes. "That's a complaint for another day. Thank you for the candy. I'll have to hide it before the grandkids come. Today's my daughter's date night, so I get to spoil them."

As Roza spoke, she set a cup of light tan coffee and a plate of cookies in front of Gina. She knew her so well.

"Tell me what happened, and not just the bright side. I want to know even the stuff your mom doesn't want anyone else to know."

So Gina did, the weird word her mom said over and over, how unsettling it was to see her face droop, the terrifying black splotch on the brain scan. She even described how and why she had to change her mom's clothes.

"Smart thinking with the skirt. You did the right thing. That poor woman, her pride must hurt as much as the stroke did." Roza bit into a cookie. "I'll visit her later today."

"She would love that." Gina reached into her pocket. "As big as that news is, that's not really why I'm here. When I brought Mom to the hospital, I had grabbed all the documents they would need to admit her. In the paperwork, I found these." She slid the birth certificate and photo across the table and tapped on the man's face. "Do you know who this man is? And why this birth certificate is wrong? I thought you might know."

Roza's lips pursed as she studied them. She picked up the photo, covering her mouth with her free hand, then set it back on the table.

"Has Lorraine seen these?" Her voice was soft.

That wasn't the response Gina had expected.

"Yes. I showed her at the hospital, but she can't speak right now, at least not words that are English."

"What did she do?"

Gina paused and remembered the look on her mother's face, both pained and happy.

"She tried to touch the picture then spoke, but it wasn't really a word. Dr. Patel said she could understand, but making her mouth say the words to respond would be the difficult part."

Roza nodded, sliding the photo back to Gina.

"I don't know who he is." The words came out quickly, like a child disavowing any responsibility for the spilled cereal.

Gina frowned. Roza was the most honest person she knew, always finding a way to tell you the worst news in the kindest way, unlike Vicky, who blurted out her opinions without any softening. When she was sixteen and crying over a boy who hadn't called, Roza let her in on a valuable truth — if he had liked her the way she liked him, he would have called. And if he hadn't, he wasn't worth her time. She deserved to be called, Roza said. It wasn't always easy, but it helped get her through some sad crushes.

But this time, something was off.

"What about the birth certificate? Why is Joseph Sandowski listed as my father? My dad's name was Floyd Price."

Roza sat back in her chair, distancing herself from the papers.

"No idea."

Yep, this time Roza was lying. Maybe she wasn't sure if Gina could take the truth. But Gina didn't even want to think that Roza would lie to her face. She'd give her one more chance before calling her out on her dishonesty.

"You're sure you don't know anything?"

"I have nothing to tell you about what you want to know."

Faced with confronting the woman who mostly raised her, Gina's determination disintegrated. She loved Roza too much to be angry at her, or worse, call her a liar to her face. If Roza wasn't telling her the truth, there must be a very good reason. She had hoped Roza would enlighten her, but she'd have to take her search elsewhere.

Gina parked her Grilled G's food truck in the usual spot near Red Arrow Park in downtown Milwaukee. Monica was already there, writing her specials on the board, and they exchanged a quick hello before getting down to business.

First things first, Gina attached her daily to-do list with a magnet to the wall.

1. ~~Talk to Roza.~~
2. Make bacon.
3. Caramelize onions.
4. Today's special?
5. Text Vicky about Roza.
6. Visit Mom.

She fired up the flat grill and set up her ingredients in an orderly line. It seemed like a month since she had last worked, when it had been only yesterday. Grateful to the routine, she lost herself in prep work, throwing bacon on the griddle, chopping onions to caramelize, and setting out the butter to soften. She needed the familiar to make sense of all the unknowns.

"Drew, what am I supposed to do with

this information? If you could even call it information." She rubbed her rings, glanced at the truck's ceiling, then returned to her prep work.

A firm knock interrupted Gina's thoughts, and she poked her head out the side door. Standing there patiently in the winter wind was a regular customer, Daniel, all six feet plus of him, bundled up in a dark fleece with a red and white winter hat. He always wore a hat, either a beanie or a baseball cap. Was he bald? Hiding a man bun? She could tell from his light brown scruff — which almost hid his dimples — that he had brown hair, not much different from her own. Not blond, not dark, but somewhere in the middle. She'd never asked his age, but Gina didn't think he was much older than her, maybe even a few years younger.

"Hey, G. I just came back from Texas and brought you this peach salsa. Think you can do something with it?"

He held out a jar with five peaches across the top, all of them on fire.

"Thank you, Daniel." She popped off the lid and gave it a sniff. Her nose burned just from the smell. "Did you try this? It seems like it might be spicy."

He shook his head, the pompom on his beanie wobbling. After he'd been a customer for a while, he started stopping by her truck a little more often, always bringing her something new to try on her sandwiches.

"Hop on in and let's see what we have."

She pulled out a few tortilla chips from a nearby shelf, dipping one deeply and popping it in her mouth, then holding out the jar so Daniel could do the same. She was hit with the summery peach and brown sugar that sweetened the tomatoes, and then the heat built, numbing her tongue from the back to the front. She swallowed, eyes watering, and looked at Daniel, who already had his mouth open trying to cool it off. Most Wisconsinites couldn't hold their heat, so she wouldn't be able to use it straight, but there were some nice flavors in there.

"Here." She handed him a yogurt smoothie she kept in the fridge for days when she didn't have time to make a sandwich for herself.

"Sorry, G. I thought it would be delicious." He had an easy manner, bordering on shy, but with a strong thoughtful streak. Gina appreciated his amiable company.

"Ye of little faith. It has great flavor. It would be a shame to waste it. Have a seat and give me a few minutes."

Daniel settled on the overturned five-gallon bucket she used as a chair when it was slow.

"Tell me about what you were doing in Texas," she said.

"My sister and her family live near Austin. I try to get down and visit her once a winter. It's a nice break from the cold."

While he spoke she worked, mixing the salsa into cream cheese to cut the heat. She had some cornbread that she had made herself so it was the right texture to cut into slices — it would be the perfect accompaniment. She warmed up a little slow-cooked pork, tossing it with the peach salsa cream cheese mix, and put it between the cornbread slices with some shredded Monterey Jack, grilling it with butter to give the bread a crisp crunch. She cut the sandwich in two and gave half to Daniel. He took a huge bite. She liked that about him, he always ate with gusto whatever she gave him.

"What do you think?"

He finished chewing.

"You're a magician with cheese. Barely any heat at all."

He let the words float. Gina suspected he had a crush on her, but he never did anything other than bring her unusual condiments. Of course, her radar was way out of use. She hadn't flirted with a man since Drew. What did adults do anyway? She heard customers talk about apps and swiping — it all sounded so impersonal. Thinking about it made her stomach twist, so she shoved those thoughts away. No need to fret over something that was never going to happen.

She took a bite of her half. It really did work; the cornbread gave it a taco vibe. She could make a side salad to go with it with black beans, cilantro, and roasted corn.

"I think we have today's special. This might be the best yet. Thank you."

Daniel smiled at her, a blush tinging his face and his dimples denting his cheeks, implying a boyish innocence.

"You're welcome." The words were barely audible. He stood to leave.

"You aren't going yet, are you? That couldn't have been enough to fill you up. What can I make you, on the house, for such a great inspiration?"

"That's not necessary."

"Sit." She pointed her spatula at the bucket. "You're not leaving here without more food. How about I make you another pork sandwich? We need to name it anyway."

He nodded and retook his seat on the bucket, and Gina got to work.

"So what do you do during the winter? Other than visit your sister in Texas, of course," Gina asked.

Daniel rubbed his hands together before answering.

"I plan the spring's landscaping jobs, get them lined up on my calendar." Daniel owned a landscape company, she could tell it was a successful one from the way he talked about his jobs, but he never bragged outright. "I do plowing for a few customers when we have snow. But I have a lot of free time." He paused and looked at the floor. "Maybe . . . sometime . . . we could . . ."

Gina paused in her movements, but she never heard the end of the question. Vicky stomped up the steps at that exact moment and stood before them, her perfect ponytail swaying against her puffy black winter coat.

"You cannot send me a text then not answer my calls." She looked down at Daniel and smiled. "Well, hi there, handsome."

Daniel turned truly red, way redder than his normal blushes. It was a just-chugged-an-entire-jar-of-five-burning-peaches-salsa kind of red. Vicky was too much for most people, let alone someone as gentle as Daniel.

"That's my cue." He slid past Vicky, who was standing in front of the stairs. "Have a nice day, G." And he was out the door.

"Wait, you forgot your sandwich."

He poked his head back in. Vicky watched in amusement as Gina quickly cut and wrapped his sandwich and handed it to him.

"You have a good day, too, Daniel."

Then he walked toward a large silver pickup truck on the edge of the park.

"That man is sweet on you."

"Sweet on me? Since when are you from the South."

"Illinois is south. Of here."

Gina rolled her eyes, and Vicky plopped onto the bucket.

"Daniel is kind, but there's nothing more going on there. He swings by because he's bored while his business is off-season."

"I'm sure he has other friends who are easier to find."

"They probably all have day jobs. And he likes to drop off fun things for me to add into sandwiches. We just both like grilled cheeses."

"He brings gifts of food and you give him sandwiches. He is sweet on you, and I think you feel the same. You should ask him out."

Gina's chest clenched at the thought. It may have been almost two years since she had lost Drew, but the idea of dating pushed her toward panic. Her mother insisted it was past time to move on. Friends were trying to set her up, and now her sister was joining in. What all of these people didn't understand is she couldn't fast-forward her grief. It wasn't another item on her checklist she could accomplish then cross out. Grief demanded to be felt on its own time. But how did you explain that to someone with a healthy husband? So she handled it the way she handled all of these types of situations: with a smile and topic change.

"I'm sure you've misread the situation and I'll do no such thing. And I didn't ask you here to talk nonsense. How is your niece?"

"She's fourteen, so a pain in the ass."

"Was she rude to you?" That girl. She needed to be polite to family, at the very least.

"Not at all. Though I'm not entirely sure she was completely conscious. I went in her room to check on her, and her blankets grumbled at me. I didn't look under them, so she could have been eaten by something."

"That's not checking."

"She's alive. What more do you want?"

"Maybe talk to her. Make sure she eats breakfast. Ask what her plans are for the day. You know, conversation. I'm sure you do it every day with your own children."

"She'll be fine. She can feed herself and doesn't need anyone to wipe her backside." Vicky picked up Gina's sandwich and took a bite. "I love my kids, but if I never wipe another tiny butt, I'll consider my life a success."

"Teens need more supervision, they can get into real trouble."

"Maggie flushing Nathan's LEGOs isn't trouble? The plumber cost five hundred dollars." She spoke around the sandwich she was still chewing. Gina snorted. That sounded like the twins.

"Hey, this is good," Vicky said. She set the sandwich back down. "This is like a minivacation for me, and I'm not going to spend it checking up on May. She's your daughter, you do it."

"Yes, all of my sandwiches are good. You don't have to sound so surprised. And you just lost the best aunt award."

"I'm her only aunt."

"That's what makes it all the more tragic."

Gina chopped and mixed the ingredients for the salad, and double-checked her list, crossing out each item she'd finished. She was ready to open for the day, with fifteen minutes to spare.

"I didn't come all the way down here to get lectured. What did you want to talk about?"

"I swung by Roza's today. She said she didn't know anything about the photo or the birth certificate."

She pulled the SPECIAL sign out and wrote up a description of her new sandwich; the From Austin, with Love Grilled Pork Taco Sandwich with spicy peach salsa cream cheese.

"Really? That's what I'm here for? I was in fuzzy pajamas that didn't have any food stains on them with a hot cup of coffee and a crossword puzzle, and you called me out into the cold to tell me Roza didn't know anything. Why would she?"

"That's just it. She knows everything about our family, even stuff she doesn't tell Mom. Remember when you had that stray kitten in your room for a week and Roza put a litter box in there."

"That was Roza? I thought Mom did it."

"Mom would have thrown the cat out the window if she had found it, let alone given you a litter box. I saw Roza do it. The point is she knows everything. I don't believe for a second she doesn't know the story behind this. Plus, you didn't see her face. She straight-up lied to me."

"Maybe it was Mom's secret lover or a neighbor she didn't like. Roza can hold a grudge if she wants." Vicky smiled, enjoying her outlandish guess.

"She's not holding a grudge. What are you

even talking about? And I'm not even going to acknowledge the idea that Mom had lovers. Ew."

"A distant relative? He kind of looks like us if you squint at the picture a bit. Or he could be one of Roza's family members? She had a lot of them, and they were always around. Do you remember any of their names?"

"No. But none of that would make sense. Roza would just tell us if it was any of those." Gina tapped her lips with a finger as she thought through the logic.

"Not if he was Mom's lover. I did say you were a secret love child from a torrid affair."

Gina raised her hand.

"Stop. If you keep bringing up that nonsense, I'm banning you from the truck forever."

Vicky laughed. Teasing Gina was still one of her favorite hobbies.

"So what do you want to do?"

"I thought you could ask Roza. You're better at getting people to tell you things."

"You mean I'm better at being a bitch and demanding answers."

"Your words, not mine." Gina held up her hands.

"I haven't seen her in ages. I'm due for a

chat. Was she baking anything?"

"There were chocolate chip cookies everywhere."

"Done deal. I'll go. I'll text you after."

Gina gave her sister a quick kiss on the cheek.

"What was that for?"

"Thank you for being here. Everything is always less overwhelming when I see you."

After Vicky left, she opened her window and propped up her sign with the day's special. Back to her routine. She may not know how she was going to help her mom recover, or the mystery of the photo, or why Roza had lied, but she did know how to make her customers happy — gooey cheese and lots of it.

Chapter Eleven

May left a note on the kitchen table.

Gone to Olivia's. Text if you need me home.

She knew she wouldn't hear from her mom — between her grandma and the food truck, her mom didn't have time for her. May had texted Olivia that she had BIG news that morning, and even though they hadn't texted since September, according to her iPhone, Olivia responded as expected.

YAM!

Olivia had called her Yam ever since kindergarten, when she had overheard May's dad call her that during a playdate. Olivia had thought it was hilarious and had used it ever since. It had been too long since anyone had called her that.

GET OVER HERE NOW!

So she was getting over there now.

Olivia lived a few blocks over in the opposite direction of Connor's house. May didn't bother with gloves or a hat or boots: tucking her hands into her pockets would suffice, and she had a hood if the wind picked up. No reason to bring extra things that she would have to keep track of. It had snowed last night, too, so the neighborhood was quieter than normal, except for the distant snowblowers. There wasn't much of a breeze, and the cool air cleared her mind more than distracted it. The last time she hung out with her friends, it hadn't gone well.

Last year she had gone to a girl-boy party at their friend Hannah's house where a dozen thirteen-year-olds were scattered around the large basement. Some kids tried to play pool, which mainly meant knocking in the balls when the opponent wasn't paying attention. Other kids piled onto bean bags around the TV where they snark-watched episodes of *Dora the Explorer.* A third group, all girls, huddled in a corner, discussing which boys they had a crush on, the occasional giggle breaking up their loud whispering. That was the group May firmly avoided.

May sat on the outskirts of the TV group,

counting the minutes until her mom would pick her up while flicking through photos of her dad on her phone; trips to the lakefront, State Fair, and their trip to Walt Disney World. But her favorite was from a few weeks before he died. She and her dad had been sitting on top of the picnic table in the backyard. It had been late afternoon, and the sun was low in front of them. She had leaned her head on his shoulder as he kissed the top of it. They were talking about their plans for the upcoming summer. He was going to teach her more about motorcycles — he swore all his favorite ladies knew about things like that. May's mom had taken her phone and snapped the picture without either of them realizing. Now she would never learn about motorcycles, and she never wanted to.

Just like she didn't want to be at this stupid party, but it made her mom happy when she did things with other people. One more hour to go. She had moved on to the next picture when the couch cushions dipped next to her. Olivia sat down.

"What's up?"

May shrugged and turned her phone facedown. Olivia took that as a sign to keep talking.

"Hannah said she like-liked Connor. Can

you believe it?" May looked across the room, where Connor was bent over the pool table, trying to aim into a side pocket. Hannah stood next to him, clearly in his way, but he was too nice to tell her to move. She pulled her blond curls over one shoulder, then tilted her head so far that it looked like she might actually fall over. May rolled her eyes, and Olivia continued.

"Could she be more obvious? So which boy are you watching?"

Olivia scanned the room as if to pick out which person May might be interested in.

"No one."

Olivia leaned in closer. "Come on. There has to be someone you have a tiny crush on. Is it Ben? Or Mikey?"

May didn't want to be having this conversation. She wanted to be in her bed, under her covers, in peace.

"Were you taking pictures of anyone?" Olivia grabbed May's phone before she could stop her, turning it over to see a picture of her dad. Olivia went still, clearly not expecting this reminder of May's loss. Ugh. May grabbed the phone and turned off the screen.

"I wasn't taking pictures." The words came out harsh and louder than she meant. A few of their friends turned to see what was going on.

"Sorry. I guess . . . I thought . . ."

Olivia's voice was hushed and she seemed suddenly uncomfortable when moments before she had been giggly and relaxed.

"What?"

"I guess, since you're here, I thought you were ready to be normal again."

Harsh. May didn't need a reminder how nonnormal she was.

"I can't just forget my dad died. Making fun of Swiper or talking about stupid crushes certainly isn't going to make me feel better." Her voice was loud again, but not everyone was looking. "So no, I'm not ready to be normal again." She stood and walked up the stairs, thankful no one followed. She called her mom to get her, and that was the last time she had tried to be social outside of school. At first, she was angry that none of them seemed to understand, but then she didn't know how to jump back in.

But for the first time in forever, she had something exciting to share, something that had nothing to do with her dad. Her feet stumbled at the thought. Kissing Connor had nothing to do with her dad. She didn't think her dad had even met Connor — he was always "one of the boys from school," nameless and faceless. It made her sad that he would never know him, but it also was something to cling to. Connor wouldn't bring up old memories. He was new and shiny, like a toy on Christmas morning. She probably shouldn't compare a person to a toy, but whatever.

She pushed aside the lingering sadness and clung to the shiny newness. She was going to tell her friend about her first kiss and she wasn't going to feel bad about it.

She walked up the steps to Olivia's house, and before she could ring the doorbell, Olivia threw it open and yanked her in. Her long dark hair was straight and shiny, like a black waterfall, except for vibrant purple streaks that would pop up as she moved. When she wore her hair up in a ponytail for gym, her head looked like a purple-and-black-striped circus tent.

"Brendan said Connor was at your house all day yesterday. Spill!"

Like most of their classmates, Olivia's parents worked long hours at the enormous hospital complex down the road, so they had the house to themselves. Her younger brothers had been farmed out to various friends during break, while Olivia was deemed old enough to be at home alone, but not old enough to watch her brothers.

It was a win all the way around, as Olivia explained on their way to the kitchen, where two mugs of cocoa waited for them.

"I thought you might be chilly," Olivia said as she pulled a foil cylinder out of the freezer and tore it open. May grinned. Thin Mints, just like always. They both pulled one out, took a small bite to expose the cookie, then dipped them into their drinks. Just enough hot chocolate got absorbed into the cookies to make them even more delicious. Maybe Olivia wanted their old friendship back, too. May warmed more from Olivia's gesture than from the hot chocolate. "Okay, back to Connor. Now talk."

"Not much to tell." May decided to play it like it was no big deal. "He texted and came over. We played Wii bowling. I crushed him. We made out."

Olivia nodded along to her summary until her eyes shot wide at the surprise ending.

"HE KISSED YOU!? How could you not lead with that? Oh my God, Hannah is going to be so jealous. She's liked him all year. I knew he liked you. He's always looking at you in math class."

"He is?"

"Yeah, everyone knows. I suppose you can't see because he's behind you."

"Everyone knows? You guys talk about it?"

"Well, sometimes." Olivia took another cookie. "But only in a nice way. We've been encouraging him to ask you out. Bring you out of hiding." May's new, shiny information was barely news, only a happy ending to her friends' meddling. Olivia leaned forward as May leaned back in her chair. "It wasn't anything bad, swear. We miss you." She nudged the cookies closer to May. "Now, how was the makeout?"

May could get pissed they were talking about her, or she could ignore it. They weren't being mean. She knew they didn't understand what was going on with her. How could they? May took another peace-offering cookie and chewed before answering.

"It was nice. Then weird. He used tongue."

Olivia leaned in.

"He did? Brendan hasn't tried that."

She and Brendan were kissing? When did that happen?

"I might have laughed in his face."

Olivia laughed so hard she could barely breathe. With each cookie, May felt more and more like her old self, someone who laughed and got excited about who liked who. She felt normal.

Chapter Twelve

Lorraine knew before she opened her eyes who was sitting at the side of her bed. She would know that scent anywhere — the warm spicy perfume Lorraine had introduced her to so many years ago, and the Polish caramels she always munched on. The girls had told Roza about her stroke. A strong, familiar hand enveloped her own.

"You old fool. What have you gotten yourself into now?" Roza rubbed her wrinkled hand on Lorraine's. She didn't look a day older than Lorraine, even though she was her senior by fifteen years. Lorraine squeezed her hand, letting her know she understood.

"The girls have been to see me — on two separate trips. Gina tried to bribe me with candy — and, I tell you, it almost worked." Roza launched into a conversation as if Lorraine could answer her. It was nice to have someone treat her like nothing had changed. Lorraine focused on the words and did her best to ignore her own inability to respond. "Vicky has gotten quite a mouth on her. I'm sure you've told her about it."

Roza chuckled. "They are strong women, like you. When they are determined, they get what they want."

Roza was right, her girls would discover the truth soon enough. She'd kept her memories so secret, Lorraine didn't know what would happen when she let them free. They were a swirling cloak that kept her warm during the darkest of nights, on mornings when she'd crawled out of bed and painted on a presentable face, in moments when Joe's loss sucked the oxygen from the room. They were the glue that had held her together, the shield that only she could use. If she loosened her hold on them after all this time, would she fall apart?

Roza knew the truth, too. Roza was a time capsule of all Lorraine's best and worst moments, and she had always been there when Lorraine needed her.

Lorraine left Regina with her mother while she returned to her and Joe's cozy little apartment to pack up her belongings.

It wasn't long ago that she had stood in the living room, with its red, blue, and yellow plaid carpet, and kissed her Joe goodbye, thinking their future was rolled out like a never-ending red carpet. Now he was under a rock, and she was about to marry a man who she didn't even know. Her first marriage had been like a sunny day in March, the Northern Lights on a summer night, snow in June — rare and precious, but not impossible. She didn't know what marriage with Floyd would hold. He may even have been all of those things, but he never would be to her.

She had loved Joe with every part of her. In a scant four years, she had met him, married him, made babies with him, then buried him. It had all seemed surreal until now, when she had to make practical decisions about the most horrific of tragedies. Should she donate the coffee mugs? He'd drunk his black coffee out of them, his lips had touched their rims. She left them in the cupboard for the next tenant. Should she keep the shampoo? It was her favorite, yes, but he always used it, too, and now the smell reminded her of him. She tossed it in the garbage. She ripped the bed linens off and threw them in a heap with all the pillows and comforters. She added the towels to the pile — anything that had touched him went in. She should donate them, but the thought of anyone else using his things broke her.

Her knees buckled, and she sank into the pile like it was a nest, tears uncontrolled. If she breathed deep enough, she could still smell his aftershave, a woodsy smoky scent. Once these sheets and towels were gone, would she never smell him again? A tornado of hate caught her up, first at him for leaving her, then at herself for thinking such a traitorous thought. Her entire body clenched as more tears poured out of her, like a towel being wrung dry over and over again. Wilted, she lay on the sheets, using a pillowcase to wipe her face. She would never move again.

But then the baby in her belly squirmed, reminding her this was not only about her. Her darling Regina needed her. This new baby needed her.

Sheer force of will got her moving again. Lorraine shoved the despair down and clambered to her feet, her pregnant belly a bigger encumbrance than she'd expected. She couldn't keep breaking down like this, not when there was work to be done. Focus on a task. Complete it. Move to the next task. One could fill a life that way.

She numbly filled boxes with her own clothes and toiletries, stuffing the bedding into garbage bags. Important memories of Joe — the flag from his funeral, all of the pictures from their happy times, each item chipped at her heart until it felt like one more blow would shatter it — went into a separate box. She looked at each item one last time, pausing on the photo Roza had taken right before he'd left for duty. She took it and Regina's birth certificate, pulled back the lining on her coat, and put them there, close to her. Once she was settled, she would hide it in her new bedroom — a place Floyd would never look. She could have this one small memory to look at when she became too lonely.

She slid her boxes into the blue VW Beetle, and walked the box containing her Joe memories to Roza's flat upstairs. When Roza answered, she motioned Lorraine into the kitchen, one of her tall, blond sons taking the box before she could even say hello.

"Why didn't you tell me you were packing things up? I would have helped you." Roza guided her to the table, noticing her raw face, but not commenting, thank goodness. "You need to take care of yourself and the baby. She'll be here any day."

Lorraine couldn't help but smile. Roza had been claiming she was carrying a girl since the moment Lorraine told her she was expecting.

"You've already done so much for me, for us." Lorraine sipped the water that appeared in front of her after she eased herself to a seat at the table. "And I need to ask you for two more favors."

"Anything."

Lorraine studied Roza's face, her dark hair streaked with gray pulled into a bun, her skin still smooth around alert blue eyes. She had no reason, really, to ask anything of Roza other than she had been a kind neighbor who had become a friend. Roza wasn't obligated to share Lorraine's burdens. Only self-preservation allowed her to humble herself enough to say the words. After losing and giving up so much, she needed to ask for help. It was selfish. It was necessary.

Lorraine dug deep, pulling her protective shell around her. She could no longer be ruled by emotions. No more breakdowns.

"First, can you keep the box of Joe's things at your house, someplace safe? I can't bring them with me and I can't throw them out." Roza nodded, as Lorraine had expected. That was the small favor. Now for the big one. "Second, I'm getting married in a few days, and my new husband has agreed I should have a nanny for Regina and the new baby. Will you be their nanny?

You'll be paid well. But —"

"Of course, I'll help with the children."

"Let me finish, please. If you agree to this, we can't talk about Joe or acknowledge our previous history. You would just be a qualified nanny that I interviewed and hired. I don't want Floyd to know you knew Joe, and I need you. I am going to have to play the good society wife. But with you, I won't forget. I can't forget."

Roza clasped Lorraine's hand, so warm against her cold one. Lorraine felt numb, frozen from the inside out. But Roza's warmth was a life preserver. "You can't pretend Joe never existed. You can't ignore that he's the father of your two children. This won't help you heal, and you need to heal for the girls and yourself."

Lorraine's armor snapped around her, waking a lurking fury at her own widowhood. How dare Roza tell her she was wrong! Roza still had a husband who came home every night. Someone she could greet with a kiss on the cheek and a warm meal. Someone to whisper with late at night. Lorraine was trapped in a dark room with all the air sucked out, scrambling to find the cracks that would give her enough oxygen to make it to the next moment. Then another crack, another moment. Roza thought she knew a better way. But she knew nothing. Anger gave Lorraine a wave of strength, and she clung to it with both hands.

"Roza, this is what I need from you. I don't expect you to understand why. I don't even understand why. But knowing that you knew Joe, even if we can't talk about him, it will be the proof I need that it had really happened. But I am marrying again, to Floyd, and this is the way it has to be. I understand if you can't do it." Lorraine slumped, her little speech had tapped her remaining energy. She needed her bed and soon.

Roza sat back in her chair and stared at her. Lorraine could guess what she saw — a pale, drawn woman in a black dress from JCPenney that tented over her huge stomach, her straight brown hair dangling on each side of her face. Dark stains shadowed her blank eyes. A woman whose future had crumbled and who had to carve a new one from the remaining rubble. She was desperation and despair. A woman reaching for a life raft in an ocean of grief.

Roza's mouth opened and closed, questions visibly bubbling to the surface. Her every misgiving and worry was written on her face. When Roza made up her mind,

Lorraine could see the determination flash in her blue eyes, a fire that would light both their ways.

Lorraine took a deep breath and waited to hear what Roza had decided.

"Yes. For you and Regina, and the new baby, yes, I can do it."

Lorraine nodded, eyes welling in gratitude, and rubbed her belly.

"Thank you. I'll call you with everything you need to know, and I'll pay you so much you won't think twice. Floyd emphasized money was no object." Lorraine stood and hugged Roza, hoping her gratitude shone through in her grasp. "But, honestly, I'll never be able to repay you. You are saving me and my children. Thank you."

The women held each other, a silent agreement that would get Lorraine through the coming years. And that was before Lorraine even knew how much she'd come to rely on Roza's steadying hand.

When Regina was in first grade and Victoria ruled kindergarten like a queen, Lorraine was brushing Regina's hair, working to get it smooth so she could braid it for school, but the seven-year-old kept reaching up to scratch her head, ruffling the sleekness.

"Stop that. You're messing up your hair.

Do you want to look like a ragamuffin?" Lorraine said.

"But it's itchy."

Lorraine paused her smoothing and parted her hair to see if there was a rash. What she found was so much worse, she threw the brush into the sink and stepped back from Regina's head, hands held high while trying to keep her calm. Lice.

"Victoria, get in here."

"What is it?" Regina asked, scratching at her head again.

"Stop doing that. Don't touch anything."

Victoria appeared, and Lorraine motioned her to stand next to her sister. She was loath to touch Victoria's head, worried she'd find the disgusting things. Examining the part running down the center of Victoria's silky light-brown hair, she didn't even need to touch it to see clearly. Victoria had them, too. Suddenly, her own head erupted in the buggy sensation. Could she have them?

"Stand in the shower, both of you, and don't move."

"But we have to go to school."

"Not today. You can't." She leaned her head out the door and called, "Floyd, can you come to the girls' bathroom, please?"

While she waited for Floyd to arrive, she leaned toward the mirror, lifting up chunks of her immaculately feathered hair, looking for the telltale immovable white dots. Her roots were starting to show, so she couldn't tell. Doubly disgusting. Floyd appeared, already dressed for work in a dark gray, three-piece pinstriped suit.

"The girls have lice. Can you check my head?"

She leaned forward, head tipped, for him to look and he recoiled back, his hands up, as if he were under arrest.

"Absolutely not. Call Roza. Pay her extra if needed."

Lorraine looked at her husband of six years as though seeing him for the first time. Who was this man? He'd always been pleasant enough. A perfectly fine roommate. On time for dinner, respectful of her privacy and parenting decisions, and positively doting in public. As a family, they had all the creature comforts they could want.

But for the first time since she'd made the decision to marry him, she needed more. She needed a life partner, someone whom she could count on to check her head for lice. Floyd couldn't make it clearer that he was not, nor would he ever be, that kind of partner. *Joe would never — no.* She couldn't go down that road. *Just solve the problem, Lorraine.*

"Fine," she said, closing the door. She heard his steps retreat and the front door close as she watched her girls stand in the giant, cobalt-blue tiled shower.

Floyd had been right on one point, though — Roza would help.

"Stay there, girls."

She called Roza, who arrived to all three of the Price women scratching their heads. Under her arm she had a large tub of something white and on her face rested the self-possession of a general who knows what battle entails.

"Okay, who's first?"

Lorraine bent her head so Rose could check her scalp.

"You're all clear."

Lorraine relaxed a bit.

"You take Victoria, and I'll work on Regina's head." Roza motioned the girls to get out of the shower and stand in front of them. They listened immediately. "You didn't need to quarantine them. It's not the plague, just a few little buggies." The girls giggled.

She scooped out a large glob from the tub and plopped it onto Victoria's head, then did the same for Regina.

"Now rub it in. We'll put shower caps on them while the coconut oil suffocates the live ones. In a few hours, we'll comb through their hair. Then you need to do this every three days for three weeks."

"Isn't there someplace we can take them? Something to kill everything faster than that?"

"Do you want to put pesticide on your child?"

Roza was right, as usual, she didn't want that. Lorraine shook her head.

"You can do this."

The women got to work. As the girls waited for the bugs to die, sitting in front of the TV, Lorraine and Roza stripped their beds and washed anything a bug-infested head could have touched. The mountain in the laundry room grew, and Lorraine whimpered at the thought. Thank heavens for Roza.

Roza brushed Lorraine's hair off her face and then paused to look her in the eye, the older woman's deep wrinkles matching Lorraine's, her hair white and pulled into a low bun, the way she had worn it for years. Without Roza, Lorraine would never have made it through those early years without Joe. For the last forty years, she was the only one who'd known Lorraine's secrets.

"Your hair looks a mess. Did they take

away your mirror privileges?" She looked around for a brush and found one in the toiletry bag in the bathroom. She helped Lorraine sit up and propped her back with pillows so she could brush the messy locks. "In the forty years I've known you, I've never seen you let your hair go. But don't worry, I'll fix you up." As she brushed with slow, gentle strokes, she spoke.

"It's time, Lorraine. They are halfway there. Unless you tell me otherwise, I'm going to tell them." She paused to assess Lorraine's reaction. With all the strength her neck had, she managed to bob her head. It was the best she could do. "I'm going to take that as a yes, and God forgive me if I'm wrong." She paused her brushing to make the sign of the cross. "They are going to have so many questions. You've really chosen the worst possible time to lose your voice. But then again, you've never been one for good timing."

She smoothed Lorraine's hair one more time, then helped ease her back to a comfortable position.

"There, now you look more like yourself. I can't believe you've let them keep you in those hospital gowns. I'll have the nurse get you into one of your own nightdresses. They can't expect someone to get better when their caboose hangs out the back."

Lorraine looked at her old friend, hoping her gratitude was clear. One thing was for certain — she didn't like not being able to say the words. The stroke reminded Lorraine that time was not infinite, and some words shouldn't wait. She grasped Roza's arm with a trembling hand, squeezing it the best that she could. Roza wiped up the tears that wet both their faces.

"I know. I know." She squeezed Lorraine's arm back and returned the hairbrush to the bathroom, clearing her throat before she spoke again. "I'll stop by Gina's house tonight after she's done working. I'll bring them some pierogi. Your girls always handled bad news better with my pierogi."

It was true. Just the smell of Roza's dumplings calmed her, like the thrill of drawing a bath and anticipating the comfort to come. Or like two fingers of good bourbon after a stressful day. The two women had made pierogis a million times together, but Lorraine still didn't understand what made Roza's so much better than any she had tried elsewhere. The dough was more tender, more flavorful, the edges crispy, and the filling, no matter if it was sweet or savory, was always delicious. She had eaten them cold at midnight, straight out of the pan, and at every point between.

Now she just hoped the pierogis were delicious enough to soften the hurt Lorraine's secret could cause her daughters.

What's Been Your Greatest Joy?

Chapter Thirteen

May tossed her boring cotton sports bras onto the floor. She wished she had some pretty bras, something that would catch Connor's attention, make her seem more grown up than plain white cotton. May and Olivia had spent all day yesterday dissecting every moment of her makeout session with Connor. They both agreed he really did like her, and she wanted to show him that she liked him, too. That's what lingerie was for, right? She pulled out an old bikini with a fun turquoise and green pattern. Would this work as a replacement if he didn't notice it was a bathing suit? A knock sounded on the back door, and all her nerves sprung to the surface, a porcupine of anticipation. Too late. Boring cotton would have to do.

As May dashed out of her room, she pulled a black T-shirt over her head — this one had an adorable zombie rabbit wearing pajamas. Connor had made good time. She only had had enough time to change clothes and rub on some strawberry-scented lotion. She hoped Connor liked strawberries.

"Come in," she shouted, sliding down the hallway and into the kitchen. He opened the door, stomping his feet on the rug to get off the snow that covered his shoes from running through yards. While this was only the second time he had come over, it felt like a routine, a new routine. May liked it. He looked up, snow dotting his dark hair and fleece coat.

"Hey," he said.

"Hi." What now? Would he kiss her right away, or later? She licked her lips. She definitely should have put on lip gloss. "Are you hungry? I can make a snack?"

"No, not really. Thanks." He lined up his shoes carefully on the rug and hung his coat on an empty hook, then rubbed his hands on his jeans. His nervousness made her feel a little better about her own.

"We can watch Netflix. I started watching *Buffy,* and it's pretty good. I'm only on episode three, so I can catch you up in a few minutes."

Connor nodded and stopped fidgeting with his hands, looking relieved she had a suggestion.

"Sure, that sounds good."

They walked down the carpeted steps into the dark basement, May's nerves bouncing, light making random rectangles on the carpeting where it leaked through the snow-covered basement windows. The room was warm. It always was — the hot air got trapped in the basement, so it was always the coziest spot in the house. She needed to relax or Connor would think she was a huge dork. She needed something so he'd think she was cool. And normal. What did cool, normal people do?

Her eyes landed on a part of the room she'd never given much thought to before: a small, dark wood bar. It had enough room for two stools in front and a few shelves behind. Underneath was a small refrigerator and a few bottles of alcohol her mom never drank.

"Did you want some wine?" She went behind the bar in the corner of the basement and pulled out a dusty bottle of wine that had been stashed there for years. The label was white with a picture of a fancy building.

"Wine? Are you serious?"

She opened the bottle using the fancy cork remover she'd seen her mom use and poured some into a glass.

"Sure. Why not? It's not like we're going

to be operating any heavy machinery."

"Okay. I'm down." Connor didn't look too sure, but she poured him a glass anyway.

"Cheers." They clinked their glasses and both sipped. Connor made a face, but May used all her self-control to keep from doing the same, even though the sour liquid burned as she swallowed. She took a bigger gulp, which tasted a tiny bit better. Connor took another sip and carried it to the couch, so she poured a bit more in her glass and followed him. She knew it took time to feel drunk or whatever, but she already felt a little light-headed and rebellious. In a good way.

Leaving all the lights off, they both settled on the couch, with only a few inches between them, setting their glasses on the coffee table. She started the episode, and by the time the opening credits were over, she had updated Connor on the major characters, and they were holding hands. Her body felt a little numb, but good. By the time the theme song started on the second episode, his lips were on hers.

"You smell amazing," Connor said between kisses. One hand traced a path up and down her arm like a robot programmed to perform only that action. She turned her body toward him, giving him more room to move his hands. He leaned into her until she tipped backward, following so he was on top of her.

"I can't move," she exhaled. He rolled toward the back of the couch so they were facing each other as they lay on their sides, their legs bumping into each other as they kissed. Finally, they settled into a pattern. Three turns with her head to the right, then they would switch and do three with her head tilted left, then switch again. She didn't mind his tongue as much anymore. She knew a good chunk of time had passed because her lips started to get sore and she heard the end credits of the second episode. Should she stop? Pause Netflix? She adjusted her hips so she could get leverage to reach the remote, but Connor mistook what she was doing. His kissing became more eager, his fingers edging the bottom of her shirt, touching her back and sides with his hands. They were warm and gentle. What if? She moved her free hand to the edge of his shirt. The other hand was trapped under his body and she could only flap it against his shoulder blade. Was she doing this okay? His skin was smooth, so she moved it upward, and he didn't move away. In fact, his hips rubbed against hers. She could feel a few small pimples on his back. Suddenly,

Connor paused, his hand at the bottom of her sports bra.

"Want me to take your shirt off?" His breath was heavy, and his lips were puffy from all the kissing. Was she ready? They'd been swimming together, she figured, so seeing her in her sports bra wasn't exactly anything he hadn't seen before. Not that much different from swimming, right? But it seemed unfair for her to take her shirt off if he got to keep his.

"Okay, but you have to take off yours, too."

All elbows and knees, they removed each other's T-shirts, getting her arm stuck in a shirtsleeve and, at one point, slapping his cheek with her wrist as it popped free from an armhole. Was making out always so awkward? She guessed she shouldn't have worried he would be disappointed by just her sports bra, though — as soon as they started making out again, he traced the line where the material met her skin, and she tried not to giggle when he grazed too close to her armpit. She rubbed his back and sides, sometimes letting her thumb roam around the front of his torso until she accidentally bumped his nipple. She definitely wasn't ready for nipples.

The TV still played in the background.

Years from now, would she hear the theme song and remember getting face burn from all the kissing? Was her mind supposed to wander like this?

"What the hell is going on down here? And where are your shirts?" OhmyGod, her mom was home early from work. Shit. Why couldn't she rewind life for just a few minutes? Her mom already stood in the basement. How did she get there so quickly? They hadn't heard the upstairs door, or the steps on the stairs or anything. Connor jumped away from her, and May sprung off the couch. This was happening. They each grabbed the first shirt they could, realized they had the other person's, and switched. Connor slipped his on even though it was inside out and backward. May used hers to cover her front like a bedsheet and glared at her mother, anger quickly taking the place of embarrassment. How dare she?

Then she saw her mom's face, which wore an expression May had never seen before. Her mom's nostrils were so flared, cocktail weenies would fit in them, while her lips pressed together so tightly, they disappeared into each other. It seriously looked like she didn't even have lips.

"Mrs. Zoberski . . . ," Connor said.

"Go. Now." Connor ran from the room.

As his footsteps echoed up the stairs she shouted after him, "And don't think I won't be calling your mother about this, young man."

"Don't call his —" May said.

"No. You don't get to speak. Maybe not ever again." She rubbed her hands on her face like she was trying to remove mud, or maybe erase the memory of what she just saw. Then May saw her notice the bottle of wine. She floated to the table and gently picked it up. She cradled the bottle in one hand and ran her fingers over the stone building on the label. "You were *drinking this*?" Her voice was soft and scarier. Tears brimmed in her eyes. This was different and way worse than just anger. Her mom picked up the two glasses. "Put your shirt on, turn off the TV, and meet me in the kitchen. If you aren't there in two minutes, you'll be lucky to ever see the inside of any building but school and this house until you graduate high school."

She turned and left, her feet silent on the steps. No wonder they didn't hear her come down — she was like a freakin' cat burglar. May stuffed her head into her T-shirt, finding the armholes and turning off the TV as she straightened her top. A headache thumped behind her forehead. If her mom was threatening a permanent grounding, she wasn't messing around. As she walked up the steps, she fixed her ponytail, which had come loose during all the making out. Her mom waited at the kitchen table with the two glasses and the bottle of wine. She took a sip out of one of the glasses and pushed it away.

Avoiding eye contact, May opened the fridge to grab a bottle of water.

"No. No drinks. Sit."

"What next? Are you going to shine a bright light on me?"

"You don't get to be funny right now. Sit."

May slid into the seat across from her mother. Now that she couldn't have water, she was really thirsty. Her mom picked at a paper towel that had been left on the table from breakfast, and the leftover crumbs fell onto the table. Why didn't she get started already?

"Are we just going to sit here?"

Her mom's eyes lasered in on her face.

"Young lady, you have no idea. I'm trying to organize my thoughts so I don't say something I'll regret and scar you forever."

"You think I'm not already scarred? That ship sailed two years ago when Dad died." Her mom flinched. "And we weren't doing anything bad, anyway."

"Sitting in the dark and watching a movie isn't bad. Baking brownies and making a mess in the kitchen isn't bad. Heck, lying to me about not eating meat isn't even that big of a deal. But fourteen-year-olds drinking that bottle of wine and lying half naked on the couch with your tongues down each other's throat *is* bad." May guessed her mom wasn't worried about scarring her anymore. "I have always trusted you to do the right thing and given you the freedom I thought you earned."

"Ignoring me isn't freedom. Dad never —"

"Ignoring you? Anytime I try to talk to you, you brush me off. You ignore me." Her mom took a deep breath. "But that is not the point. The point is that you are fourteen and simply not ready for wine and sex and all the responsibilities that come with those two things."

"We hardly drank the wine, and we weren't having sex. We were just kissing." Her head thumped. If Dad were alive, he'd never let her mom yell like this. He'd ask her what she thought and listen to her, not just pop a can of crazy. *What had Dad even seen in* her?

"With clothes off. Where did you think that was headed? I was a teenager once, you know. It might not have been today or tomorrow or even next week. But that's how it starts. Lying on a couch in a dark basement with no shirts on."

"That wasn't going to happen. God!" This was stupid. She wasn't going to have sex and she didn't even like the wine. Regina was overreacting. May stood. "Connor isn't like that. He only took a sip of the wine. I was the one who drank it."

"Who's blaming Connor? But great, it's good to know you were the one peer-pressuring him." She smacked the table with both hands and stood, pacing the room. "Good to know. His parents can deal with him how they see fit. You are the one who's my problem."

There. Her mom had *finally* said what May always knew she was thinking.

"That's right. That's all I am. Your problem." She stormed to her room and slammed the door.

Chapter Fourteen

The slammed door vibrated through the house, sending ripples across the wine like *Jurassic Park,* then absolute silence. Gina slumped into the chair at the table, took another sip of wine, and spit it back out. Fuck. It had turned. She and Drew had waited too long, and now their babymoon wine was expensive vinegar. That seemed to be her life now — waiting too long only to find out it was too late.

She didn't even know why that phrase came out of her mouth. She never thought of May as a problem. The problem was that Drew had died and now her mother was in the hospital and her teenage daughter was halfway to alcoholism and pregnancy. She picked up the wine bottle and dumped its contents into the sink. She ran her fingers over the label, remembering the day they had bought it.

It had been their last vacation before

May's birth. They booked it months prior as a romantic wine-tasting getaway in California, before they'd found out Gina was pregnant. By the time they realized, it was too late to back out without losing money on the package, so they went. They spent more time walking and dreaming about their baby than wine tasting — especially because she couldn't drink, but at one winery, they bought a special bottle — something to celebrate their new family. They intended to drink it after May was born but kept putting it off. First because Gina was nursing, and then because there were other milestones to celebrate. There had always been something bigger coming down the road.

"Dammit Drew, this is when I need you. You always understood her and how she saw the world. I can't do this without you." Instead of throwing it away, she hugged the bottle to her chest, the emptiness rocking her. She wished there was someone she could bargain with for one more day, one more conversation with him, to see his reassuring smile that would let her know she was making the right decisions for their daughter. But she was alone. And she had just driven another wedge between them.

The silent house pressed on her. She slid

to the floor under its pressure, the bottle nestled between her chest and her knees so she could set her forehead on top of it. Tears fell from her cheeks and trickled down the sides of the green glass, mingling with the few wine droplets still clinging to it.

She wanted to go to May. She wanted to shout at her for doing such stupid things, and she wanted to apologize for letting her think for even a second that she was a problem. May was half-Drew — how could she be anything but perfect? Even when she was acting like a little shit.

She lifted her face to the ceiling, and her eyes stopped on the flower crown hanging on the far wall, its red and white ribbons trailing down the wall. When May had been little, she would be allowed to play with it when she had been extra good and only after she vowed to be very careful. The circle of fake flowers represented the beginning, and like it or not, it was the moment that set their family on the path to this exact day. It was the moment Gina had known Drew was hers forever.

After finding out Gina had lived in Milwaukee her entire life and never been to Polish Fest, Drew had insisted that be remedied immediately. They parked in the huge lot under the Hoan Bridge and followed the throng toward the main gate. It wasn't too crowded or noisy, but the people smiled and danced to the ever-present polka music. Stands sold Polish food ranging from cabbage rolls to a wide variety of pastries. You could even do vodka tastings and pet beautiful white Polish sheepdogs. One tent had tables full of vibrant Polish pottery, with intricate patterns hand painted in bold colors.

"I can't believe you've never been to Polish Fest. Didn't you say Roza lives in the old neighborhood?" Drew asked, referring to the area south of downtown where the largest number of Polish immigrants had settled when they had first come to Milwaukee.

"My mom would never have let her take us," Gina said. "I've never been to any of the Fests. You'll see when you meet them, this isn't their scene. Anyone can come here. They prefer less plebeian pursuits."

Drew stopped on the sidewalk, causing a few people behind them to grumble and walk around.

"How is that possible? The Fests are one of the top five . . ." He paused and touched his fingers as if counting. "No, top three best things about Milwaukee, behind the

Brewers and Harleys. For the rest of the summer, this is what we're doing. But you should know Polish Fest is the best, so the rest will disappoint."

They began walking again, moving with the foot traffic, many clad in red and white. If Gina didn't know better, she'd think they were on their way to a Badger game.

"Your bias toward Polish Fest doesn't have anything to do with your last name being Zoberski, does it?"

Drew smiled and pulled her in close, kissed the top of her head, and pointed to the tattoo on his arm. The two flags on the motorcycle were an American flag and the red and white Polish flag. She'd never noticed it, too distracted by what was under the ink, but there it was — his Polish pride.

"I don't need to be biased. I'm giving you the facts here, lady."

He smiled at her, all golden hair and sparkling blue eyes. He was so different from any of the boys she'd ever dated. He was less inhibited, more kind, and harder working. And she was falling fast.

They joined the crowds of families and older couples — a few already dancing to the polka music echoing from multiple stages, shuffling around in circles as if they had been doing it for years, and they probably had. Gina could see why her parents would never feel at home here. It was so unpretentious, attendees relishing the good food, lively music, smiling faces. Everyone sat elbow to elbow at picnic tables and stood in line for simple food like pierogis and polish sausages, wearing their comfortable Polska T-shirts and shorts. Her parents would hate it here, if for no other reason than their Waspy selves couldn't get a gin and tonic — she'd never seen either one drink beer, let alone out of a plastic cup. Her parents would be the outsiders here. That made her love it all the more.

They stopped at a small booth tucked into a tent where a few older women attached fake flowers to plastic rings, then tied on ribbons to dangle off the back. Gina had seen other women wearing them in the crowds.

"Pick one," Drew said, his eyes twinkling.

"What are they?" Gina loved their festive, bright colors — blues, teals, purples, reds, and yellows. She touched a pink ribbon dangling in front of her, letting the satiny material slide through her fingertips.

"Wianki." He pointed to a small sign on the table where, under the word, the phonetic pronunciation was written out — VEE ON KEY.

"You still haven't answered the question. What are they?"

"Pick the one you like, and I'll explain later." He gave a wink to the short older woman behind the table.

Gina rolled her eyes, but she loved his mysteriousness. She pointed to one with white flowers and red roses. If she was going to wear a wianki, it may as well be made up of the Polish colors. Drew paid, and they walked out of the tent into the June sunshine. After moving onto a nearby patch of grass, Drew settled the crown on Gina's head, straightening the ribbons so they could flutter freely behind her and tucking in a few stray strands of her hair.

"You look beautiful in a wianki, but that's no surprise." He studied her face, as if memorizing the moment. This is what made Drew so special, so different from anyone else she'd ever dated. He treated her as a gift in his life, someone to treasure, not as an afterthought or employee. Her parents treated marriage as a business proposition. If she had lived a century earlier, she probably would have been married off at thirteen to whatever club member's son had the best prospects. But with Drew, she knew in her bones that he wanted to know all of her and for her to know all of him. He wanted her to feel special because, in his heart, he believed that she was. At last, he answered her question.

"Wianki are traditionally worn by maidens at festivals, especially on St. John's Eve, which was always near Midsummer's Eve. At the end of the festival, the maidens would throw their flower wreaths into the water. If yours became tangled with another girl's, then you were destined to be best friends. If it sank, then you would likely never get married and probably have a lot of cats. But, if a young man snatched your wreath from the water, then the two of you were destined to be married." Drew took her hands and wrapped them around his own neck, pulling her close to him. "I would dive into any river in the world to catch yours."

His lips settled on hers in the softest of whispers, then pulled back, their faces only inches apart.

"I love you, Gina Price."

Standing in the shade, surrounded by hundreds of people, the waft of sauerkraut in the air, Gina gave her heart away forever. She would follow him anywhere, do whatever it took to make him happy. Her joy shone in the smile that took over her face.

"I love you, too, Drew Zoberski."

The words weren't nearly enough. She wanted to get him home, to show him just how much she loved him, but now was not the time. First, they needed to make it through cocktails with her parents.

"Now you're Polish like the rest of us," Drew said.

If only that were true. Being here with Drew, Gina had never felt she belonged somewhere more.

Now she didn't even belong in her own home. "I'm screwing this up so badly, Drew. I need you right now. More than ever. I'm losing her. I'm going to turn into my mom without you here. May's going to hate me."

She let the tears take her. Gina had learned long ago that once they broke, she had to let them dry themselves up. Then she could stuff all the anguish back inside its bottle until the next time the cork popped off. A rush of cold air sent a shiver through her already shaking body.

"What happened? Is Mom okay? I was only on the road for a few minutes!" Vicky had burst through the kitchen door.

Gina took a deep breath and shook her head in response to Vicky's question before she began re-corking her pain, wiping her tears with the kitchen towel hanging off a hook near her face.

"Mom's fine," she said, her voice scratchy.

Vicky knelt beside her and pulled her in for a hug.

"May?"

Gina nodded. "And Drew. I can't do this alone."

"Yes, you can. You already are, and you're doing brilliantly. You aren't ever really alone, but it's okay to feel overwhelmed."

She smoothed Gina's hair away from her face as Gina explained what had happened.

"Way to go, May!"

Gina glared at Vicky.

"That was not the reaction I had."

"Of course not. You're her mom. I'm her cool aunt Vicky. Wait until one of my kids does something stupid, then you can laugh about it. You only have one — I have four glorious deviants in training."

Gina managed a chuckle at Vicky's logic. Her kids were going to be a handful, if only because they outnumbered their parents. The laughter eased her tension, clearing some room for rational thought. She was no longer buried and immobile from her guilt and failure. Grateful, she hugged her sister, stood, and helped pull up Vicky.

"Thanks, Vic."

"That's what I'm here for. Besides, at her

age, I'd already graduated to amaretto sours and tequila shots."

Gina raised an eyebrow. "That's less helpful."

"You're a good mom, just follow your instincts," Vicky said as they both sat down at the table. "You know, I've always been a little jealous of you." Gina rolled her eyes. "No, really. You married the man of your dreams no matter what Mom said. You loved each other to the point of stupid. I can barely imagine the pain you've experienced, and I'm sure that still isn't even close to the reality, but you had perfection once. That's amazing. I followed the Mom-approved route of marrying for financial security. It's . . . a less optimal plan."

Vicky picked up one of the wineglasses and took a sip, made a face, then drained the glass into the sink. "That's awful." She set the empty glass next to the sink. "FYI, Jeff called. He's bringing the kids up tomorrow morning. Apparently being in charge of them for thirty-six hours is too much for him. He said he didn't marry me so he could manage the kids and make all the money. Charming, right?"

Gina's heart clenched for Vicky. Jeff could be a real dick. She stood and hugged Vicky, who was staring out the kitchen window, then left her alone with her thoughts. Making a mental note to pull out the air mattresses after she spoke to May, Gina took a deep breath and walked down the hall toward her daughter's room. She tapped lightly on her bedroom door, then opened it, knowing she wasn't going to get a response. May sat on the one spot of open floor, her clothes pushed back to form a ridge, like a crater after a bomb detonation. Gina nudged an edge to expand the area and sat down in front of her, grabbing one of her hands. May didn't pull back, which Gina took as a good sign.

"I'm sorry I said you were my problem. You have never, ever been a problem, and I'm sick over you thinking I feel that way. You believing that, even for a second, is my problem. I love you, May, more than you even know. I know I don't always say or do the right things, but I am trying. Do you believe me?"

May shrugged her shoulders, her cheeks red and her lashes wet. This was going better than expected — maybe Drew was helping her somehow.

"Drinking and getting naked —"

"We weren't naked. Or getting naked." May's head popped up and she tried to pull her hand back, but Gina held tight.

"Fine. Drinking and making out. Is that better?"

She shrugged again.

"That is a problem," Gina continued. "You are fourteen and much too young to be drinking."

"I hardly had any. It was gross. Besides, you drink all the time."

Gina didn't reveal that the wine had soured. Let her daughter believe wine always tasted that bad.

"I drive a car, too. And work all day. Does that mean you're going to do those things, too?"

"I've had to deal with a lot of stuff that most grown-ups don't deal with."

"I know, baby. But you don't have to anymore. You're a kid. Enjoy being a kid." There, that was a good, parentally sound message. "And besides the wine, I'm not okay with shirtless making out either. I believe you that you didn't intend for it to go further, but you're my little girl and I'm not ready." Gina reached over and rubbed May's leg. "For the rest of break, you are with me all day. You're helping me on the food truck, you're coming to visit Grandma in the hospital —"

"But —" May started to say.

Gina put her hand up.

"Let me finish. I've been letting you do what you want, not demanding anything of you, and that's not what a good mother does. You're a teen, so it's normal for you to have days like today. But the consequences of those choices are that I'm going to try to teach you why those weren't the right decisions. It's time we spent a lot more time together. I don't know you anymore, and that's on me. You have never been, nor ever will be, a problem to me. You are what I get out of bed for. So while this might feel like torture to you, I'm really looking forward to spending more time with you. Maybe hearing a bit more about Connor . . ."

May scrunched her face. "Grandma will probably yell at me because I haven't been to see her yet."

"Actually, with the stroke, she can't say much of anything. It makes her a little more pleasant to be around."

"Mom! I can't believe you said that." Gina skootched around so they were leaning against the bed, side by side.

"Maybe I need to be a little more honest about things. Grandma and I never got along well when I was your age. I never could live up to her standards — always a disappointment to her. I don't want that to happen to us." She held out her hand. "One last thing: I'm going to need your phone. You'll get it back when winter break is over."

May winced, started to protest, obviously thought better of it, and plopped it in her open hand. Gina knew this would be the worst part of May's punishment — but a little tech-free time would be good for her. For them. She put her arm around May, who leaned her head on Gina's shoulder. It was a start.

After the day they all had, it was definitely a pizza delivery kind of night. A half bacon and half pepperoni was on its way, and May mixed up a batch of brownies with chunks of peanut butter cup. Gina was so proud of her flare for baking and loved sampling her fun creations. Plus, as the mom, she got first dibs on the corner pieces.

As Gina hung up the phone after a status report from the nurse on Lorraine's floor, Vicky ran into the kitchen, her hair wrapped in a towel, and she flung open the back door.

"Look who's sneaking up on us," Vicky said.

Roza stood on the back stoop, holding a large foil-covered pan.

"Are those what I think they are, Aunt Roza?" May asked, swiping the pan, plopping it on the counter, and tearing off the foil to reveal the mountain of brown-speckled pierogis.

Before May could get the plates on the table, Gina and Vicky had each grabbed one straight from the pan, like they were still teenagers themselves. The dumplings were still warm. Gina had closed her eyes to savor the onion and potato goodness in her mouth when the doorbell chimed. The pizza guy. She paid him without a word, unable to speak with her mouth full, and put it straight in the fridge for tomorrow. With Roza's pierogis around, who could want pizza?

The four women all gathered around the table, eating and wiping their buttery fingers on paper towels. Most families were more civilized and ate pierogis with a plate and fork, but they were always such a treat, formality would have only gotten in the way.

"No one would ever accuse you three of being ladies." Roza stepped out of their way. "A person could lose a limb in the stampede. Is no one feeding you all properly? Gina, what sort of house are you running?" She went to the fridge and poured them each a glass of milk, not able to turn off her caretaking, even at another person's house.

"Your pierogis are the best, Aunt Roza." May leaned into her side for a hug and kiss, then walked around to sit next to Vicky, the farthest chair from Gina.

"I'm not questioning this wonderful surprise, but what brings you over bearing our favorite food?"

Roza wiped her already pristine hands on a paper towel, not meeting Gina's and Vicky's eyes.

"Do you still have that picture and birth certificate you brought to my house?"

"Yes." Gina wiped her hands carefully and leaned over to pull them from her purse and hand them to Roza.

She pointed to the uniformed man in the photo. "This is your father." No nonsense, as ever.

"I knew you were a love child!" Vicky said.

"Both of yours."

She pointed at both Vicky and Gina, and Vicky stopped crowing to let the truth hit her, too.

Gina shook her head forcefully, resisting this blunt fact. "You said you didn't know who this was — and that guy looks nothing like our dad."

"I lied to you earlier. I was protecting your mother, but she and I came to an agreement this afternoon. The man in this photo is your biological father. This is Joseph Sandowski. Joe." She tapped the birth certificate where his name was. May leaned in to look, but Gina picked up the photo, trying to find the words to respond. What Roza was saying was like two puzzle pieces that wouldn't connect. No matter which way she moved them, they wouldn't go together. Floyd Price. Joe Sandowski. Father. The picture. The baby in the picture.

Her dad had never been father of the year, sure, but she had never doubted that the man she grew up with was her father. She'd always taken her family at face value. Now, everything about their family had imploded. Or exploded, she didn't know which. She didn't doubt Roza — she'd known the older woman had been hiding something earlier. Now she couldn't find the questions to ask, because suddenly there was an entirely new history she had never known about. The room wavered, and she grabbed the table.

"How? Why?" She went with the basics. Vicky nodded in agreement at these simple questions.

Roza folded the paper towel in half, then in half again, smoothing it out with her fingers.

"This was a long time ago, girls, and things were different. Lorraine and Joe — your father — used to live in the apartment underneath me. We would have Sunday dinners on the lawn during the summer, and cozy meals upstairs in the winter. Your mom would help clean up after. Joe, bless him, would fix broken screens and squeaky doors, tasks that my husband didn't have a chance to do because he was working long hours at the store. They were young and in love, and alone. Your grandparents had cut your mother off for marrying someone they deemed unworthy."

That sounded like them, from Gina's scant memories of her grandparents — but it also sounded like Lorraine herself: judgmental, quick to issue edicts.

"Joe went off to the Vietnam War. So many like him did — young, hardworking, poor. They thought, naively, he would do his tour then be back before you girls even knew he'd been gone. I took this picture the day he left. He never came home."

"But I don't understand why Mom wouldn't . . ." Vicky started.

"Your mom was unskilled, with a small baby, a second on the way, and no way to earn a living. Your dad was killed in combat, so she was entitled to a little money from the government, but it wasn't enough to live on, especially since he was an enlisted man and not an officer."

Gina opened her mouth to protest, but nothing came out. There were so many options. She could have worked at a restaurant, gotten government assistance, what about Joe's Social Security benefits?

"Why didn't she get a job?" May asked the question Gina was thinking.

"Think about it," Roza continued. "Can you really envision Lorraine working as a receptionist or in a restaurant, living paycheck to paycheck and sweating through her days? She would have been happy with Joe by her side, but without him — well, she wasn't raised like that. And if you ask me, she was scared to be on her own, especially with two little ones — or, one little one and one on the way. So she went home to what she did know. Within a few days, her father had found Floyd, the man who raised you. He was a solution to her problems. Floyd agreed to the marriage, though, only as long as no one knew you and Vicky weren't his biological children."

"If you knew Mom before she married my dad, I mean Floyd, then why were you our nanny?" Vicky asked.

"Your mom needed help, and she asked me."

Still wordless, Gina bit into another pierogi, letting the familiar ease her into this new information. Should she be angry? Hurt? Relieved? She had so many emotions and questions competing for attention in her brain. What was Joe like? Who really was her mother, to keep such a big secret from them their whole lives? There was so much to ask her mother she didn't know — so much that she should know.

"Your mom wasn't unhappy, but those early years shaped her. If she wasn't going to have Joe as her husband, she had to put you first. Never forget that she loved you girls and wanted the best for you. Marrying Floyd let her give you the most promising upbringing, great schools, and social connections."

"You," Gina said.

"Yes, me. Being a part of your lives has been one of my life's greatest joys. You girls were a second family for me, and you can never have a big enough family. She gave you the best she could."

"But she married someone she didn't love. And don't tell me she and Dad loved each other. I'm not stupid. I could almost hear her sigh with relief at his funeral," Vicky said.

"Theirs was a . . . complicated marriage."

Roza didn't say another word, but Gina had questions about that, too. She'd always known her parents had never shared a bedroom. It had seemed normal until she started visiting friends and saw that their parents all shared the one room. Her mom had always claimed it was because Dad snored and she was a light sleeper. As Gina got older, though, she wondered if there wasn't a simpler explanation.

"Well, now the pierogis make sense," Vicky said, swiping another one in the butter before popping it into her mouth. "Shocking news is always better with your cooking."

After they finished the pierogis, Gina washed the plate and Roza left, quickly followed by May heading off to her room. At least she and May seemed to be in a better place. One less relationship to worry over. Vicky pulled a bottle of wine from her purse, unscrewed the cap, and poured wine into two coffee mugs she retrieved from the clean dishwasher. She slid the white chipped mug across the table to Gina.

"Well, cheers to our expanded family tree."

Gina picked up her mug and clinked it against Vicky's.

"I don't even know how to feel," Gina said.

"Oh, I'm pissed. All those years of playing the perfect society matriarch and our mother had run off with a man who also happens to be our real father. We're a bad soap opera plot. She has lost all credibility."

Gina took a long gulp of the red wine. It was tart and burned down her throat. She took another swallow and it went down easier. Like this new information, the longer she tasted it, the more she accepted it, but it still wasn't good.

"I'm hurt, but I'm relieved, too. Dad always seemed so distant and I was jealous of friends whose dads doted on them. At least now there's an explanation."

"I don't care. We should have grown up knowing he was a stepfather."

"If what Roza said is right, Mom was making these decisions right after Joe died. I can't imagine having to make life-altering choices during that immediate wave of loss. I could barely get out of bed, and she did what she had to do to put us first. She's tougher than I thought."

"Stop trying to put a positive spin on this. You aren't going to convince me not to be angry. And I don't understand why you aren't, too. She made things so difficult when you decided to marry a Polish boy and she had done exactly the same thing. Hell, we're both half-Polish."

Gina hadn't thought of that. Her eyes strayed to the Wianki on the wall and she briefly smiled at the memory, but it quickly turned back to a frown. It was true. Her mother had done exactly as she had once, but instead of understanding, her mother had criticized and rejected her for it.

"Why did you have to say that? Now I'm pissed, too. I can understand why she did it, but now I don't want to forgive her. But I'm also really curious about Joe, and what he was like."

Eager for some alone time, Gina drank the last of her wine, rinsed the mug out in the sink, and kissed her sister on the top of her head. "Night."

"Night." Her sister dumped the rest of the bottle into her mug and disappeared into the guest bedroom.

After such a day, Gina sat down looking forward to writing her end-of-day list. She found it cleared her mind before sleep, giving her a plan to wake up to the next day. The smooth pen and the way it whispered as it flew over the paper was better than any meditation: the sound of order and productivity and control. It kept her focused on moving forward rather than risking moving backward, or dwelling on the past. Gina really needed to feel in control of something.

Tonight's list started with the usual items:

1. Shower.
2. Costco — supplies for G's (cheddar, Brie, white bread, onions, pork, bacon, napkins, aluminum foil squares) with May!!!!
3. City hall, with May.
4. Visit Mom, with May.

She smiled at getting to spend so much time with her daughter, even though it was technically a punishment.

As she turned the notebook page, all the blank holes in the story Roza had told cluttered her thoughts, and her list evolved into questions — questions she hoped would help her sort out her muddled emotions. It was so hard to know where to start. But if Dr. Patel was right, there was a possibility her mom might have another, more lethal stroke, and there was so much she still didn't know. She settled back into the fluffy pillows of her bed, her notebook propped up on her knees and opened to a fresh page.

1. What is one fact you know to be true?
2. Have I lived up to your expectations?

3. How did you meet my father?
4. How are we alike? Different?
5. What's been your greatest joy?
6. Have you ever felt overwhelmed and wanted to give up?
7. What is your greatest heartbreak?
8. What is your biggest regret?
9. What is the best part of being my mom?
10 What do you need me to know?

All Gina's life, Lorraine had been the wall she needed to get around before she could live. Her mom was a jailer, an enforcer, a life-ruiner. She was a job description, never a person. Even when Gina had called crying in the night because May had colic as a baby, talking to Lorraine had been less helpful than reading Dr. Spock.

Looking over the list of questions she'd scrawled, she realized she really knew nothing about her mom — she didn't understand the complicated person hiding behind the persona. She wasn't merely someone who kept Gina's freedom at bay during her teen years, or the fussy older woman who ran guilt on an open tap when she became an adult. She had always viewed her mother as someone to placate, keep happy, try to please. She never thought of her as someone she wanted to know. But for the first time, she did want to know her mother. It was time to ask some questions.

Chapter Fifteen

Lorraine knew the second the sad-face train entered her hospital room that Roza had followed through on her promise to tell the girls about Joe. Regina, Victoria, and May stared at her like some tragic figure, a victim of circumstance. After an obligatory kiss on the cheek, May slumped into the chair farthest from her, her clothes wrinkled, and proceeded to avoid eye contact by enlarging the ragged hole in her jeans, making a haystack from the threads she pulled out. At least the girl didn't have her face buried in her phone, but she did have an orange stripe in her beautiful brown hair. What had that child done to her head? And why was Regina letting her out in public like that?

Victoria went straight for the most comfortable chair, pushing back on the arms to kick out the footrest. She was treating her own mother's hospitalization like a personal vacation.

Regina pulled up the last chair and sat next to Lorraine, pulling a piece of paper from her pocket. Lorraine stared at her, wishing she could speak, wishing she hadn't waited so long. Gina hadn't put any makeup on — after all the times she explained the importance of always looking one's best. Heaven forbid. She could have at least put some moisturizer on. Or coconut oil. Yes, Regina needed coconut oil. She could see the tub on the windowsill.

"Yerba lay." Her lips and tongue felt swollen, making it impossible to make the right sounds. That morning, Lorraine had practiced for an hour with a therapist. Sounds were coming better now, yes, but not even close to the right words. She stretched her tongue. Her therapist said she needed to retrain her mouth to speak, and it would take time. But Lorraine did not have time. There were important things to discuss. She licked her lips and tried again, wrapping her mouth around the sounds, slowing them down. "Yeeerrrr-baaaaaaa laaaaaay." Even to her own ear, she knew that wasn't right.

"Do you want to lie down, Mom? Are you tired?" Regina asked, standing to look for the bed's controls.

Lorraine shook her head from side to side in slow sweeping motions. That was her one success. With a lot of concentration, she could shake her head yes and no. She looked at the window, even moving a hand in that direction.

"Yer. Ba. Lay."

"What?" Regina looked around the bed to see what Lorraine could possibly want.

"Gina." Victoria made a lot of unnecessary noise folding the footstool back into the chair, clomping to the windowsill, and grabbing the jar of coconut oil to hold out to Regina. "She wants this."

Lorraine nodded. "Yerba lay."

"How did you get that from 'yerba lay'?" Regina asked, reaching for it from her sister.

"Because she always wants coconut oil. The odds were in its favor."

Regina opened the lid and scooped out some.

"Can you point to where you want it?" Regina asked.

How could she not feel her own skin begging for some moisture? Lorraine lifted her hand toward Regina's face. "Okay, your hands." She took Lorraine's hand and rubbed it in, which did feel nice, but Lorraine shook her head and put her hand on Regina's face, leaving a greasy smear.

Victoria laughed. "She thinks you need it.

Good to know some things never change, Mom."

Lorraine nodded as Regina pulled away from her, using a tissue to wipe the coconut oil from her face. What a waste. Regina flattened her paper again, her eyes growing sadder.

"How could you never tell us that Floyd wasn't our biological dad? How could you hide that from us? Something so big?"

Victoria flopped back in her chair. "How do you expect her to answer?"

Lorraine looked at both their dear faces. How could she explain when she literally had no words? Losing a beloved spouse was like losing an arm. Regina should understand that. You could carry on, but everything was simply harder than it used to be. Then, just when you thought you had adjusted to your new reality, you'd lose a leg. Lorraine would turn to tell Joe something the girls had done, and the bed would be empty. Moving on hadn't meant forgetting Joe — it had meant carving out a special place in her heart so he could be a part of everything in secret. She wouldn't have traded anything for the few years she got to spend as his wife, and that's what she could never explain to the women standing over her bed — what choosing Joe had cost her.

■ ■ ■ ■

The restaurant was perched on a cliff overlooking Lake Michigan where they could see the whitecaps dotting the surface of the water, breaking up the monotony of the icy gray-blue. White-clothed tables dotted a golden wood floor. Joe's strong hands shook as he pulled out her chair, having shooed the waiter away from the task he viewed as an honor rather than a responsibility. He wore what she knew was his best — well, only — suit, a classic dark gray with a wide blue tie. He looked even more dashing than usual, and Lorraine was floating on air, even as she was curious about his formality.

"Are you okay?" Lorraine asked.

"More than." He smiled to her as he sat across the table. He straightened a fork he had knocked askew and spread his napkin on his lap, then sipped from the sweating ice water goblet. He looked around the restaurant and cleared his throat. "Tell me about your day."

Odd. She had just spent the entire car ride telling him about her day.

"I'm not sure what else to tell you that I didn't already say in the car. Mom is still determined to marry me off to Benny Miller."

Joe scowled at the mention of the name.

"I am not a fan of that plan. If he ever touches you, I'll . . ."

She reached across the table and held his hand, amused that he didn't think she could handle herself. The waiter arrived and took their orders, bringing a bottle of champagne that Joe must have ordered before they arrived.

"Are we celebrating something?" she asked. Her stomach fluttered as an idea — a hope — as to what they might be celebrating rose.

Joe rubbed his hands together and nodded his head.

"I was going to wait for dessert to do this, but that seems ridiculous. I'm so nervous I can't even think straight and I want to remember every second of this night."

He stood, reaching into his jacket pocket, and pulled out a box, then took a knee in front of her. The room went black except for him, as if he knelt in a spotlight on a dark stage. She had envisioned this moment a million times in the few months they'd been dating. Before his knee even hit the restaurant's wooden floor, she knew her answer.

"The day we met, the world changed for me. Colors became brighter, jokes were funnier, and food tasted better. Just knowing you breathed the same air and walked the same earth as me, gave me hope I didn't know I was looking for. And then you smiled at me and I was done. I pray every day that what you want is me, because I know I want you. I promise to spend the rest of my life trying to be worthy of that honor. My lovely Lorraine, will you do me the great privilege of becoming my bride?"

Lorraine was lost in his clear brown eyes, so certain of their future, yet so reliant on her for his happiness. She felt the same. In such a short time, he had become her everything, her strength. She didn't care that he was poor, or that her parents disapproved. She wanted to spend the rest of her life making him smile like that. He made her a better person, helping her realize she didn't need to rely on her parents for everything. As long as his eyes were on her, she didn't need anything else. Tears formed along with a smile, as the vision of the many years in front of them danced in her mind.

"Lorraine?" Joe whispered. "I'm going to need an answer so I can slip this ring on your finger and give you a proper kiss."

"Yes, of course, yes." She grabbed him by

the neck and pulled him close, kissing him with all the promise of a woman madly in love. The restaurant broke into applause, and Lorraine blushed, having forgotten about their audience. Joe slid the simple, modest solitaire onto her finger, kissing it, and moved his chair so he'd be sitting next to her instead of across the table, leaving his back to the restaurant.

Under the table, their legs and feet mingled, his hands holding hers as he brought them to his lips for tender kisses.

"I think I see a flaw in my plan now. You see, I'm no longer very hungry for dinner or for an audience."

They took their dinners to go.

"We should tell your parents tonight," Joe said. They were parked in her blue Beetle, saying their good nights outside his small apartment. She had managed to climb onto his lap so her back leaned against the open window of the door.

"And ruin this perfect night? Why would you suggest such a thing?"

"The sooner they know, the sooner we can start planning the wedding." He was right, of course, but she wanted to stay in this cocoon of bliss a bit longer. As if he knew what she was thinking, he continued. "If you think this is nice, imagine when we can share the same home. The same bed."

Oh, she'd imagined it. Much to her dismay, he'd been the perfect gentleman toward her during the entire time they'd been together. She thought things might change when they took their dinner to go, but they only kissed until he pulled back — like always. He had the self-control of a vegetarian at a barbecue, while she would be stuffing burgers in her face with abandon. Unbuttoning Joe's shirt, she trailed kisses down his neck and let her hands roam over his chest. He leaned his head back as her hands found their way to his sides, trailing up and down along his ribs as she worked her lips up to his ear, giving a little nibble. His breathing came quicker, proving he wasn't immune to her. She enjoyed the power she had over him, seeing how far she could push him before his brakes kicked in, and wondered if she could crack his self-control tonight.

With a quick sucking in of air, he picked her up and moved her back to the driver's seat. When they took her car, he always let her drive — something she'd never seen her father let her mother do — and she liked that.

"It's time, my lovely."

"You sure?" Lorraine let her lip pout. She wasn't above using all her tools to get her way.

"No, I'm not sure in the least, which tells me everything I need to know. When we're married, and not a moment before, I'm going to take my time exploring every inch of you. So the sooner we get married, the better. And that can't happen until we tell your parents."

She nodded in reluctant agreement, started up the car, and drove to her parents' house. They waited, hand in hand, for her parents to return from the club, in the dark, wood-paneled living room, on the bright orange sofa that matched the plaid carpet. The goldenrod drapes tied it all together, or so her mom said. Nothing in this room was comfortable. It was meant to be looked at and not enjoyed, like everything else in her parents' world — it was all for appearances.

They didn't have to wait long. When they heard the door close, Lorraine rose to greet them in the hallway.

"Darling, I didn't expect you to be up. Are you feeling better?" her mother asked, moving to place the back of a hand on her forehead. Lorraine ignored the question and plowed on with purpose.

"Mom, Dad. Can you join me in the living room? I have something I need to tell you."

Her mother's face scrunched in confusion while her father's turned to stone. He knew. Maybe not exactly what, but he knew that something was amiss under his roof the way a wolf knows there is an intruder in his territory. Lorraine moved quickly to stand next to Joe in front of the lannon stone fireplace they never used. Her parents paused, startled.

"Who is this young man?" her mother asked. Lorraine had completely forgotten that her mother had never met the man who consumed her entire being, but it was clear from his expression that her dad remembered Joe. His nostrils flared at Lorraine's disobedience, but he remained silent. Lorraine knew her mother was the weak link: if she could gain her support, her father might tolerate the union.

"Mom, this is Joseph Sandowski. We've been dating for a few months, and it's gotten serious. He proposed to me tonight. I said yes. We're getting married." As Lorraine said the words, her heart wanted to squeal with joy. She was going to marry Joe!

Joe stepped forward with his right arm extended to shake her hand. Her mom didn't move forward to meet him. Not a good sign.

"I don't understand," her mother said as her dad finally found his voice, roaring over his wife's soft-spoken tone.

"Get out of this house. You are not marrying my daughter." He grabbed Joe by the arm and pulled him toward the exit. "I already told her you weren't good enough for her. I still mean it. I forbid it."

Joe yanked his arm free and stepped out of arm's reach. Even now, he was unintimidated by her father's thunder.

"Stop it, Dad!" Lorraine shouted. "I am marrying him, whether you like it or not. I love him. He loves me. If anyone is not good enough, it's me. Look at how my family is treating him. You're trying to shove him out the door, and Mom can't finish a thought. You'll just need to get used to the idea and then you'll see."

"He is a used-car salesman, young lady. You will not marry a glorified grease monkey and struggle for the rest of your life. I didn't work this hard to see my daughter have a worse life than my own." Her father's face reddened with each word as her mom stood still in his shadow. Tears sizzled on Lorraine's cheeks.

Joe's nostrils flared, but he let Lorraine

take the lead. She loved him all the more for it.

"I'm marrying Joe. Accept it."

"Then get out from under my roof. You marry that man and you are no longer my daughter." Her mom opened her mouth to protest, but her father pointed a finger in her direction. "Not one word." Her mother started to cry silently — a skill she had learned over the years. Today was not the day her mother was going to stand up for herself. "You have fifteen minutes to gather some clothes."

He slammed the door to his office.

"Mom?" Lorraine couldn't believe he would actually kick her out, make her choose between her fiancé and her parents. How could he disown her? Her mom only shook her head and left the room. They were really letting her go, just like that. Joe laced his fingers with hers.

"I can't ask you to give up your family. I understand."

His face told her he meant it. He would let her go if that was what she wanted.

She looked directly into the face of her future. "How could I choose them over you?" She kissed him softly on the lips, letting her loss and joy mix together. "I'll be down in ten minutes."

She stuffed clothes and a few treasured books into her matching powder blue suitcases and they were married a few days later. Joe was a partner, not a provider, their marriage would never be the cold, uneven relationship her parents shared.

Together, they'd walked out the door and into their new life, the life that would bring Lorraine's two beautiful girls to this moment by her hospital bed, wanting answers to questions she couldn't give voice to.

■ ■ ■ ■

Have You Ever Felt Overwhelmed and Wanted to Give Up?

■ ■ ■ ■

Chapter Sixteen

May hated it here. Everything about the hospital reminded her of her dad and the day he died. The air so filtered it didn't smell like anything. The stark, easy-to-clean surfaces everywhere. The cords. The machines. The odd spigots on the walls. Sure, they all had a purpose. Not enough air, breathe here. Not enough fluid, hook up here. Can't pee on your own, there's a tube for that. It made her skin crawl.

Using an earring post she'd taken from her ear, she yanked at another thread from her jeans, carefully unweaving it rather than pulling it out. She hadn't looked at Grandma Lorraine since the first quick greeting when they walked in the room. Grandma had never been the type of grandma who would bake cookies or color at the kitchen table. That was more like Grandma Zoberski, her dad's mom. She lived near Aunt Roza but spent the winters in Arizona at a giant resort for old people.

May always felt like Grandma Lorraine was studying her, looking for what she was doing wrong, like not standing straight or not speaking clearly. So, she tried to stay out of Grandma Lorraine's line of sight when they were in the same room. May thought she'd be glad that Grandma Lorraine couldn't bark suggestions at her, but instead, it made her sad. It meant something had changed, and change was never good. Change combined with a hospital? The worst.

The only upside was that her mom was too focused on Grandma Lorraine to pay any attention to her. If they had to spend all day together, she didn't want to have to pretend everything was better. It wasn't, not really. How could it be when she couldn't text Connor or Olivia? They probably thought she was going dark again.

Oh my God, Connor's mom was here.

"Good morning." Dr. Patel zoomed into the room, her hair pulled into a neat ponytail, showing off her freckles. Connor had a few, but they were difficult to see on his much darker skin. May had seriously been hoping to avoid his mom. She slouched in her chair but could feel Dr. Patel's crisp blue eyes on her.

"Morning," her mom said back. "May, don't you have something you wanted to say to Dr. Patel?" They had talked about this on the way to the hospital. But she didn't want to say anything. The silence stretched out like taffy. Her mom gave her the Mom-sending-message-look. Fine.

"I'm sorry for giving wine to Connor. That was wrong and inappropriate. And for having him over without supervision." She didn't really want to get into too many details, not with so many adult eyes on her. She had practiced in her head once her mother had decreed she would need to apologize. The words were well rehearsed and clear, though she really didn't regret his unsupervised visit. The wine — yes.

"Thank you for saying so, May. That means a lot. But I'm sure Connor played his part, too."

May wasn't going to respond to that. She knew that they knew about Connor and her making out, but she didn't want to talk about it with them or near them, ever.

"May and I are going to be inseparable this week, like peas and carrots. Like peanut butter and jelly. Like melted cheese and crispy bread." May rolled her eyes and her mom saw it and looked hurt. May only felt a little guilty. "Anyway, she'll be with me, so there won't be any more shenanigans. I used to think chasing them around to make sure they didn't run into traffic was the hard part," her mom said.

"Right? I feel like we need to watch them more now." Dr. Patel pulled out her iPad, signaling she was moving into doctor mode. Thank God. "Now, Lorraine, let's see how you're doing."

She proceeded to ask her grandma yes and no questions, but May drifted off, thrilled that the uncomfortable portion of the day was officially over. She wished she could text Connor to see what his punishment was, if he was even getting punished. She may have avoided her friends for a year, but that had been by choice. It was totally different when the isolation was parent-induced.

"Okay," Dr. Patel said. "Your mom has made a bit of progress today. We'll keep her here for a few more days to do more follow-up tests, then move her to a long-term rehab facility."

"Why can't she come home with one of us?" her mom asked.

Dr. Patel smiled, and Aunt Vicky looked a little alarmed. May seconded that opinion. *Please say that's a bad idea, please say that's a bad idea.* She knew who would be expected to help whenever she wasn't at school.

"I understand your wanting to help, but it's too much. Trust me. You'd have to bring her to physical therapy every day for several hours, then be around to help her all night. You wouldn't be able to work. Her insurance is good and covers the cost, so the best course of action is to take advantage of it, for everyone's sanity and your mom's safety."

Whew.

She left and May returned to picking at her jeans. Her mom went back to asking Grandma questions she couldn't answer. Why bother? How did no one else get that but her? Especially when she had hid their real dad from her mom and Aunt Vicky all their lives. She had heard stories about Grandpa Price but couldn't really remember him. He died when she was still very young, but he sounded like a dud. Not mean, just not good grandpa material. She was glad she didn't remember him. But Joe Sandowski. From what Aunt Roza said, he sounded like the kind of grandpa who would have picked up teaching her about engines now that her dad couldn't.

She pulled out the threads, listening as the grown-ups talked. Sometimes they would forget about her if she was quiet enough. She picked up a lot that way.

"Are you going to spend the rest of the day here?" her mom asked Aunt Vicky.

"It depends when Jeff gets here with the kids. Once they arrive, they can only maintain their best behavior for forty-five minutes. After that, they'll need a change of scenery." She got up from the comfy chair and walked to the windows. "I could take them to the park down there. They'll need to get their wiggles out after the drive."

"He's driving them up here?"

"Apparently driving four hours round-trip is preferable to managing playdates and feeding them. Now that he'll be on his own, I'll be surprised if he even bothers to leave the office at all."

Her mom got up to stand next to Aunt Vicky.

"I thought things were better?"

"According to Victoria's Secret, lingerie solves all the world's problems. Their ads are lies."

"I'm sorry." Her mom wrapped her arms around Aunt Vicky. "You let me know what you need."

"Nothing to need. The kids and I will keep doing our thing. I have a beautiful house, beautiful — if not slightly spoiled — children, and I don't have to worry about paying bills."

"You deserve more than just security."

Aunt Vicky shrugged and stepped away from the window. It seemed like Uncle Jeff was being a jerk, but May was excited to see her cousins. Greta and Jake were old enough to play games with her, and the twins Maggie and Nathan were adorably snuggly and cute. Plus, they thought she was the coolest and basically did whatever she said. It was fun being idolized. Maybe she'd make some brownies with them.

"I don't think I have the energy for more. Some days, I'm barely handling this."

Grandma Lorraine watched. Her eyes following the conversation. *I bet she would have a lot to say about Uncle Jeff if she could talk.*

"Why don't you go grab a snack from the vending machine?" Aunt Vicky stood in front of her, holding out a few dollars and May's phone. She must have swiped it from Mom's hiding spot. "Maybe see what's happening outside this room." She winked. Aunt Vicky was the best! May grabbed the phone and escaped.

She found the vending machines and bought a Twix and a water. She found the visitors' lounge and tucked her feet under her. Having her phone back felt like a lifeline to the outside world, or eating ice cream after hours in a pool. She was whole again. Opening the Twix wrapper, she pulled out one of the sticks, nibbling off the chocolate and caramel on the top before gnawing the chocolate on the narrow sides of the cookie. Last, she would eat the nearly naked cookie, but only because she hadn't yet found a good way to get the thin layer of remaining chocolate on the bottom. Her dad had taught her to eat Twix this way. They would share all the small ones she would get from trick-or-treating. Her mom would eat a Twix in two bites, like a savage.

She had pulled out the second stick by the time her phone came back on and had started to receive messages. She had a screen full of texts, most from Connor and the rest from Olivia.

Connor: U okay? What did your mom say?
Connor: Let me know what's up?
Connor: RU grounded?
Connor: I'm grounded for the rest of break. I regret nothing. Except the wine, that was gross. 🍷😵
Connor: RU mad?
Olivia: What happened!?!?!?!?! Connor

said u aren't talking to him???????
Olivia: TEXT ME!!
Olivia: YAM.
Olivia: YAM.
Olivia: YAAAAAAAMMMMMMM. 🍆🍆🍆🍆🍆🍆🍆🍆🍆🍆

May rolled her eyes.

Connor: Did u lose your phone?
Connor: I want to watch more Buffy. 😉

May smiled at that last one. Did he really want to watch, or just kiss more? She wanted to kiss more.

May to Conner: I do, too. 😉 Phone confiscated, but I have it for a second.
May: Grounded, too. Mom was not happy and I had to apologize to your mom for making you drink wine. I'm sorry to you, too.
Connor: Totally okay. Glad you aren't mad at me. 🎉
May: Definitely not mad.

She wouldn't text Olivia back yet. Having something special with Connor was like a secret. Even though she'd lost the rest of her break, it was nice to be alone with him, to feel normal, even to get in trouble.

"May." Aunt Vicky was walking toward her, her eyes wide, like she was trying to send a secret message. "Your mom wants to go." Her mom was right behind her, leaving the room carrying their coats. May got the hint — she needed to get the phone back to Aunt Vicky without her mom seeing. She turned it off and walked toward Aunt Vicky, blocking her hands with her body, handed it off in the space between them where her mom couldn't see.

"Thanks," she whispered.

With her cousins, Aunt Vicky had a lot of rules, like no eating on the carpeting or Play-Doh on the carpeting, or any drinks on the carpeting. A lot of her rules had to do with carpeting, now that May thought about it. But Aunt Vicky bent the rules for her, which was awesome.

May hated it here, too. Grilled G's was set up outside Wauwatosa's city hall, along with a few other trucks they saw often. She didn't know how her mom stood working inside of a constant reminder of her dad. He had touched every surface. It smelled a little like him, too. She didn't even like looking at the truck when it was in their driveway, and now she needed to spend hours in it.

May hadn't helped in the truck since last

summer. Lunch was always short and frantic, two hours of hustling. In the summer, they sometimes did extend the hours at fests, but for a lunch, it was two hours, in and out.

"You'll be taking orders, register, and expediting, I'll handle all the cooking, okay?" her mom said.

"Fine."

"Do you remember how to run the register?"

It was just an app. A chihuahua could be trained to use it.

"Yeah."

"I'm excited about having you here. It's been too long since you've worked with me."

Her mom smiled like everything was perfect, but she wasn't the one grounded and without a phone. Could her mom really be so delusional that she thought one little apology would fix everything?

May didn't respond.

People were already lined up outside. Her mom had a pretty good system for prep, so May mostly stayed out of her way, stealing shreds of cheese.

"It's go time!" her mom said, opening the order window and pushing up the corners of her mouth to remind May to smile.

May began taking orders and handing

them to the waiting customers. She didn't really mind this part, making sure each order had the right components. Her mom didn't often miss something, but she loved catching her when she did.

An older woman ordered a Classic grilled cheese and slid her the crumpled money to pay for it. Her mom looked over from the grill, suddenly alert to the customers.

"Hey, Charlotte. How are you?"

Wisps of hair stuck out from under her hat. May took the money, her mom already making the order before she'd even entered it into the register. When she slid the grilled cheese over, a corner was almost black. Her mom never burned food.

"Mom? I think . . ."

"Just give it to her."

Weird, but whatever. Maybe that was how the woman — Charlotte — liked them. May shrugged and handed it over.

Charlotte took the sandwich without commenting on the black edge and stepped to the side to start eating. Her mom slid May two more aluminum foil-wrapped sandwiches that hadn't been on anyone's order.

"When she complains that the sandwich is burned, give her these."

"What?"

"I'll explain later."

Sure enough, Charlotte's head appeared in front of May two seconds later.

"This one's burned." She didn't say please, and she'd eaten half the sandwich — the part with the burned spot. May wanted to tell her off for taking advantage of her mom.

"May." Her mom said her name, clipped, like a command.

Her mom was giving away free food to this cranky old lady? Who knows. May gave her the sandwiches. Charlotte tucked them into a plastic bag looped on her arm and walked toward the truck next to them, On a Roll. *What the hell?*

She turned to ask her mom about it, but her question was interrupted.

"Hey, Yam!" Olivia said.

Olivia and Hannah joined the line, wearing unzipped winter jackets with their hands jammed into their coat pockets. May waved to them before helping the next customer. Olivia smiled back at her, but Hannah's lips were pursed, and she squinted at May. Or glared, would be more accurate. May felt the same about Hannah, because she guessed Olivia had told her about the kiss. News traveled fast.

"Hi!" May said when they got to the front of the line. She was mostly happy to see

Olivia — though she would have preferred a little less gossiping about her and Connor.

"Hey, girls." Her mom poked her head out the window. "Having a nice break?"

They both nodded, and she went back to the grill.

"What can I get you?"

"I'll take a grilled Mac n Chz. No pickle," Olivia said.

"Same. But, May" — Hannah dropped her voice to a whisper — "we don't have money." Olivia looked at Hannah, her eyes wide. "That's okay, right? Because we're friends?"

May checked to make sure her mom wasn't paying attention, her pits suddenly a little sweaty. Gross. She wasn't supposed to give out free stuff, even to Aunt Vicky. But she also couldn't say no. She had just started talking to Olivia again. And her mom did just give that old lady extra sandwiches for free. Maybe it wasn't such a big deal?

"Sure. On the house." She rang in the order so the order printed, then entered that they'd paid with cash. The drawer popped open, and she shut it again before it could open all the way. "Your number is twenty-five." She handed them a laminated number. Hannah smiled like she had won, causing

Olivia's frown to deepen. Maybe May would spit on her sandwich.

When she handed them their orders a few minutes later, spit-free, Olivia mouthed "Sorry" and they walked to the nearby park. She didn't like how Hannah was bossing Olivia around, but May just hoped her mom hadn't seen or she'd be in even more trouble.

They finished the lunch rush, each eating a grilled cheese as May wiped down the surfaces and put away the ingredients, checking off her mom's inventory list as she went. It was important everything went back where it belonged — knowing every item's location was the only way her mom could work the truck by herself. Begrudgingly, May was a little impressed that her mom could do it alone.

Her mom printed out the report for the day while counting the cash and reading the numbers as she munched, a string of cheese stretching from her mouth to the sandwich.

"Why are we short? We only had one cash transaction today, but the cash isn't there."

Crap, she'd forgotten to delete their order after it was done.

"Huh?" May stalled for time.

"Did you give free food to your friends?" Her mom tilted her head at her. "You know you can't do that, right?"

"But you did it." The words were already out. She hadn't wanted to do it, but she didn't want Hannah to make a scene and call her uncool in front of Olivia and the line of customers. But she couldn't tell her mom that. "You gave the cranky lady two free sandwiches. And she'd already eaten the burned part."

Her mom pinched the bridge of her nose. She only did that when she was really stressed.

"Charlotte gives those extra sandwiches to people who don't have food to eat, but she won't accept handouts herself. I've tried. So this is how I try to help her. She is helping other people who really, really need it. Not giving sandwiches away to friends that probably had money in their pockets. The phone is mine for an extra week. No complaints."

Her mom turned her back to her, and May kept cleaning up in silence, frustrated that she hadn't known how to handle Hannah, frustrated that she was now in even more trouble for something that wasn't even that big of a deal, and frustrated she couldn't explain it all to her mom.

Chapter Seventeen

Gina couldn't wait for this day to be over. Between her mom finding a way to tell her that she had wrinkles even though she couldn't actually speak, to her daughter giving away free food to her friends, she was done. Never mind that her dad was not actually her dad, but some other guy she had never even heard of, and her mom couldn't elaborate on this beyond simple yes and no questions. Plus, Vicky thought she hadn't noticed her sneak May her phone — but she had. She had let it slide at the time, thinking what's the harm, but that girl was pushing one too many of her buttons today.

Her entire body vibrated with rage or anxiety or irritation or all three. Gina leaned her head against the cool wall of the truck, hoping the chill stainless steel would ease the headache throbbing behind her eyes.

She took a deep breath and focused on

the biggest issue: Joseph Sandowski. Roza had told them only a little, clearly wanting to leave the full story to Lorraine. But Mother couldn't speak, and Dr. Patel suggested she might never fully recover. Hell, she might not even live that much longer, given the statistics. How was she supposed to learn more about her real father if her mother couldn't speak, or worse, died? The more she thought about it, the angrier she became. How could her mother lie to her for years and years and years on end?

Her entire life, Gina had made excuses for why her mom never seemed happy — was never warm, was never satisfied. But she couldn't make excuses for her anymore. This betrayal was too much.

"Hey, G." Daniel's smiling face appeared in the window. "Am I too late?"

Gina smiled. What a treat to see someone who wasn't going to complicate her already complicated day. She'd already turned the grill off, but Daniel's cheerful attitude might be exactly what she needed.

"We turned off the grill," May said before Gina could answer. Daniel's smile melted like snow in April.

"I can turn it back on for my best customer." She flicked the switch. "Daniel, this is my daughter, May."

He waved at May, and she lifted a limp hand then turned her back to him. The teen years couldn't finish soon enough.

"I don't want to keep you." He looked back to Gina, seeming unfazed by May's lack of civility.

"Don't worry, it won't take long to get back up to temperature."

He smiled again.

"You know, Daniel, I love that it doesn't take much to make you happy. Unlike some people." She looked over her shoulder at May, who slammed shut one of the cabinets with a clang. "I sure do need that today."

"A rough one?"

"You have no idea." She dropped some butter to melt on the griddle as it heated. "So, what can I get you?" She leaned on the counter so her face was more level with his. He set a jar next to her elbow — sriracha bacon jam. Brave man, to try spicy again. Gina smiled.

"This one won't even be difficult." She slathered the jam on two pieces of thick white bread, then topped each side with American cheese slices, giving one slice a scoop of macaroni and cheese. While she waited for it to melt together, Daniel piped up.

"You know." Daniel's eyes flicked between

her and May. "If you ever need someone to talk to, I'm all-ears."

"That's very kind. I might take you up on that someday when it's quieter."

May snapped around.

"Sure, talk to some random guy about your daughter like I'm not even standing right here. Does he even know about Dad?"

Gina had hoped to get through the rest of the day without another fight. Obviously, that wasn't going to happen. Her mouth froze in an awkward smile, at war with her own impulse to smooth everything over and make nice. Gina didn't know what to do first, yell at May for her rudeness or apologize to Daniel. Manners, of course, won.

"I am so sorry, Daniel. I didn't raise her to behave this way."

Daniel put a gloved hand on hers where she had braced it on the counter.

"I'm right here, Regina. I can hear you," May said. Her voice was much too loud for the confined space. "And stop touching her, dude."

Gina straightened and pulled her hand away from Daniel, then turned to May.

"Control yourself, please. You . . ." Gina paused, then sniffed. Something was burning. She turned to the griddle, where the buttered toast was singed along the edge and smoke wafted off of it. She quickly scooped up the slices with a spatula and peeked at the underside. Completely black. "Mother fudge. Give me a few more minutes, Daniel. I'll get another one going."

"No need. Another time." He gave her a quick nod and wave and walked out of sight. Gina threw the burned sandwich into the trash, turned off the griddle again, and faced May, who still stood with arms crossed on her chest. If their mutual anger could catch fire, they'd be standing in an inferno. All thoughts of good parenting and understanding teens evaporated. Gina was pissed.

"What in the hell was all that about?"

"Are you dating him? Is he, like, your boyfriend or something?" May's arms dropped straight to her sides, her hands in fists like she used to make as a toddler right before flopping to the ground. At least back then Gina could pick her up and carry her to her room for a time-out.

Boyfriend. Gina gaped at her daughter.

"Where is this coming from? He's one of my best customers. Not that it's relevant, but no, I'm not dating him. And even if I were, you do not speak to me or our customers like that. This is how I pay the bills, our bills. If I lose customers, especially regular ones like Daniel, then I can't pay them. If I can't pay bills, then we can't have things like cell phones, or those fancy leggings you like, or a house. Do you want to move to Illinois with your aunt and uncle? Lose the house where we lived with your dad? Because I sure as hell don't."

Gina scowled at the burn marks on the cooktop and turned the vent up to clear out the smoky odor.

"You can scrub that back to pristine and think about your actions today . . . and, yesterday." She pulled out a bottle of vinegar and scouring pads. "I know you're not happy about spending time with me, but if you're going to be difficult, I can make it difficult right back at you. Get the gloves, because this is going to get hot."

May put the thick leather gloves on and grabbed the scouring pads, her eyes narrowed and lips thin, but at least she obeyed. Gina didn't care if she didn't like it. She could be angry, sure — but these outbursts had to stop.

Gina splashed the vinegar on the hot cooktop, where it sizzled and sputtered.

"Now scrub quickly before it all evaporates."

May glared at her but attacked the stove. At least she got to work out her anger. Gina still wanted to scream. Instead, she stared at the wall and took deep breaths, trying to find some peace, her eyes landing above the stove. Next to a framed Al Waters restaurant review of Grilled G's hung a picture of Gina and Drew on their wedding day. *Happy thought.*

In the photo, Drew wore a slightly too big black suit while she wore a simple sleeveless cream dress with a brocade pattern, and a bouquet of red roses tied up with a matching ribbon. It had been a small ceremony with only a few friends and his parents. Her own had refused to come. Well, to be fair, she hadn't invited them. After the way they'd rejected Drew, she hadn't wanted anything to do with them.

On the same day he'd shown her Polish Fest, Gina drove them to the country club after they'd changed their clothes. She wore a bright pink shift dress, pearls, and cream kitten-heeled sandals. Drew stoically wore the unofficial club uniform of pressed khaki pants, a white button-down shirt, and a navy-blue sports jacket. Locks of golden hair kept falling onto his forehead that he tried to push back, but Gina loved those unruly strands. He'd spent an extra fifteen minutes making sure all the grease was gone from under his fingernails. He was determined to win over her parents even though Gina told him it was pointless. She tried to tell him that unless he had a secret medical degree, or a few extra million in the bank, they would dismiss him out of hand, but he refused to give up hope. Yet another reason she loved him.

Her mother and father sat at one of the many dark wood tables in the even darker wood-paneled bar that overlooked the eighteenth hole. The crowd hadn't changed much since Gina was younger, just more wrinkles on the older generation. The other tables were full, as club regulars downed their cocktails before moving into the dining room for the Friday night fish fry — or in her mom's case, the baked cod and steamed vegetables. Her mother wore white, wide-legged pants, a loose-fitting silk tank top in a rich burgundy, and a white cardigan tied around her shoulders. Her hair rested in a precise light-brown line with her chin. It strategically became lighter brown with each passing year, making it easier to hide the growing number of gray hairs that were slowly winning the battle over her head. Her father wore the exact same outfit as Drew, except his shirt was a light blue — the one acceptable deviation. The main difference between them was that everything Floyd wore was custom fit by a tailor. Her father's high cheekbones were cleanly shaven, and his nails freshly trimmed and filed.

Mom and Dad stood to greet them, and Gina introduced everyone in a round. Drew shook her mom's hand first while her father looked him over from head to toe reaching his own hand out.

Lorraine loud-whispered to Gina, "His hair is a bit long."

Drew's lips twitched so she knew he had heard. "Please sit. We ordered a bottle of champagne," Floyd said.

A waiter poured Drew and Gina glasses from the waiting bucket, and Drew raised his glass for a toast.

"To meeting the woman of my dreams and her family, and to our first family gathering and the many more to come."

Simple and elegant, not too much. Gina happily clinked her glass with Drew's, and her parents followed suit. Even her dad looked moderately pleased as he set his champagne flute onto the center of his cocktail napkin. This might not be too bad, after all.

"So Andrew," her dad said. "Your last name is Zoberski? That's Polish, right?"

"Yes, sir. Born and raised in the old neighborhood. Not far from where Gina said her Aunt Roza lives." Her mom's eyes went to Drew's face.

"Ah." Her father tapped his fingertips together. "I hear you work at Harley. Who are you working under? A good number of the C-suite are members here."

Gina groaned to herself. He phrased the question clearly assuming Drew was an executive and worked for one of the VPs. Like smelling an incoming storm, she could sense this was the moment where the conversation would go sideways.

"Oh, I'm on the floor. I work on engines," Drew said.

"You're an engineer?" Floyd asked as he crossed his long legs, his brow at rest.

"No, sir. I'm a mechanic." Lorraine pinched her lips and sipped her champagne. How did she manage to get any into her mouth with her mouth pursed like that?

"He can fix anything. He's always assigned to the most important projects," Gina said, wanting to move quickly from this topic. "So, I hear you're planning a trip to the Bahamas. Tell us about it."

Her dad pulled out a pressed, white handkerchief and rubbed it on his right hand, ignoring Gina's prompt.

"I expected your work to be a little more . . . white-collar," her dad said.

Drew had opened his mouth to speak, but he shouldn't have to defend himself to her parents.

"Drew's fantastic with all things motor, Dad," Gina said.

"What your father is trying to say, is we just always expected you to end up with someone more like . . . us," her mom spoke. She studied Drew carefully, her eyes flicking to watch Gina, then back to Drew. The more she studied, the deeper her frown. Gina knew damn well they would have preferred she marry an executive, preferably from an Ivy League school and wealthy family, but Drew was polite, well spoken, and reliable. He didn't look out of place at the country club in his neat khakis. Was his choice of career really a deal breaker to them?

"What does that even mean? I write boring documentation so the people who do the real work, like Drew, can do it. Though in this case, Drew is the one who helps me do my job." Her mom scanned the room to see if anyone had noticed. Maxine Fuller and her husband sat at the next table and were definitely leaning in. She lowered her voice. "Just because he doesn't wear a three-piece suit to work, doesn't make him unprofessional —"

"We merely want what's best for you, for you to be protected. Financially." Her mom spoke barely above a whisper, hoping those around them would lose interest. But that was a lost cause, given the way Maxine was half off her chair — an elephant could skip through the bar and she wouldn't even notice. "Victoria is dating a nice man your father introduced to her."

"Of course, she is." Gina's hold on propriety was dissolving. Drew patted her knee under the table, reassuring her he was fine. He could be as fine as he wanted, but this was unacceptable. She had always tried to play nice and have good manners, look on the bright side and make them proud, but this time her parents were going too far.

"You . . . you're fucking kidding me, right?" The entire room went silent this time. Her mom gasped, and her dad clasped his hands on the table. The only clue he disapproved was the muscle twitching on his left jaw. Even Gina was stunned at the words that had spewed from her mouth, but she didn't care. She was done. "I don't even know where to begin with you both. I love him. I don't care if you disapprove of his career. He's hardworking, kind, and treats me like the center of his universe. That's more than Dad ever does for you." She pointed to her mom. "He asks about my day and actually listens. He thinks I look my best when we first wake up in the morning, with my horrible hair and dragon breath." She was on a roll now — nothing was going to stop her. She pushed back her chair and stood, looking down on the people who had disappointed her. Her mother's nervous fingers clenched her omnipresent gold cross necklace. "Yep, we sleep in the same bed almost every night — something you two have never done." Her dad's face reddened, and her mom stared at the tabletop, as if not looking at Gina would stop the deluge of embarrassment. Maxine stared — she'd obviously given up any attempt at subtlety. "You say you're disappointed in my choice. Well, I'm disappointed in you. He is everything to me, and you can't even be happy. We're only dating, but it's serious, and after the nonsense you've pulled tonight, I see no reason for you to be a part of our life. I hope Vicky gives you lots of perfect grandchildren, because you'll never meet our kids."

She turned and left, Drew scrambling after her, grabbing her hand as they stormed out together.

When they made it to the parking lot, Drew pulled her into a hug.

"You were glorious," he whispered into her ear. "I think you'd jump in a river for my wianki, right?" Gina chuckled into his chest, wishing her tears would stop falling. "A top-five best exit, too."

"I'm so sorry," Gina said. "That was so much worse than I expected."

He cupped her face.

"If they don't matter to you, they don't matter to me. I will always have your back."

Gina set her notepad and pen on the hospital nightstand, then pulled the warm garlic bread from the parchment paper package meant to keep the pooling butter from escaping, but it really provided the perfect dipping spot. She bit into the crusty edge, crunchy on the outside and soft on the inside, and sprinkled with the exact right amount of garlic salt. Mama Mia's garlic bread, the ultimate comfort food — all carbs and fat. After dropping May off at home on her way back to the hospital, she'd swung by for the necessary comfort-food fix. Now that she thought about it, their iconic bread would make an amazing grilled cheese sandwich. She'd have to find out who their supplier was — maybe they could work out a partnership. She'd add it to her list.

When she had dropped May at the house with Vicky, her little nieces and nephews were already building snow forts and rolling snowballs in the backyard. They had looked like mini-Yeti, snow caking the outside of their hats and snowsuits. She loved each of them, but Gina needed quiet time before engaging with little people. Besides, if she spent any more time with her daughter today, she might say something she would regret. Gina hoped that her little bit of self-awareness was a sign she wouldn't turn into her mother — though she never imagined her mother regretting anything she had ever said.

As she licked the dripping butter off her hand, her mom watched her — maybe more closely than she ever had before — one side of her mouth still drooping more than the other. Would it ever go back to normal? With her still-simmering anger and the memory of the day her mother had hurt Drew's feelings so fresh, it was difficult to see her mom as less than the strong-willed, waspish woman she normally was. She never really thought about how much her mother had changed over the last decade. Her hair was more ash-blond than light brown now, and her deep wrinkles proved that there were times she had smiled and laughed. Before the stroke, even, she'd been moving slower, less sure of her balance. When she went down stairs, she made sure both feet were solidly on a step before gently moving to the next one. Her mom had grown old. With so much distance between them, did Gina really want to go back to the way things had been between them? Or did she want to go forward?

Gina nudged her chair a bit closer to the rolling table near her mom's bed.

"I suppose you think I should use a napkin?"

Her mom shook her head. *No.*

Her mom's eyes moved to the bread.

"You want some?"

She nodded. *Yes.*

Gina had never seen her mom eat anything as fattening or as greasy as Mama Mia's garlic bread. She rolled the table out of the way and moved the chair so she was right next to the bed, then pulled a small piece off and swirled it in the butter. Her mom opened her mouth like a baby bird. Gina set the bread inside. Lorraine closed her eyes and slowly chewed. When she finished, she opened her eyes and smiled a lopsided smile.

"More?"

A nod. *Yes.*

Gina repeated the actions. It wasn't so different from feeding May when she was little — making sure the pieces were small enough she couldn't choke, making sure she chewed and swallowed before giving her another piece. Seeing her mom so dependent reminded Gina about how much she didn't know.

"I didn't know you liked Mama Mia's, Mom."

Lorraine opened her mouth again in response. Gina gave her another morsel, then took a big bite for herself. They finished the brick-size piece of bread this way — a nugget for her mom, a larger bite for herself. Gina tossed the greasy paper in the garbage can when they finished. That might have been the most pleasant meal she'd ever spent with her mom.

"Do you remember when you met Drew?"

Her mom nodded.

"I never told you, but he begged me to ask you and Dad to the wedding." She wiped the butter off her fingers with a napkin.

It was the biggest fight they had ever had. Drew sat on the edge of her bed draped in her bed sheet and nothing else while she got dressed for work.

"They deserve to see their daughter married," he said.

"They deserve nothing." Gina slid her arms into her purple button-down shirt. He'd been needling her on the subject since she had gotten out of the shower. Her head pounded from grinding her teeth at each of his stupid comments. She buttoned her shirt and turned to face him as he stood, the sheet falling off his body. Now he was fighting dirty. She turned her back to him.

"Do you really want to cut them out? Forever." He gently turned her around to face him. "You're crooked."

She looked down; the buttons were in the wrong holes. He started to unbutton and rebutton her shirt. She shoved his arms away, causing one of the buttons to tear off.

"Gah! Stop trying to fix things. My snobby parents made it clear they felt you weren't good enough for them. Well, they're not good enough for us. End of story. Full stop. Finite. I'm done with them and you are, too." She poked him in the chest. Even with her shirt wide open, angry heat boiled off her. Why wasn't he agreeing with her? Maybe he wasn't who she thought he was.

Drew rolled the button that tore off from her shirt between his fingers and nodded.

"If that is what you want, I support you. Always." He hugged her and all the anger ebbed away. It was his superpower.

"I couldn't understand why he would ever want to see you again after the way you and Dad treated us." Gina smiled. "He was right. He knew that family found a way through the tough stuff. God, I miss him."

Her mom nodded, again. The realization that her mom really did understand snapped her back to the present. Gina leaned forward, propping her elbows on her knees, her folded hands resting on the edge of the bed. She studied her mom's makeup-less face, the dark circles under her eyes, and the earlobes, drooping from years of wearing heavy earrings. Her normally smooth, straight, shoulder-length hair was ruffled, and her blue eyes were watery. This was the woman who had held a precious secret inside for forty years, never giving up any hint.

"Why did you do it? Why didn't you tell us?"

Unsteadily, Lorraine pulled Gina's notebook off the nightstand and set it on her lap. It was already open to the list of questions Gina wanted her mother to answer. With a shaky finger, she pointed at one of the questions Gina had written.

What is your biggest regret?

"You regret not telling us that our real dad was Joe Sandowski and not Dad — I mean Floyd?"

Yes.

"I do, too, Mom." Gina rubbed her hands together. "Is Joe still alive?"

Lorraine's eyes grew more watery.

No.

The answer hit her in the gut, sucking her breath away. Unexpectedly painful.

"Did he die before you married Dad?"

Yes.

"Were you married?"

Yes.

Gina's heart lurched. Her mom had been a widow, twice. She wanted to hear all the stories about how they met and what happened. How did she end up with Floyd? Why did she marry him if she loved this other man? How did Joe die? Phrasing all her questions as a Yes or a No felt like an impossible hill to climb when there was so much she wanted to know.

"Did you love him?"

Yes. Yes. Yes.

Chapter Eighteen

For once in her life, Lorraine longed to share all her secrets, but her mouth simply wouldn't cooperate. Her eldest sat next to her bed, silent, digesting all that her limited answers revealed. But it wasn't enough. She had let her down so many times, in so many ways.

Lorraine reached out with her hand, shaking as she moved each inch, concentrating to keep it moving in the right direction. At last her hand reached Regina's. Her daughter's skin was hot, almost searing to her own cold, thin skin. The warmth of connection felt good. Regina looked up.

Please don't move your hand away.

She didn't.

Lorraine saw so much of herself in Regina. They had both fallen in love with men their parents didn't approve of. They both lost those beloved men. They both had to find a way to move forward, leading the way for their own children. Seeing Regina lose Drew had brought back to the front of her mind all her memories of losing Joe, the ones she thought she had locked away. She cringed at how she had told Regina to move on quickly. She was such a hypocrite. What was that old saying? *You are most critical of the flaws in others that you have yourself.* Perhaps that was why she was so hard on Regina — because they were too much alike. Except Regina was stronger than she was. Instead of turning cold, Regina found the warmth in everything. She had never met a glass of water that wasn't half full, and Lorraine admired that. Perhaps if Lorraine had been able to share her own pain, they wouldn't be sitting silent next to each other when there was so much they should be saying.

For comfort, Lorraine rubbed her gold cross with her fingers. The soft gold looked scratched and dull now from constant wear, but under her fingers, it still felt as shiny and new as the day Joe had clasped it around her neck.

Baby Regina reached for the shiny buttons on Joe's army coat. He stood in the cheap wood-paneled living room of their tiny apartment on the other side of town from where her parents lived. It was the bottom flat of a duplex, with two bedrooms, a tiny bathroom where the faucet leaked, the tile was chipped, and the toilet required two flushes every time, and a kitchen with peeling, lime-green linoleum floors and the funk of cigarette smoke from the previous tenants. Not what she'd grown up in, but scrupulously clean, with nice neighbors, and all their own.

Joe had already hung a swing from the giant oak that shaded most of the yard, even though Regina was barely eight months old. Their landlord and upstairs neighbor, Roza, had returned little Regina after watching her while Lorraine and Joe said their goodbyes before he shipped off. And now it was time.

Lorraine rubbed her hand over the small bump that was their second little one. Her white belt cut into her growing stomach — it was already on the last notch. She should never have put it on that morning, but it helped define her rapidly disappearing waist and she wanted to look good for Joe. She'd break out the tent tops and elastic-waisted pants tomorrow.

Regina wore a pretty red dress with matching bloomers. She was an angel. As Regina reached for her dad's face, placing two chubby hands on each cheek, they all laughed at her determination to get all of his attention, as if she somehow knew she wouldn't have it for a while. Roza snapped a few pictures to remember the moment.

"I'm looking, baby girl, what do you need to say?" Joe asked. Regina put her lips together and blew bubbles — her way of saying she wanted kisses. Joe complied, covering her cherubic face until she giggled. He held her close and pulled Lorraine in to join them, breathing in her perfume and Regina's baby powder.

"I'll be back before you know it, then I'll spend the rest of my life making it up to you and Regina and Baby Boo." He set his hand on her stomach. "Don't give your mama a hard time, little one."

A horn honked outside. He handed Regina to Roza and pulled Lorraine into his arms, breathing deeply in the crook of her shoulder. He pulled back long enough to clasp something around her neck, then pulled her in even tighter once more.

"I miss you so much already. I'll win that war single-handedly so I can get back to you. Write me every day so I don't miss anything. I want daily reports on our babes."

"You'll get so many letters you'll be sick of me," Lorraine said, unable to say more for fear her voice would crack.

"Talk to your parents. They should know." He touched her stomach, and her spine stiffened. Why did he have to bring that up now, in their last moments together for months? "Promise?"

How could she not? He might never . . . she couldn't finish the thought, and nodded instead.

"My lovely Lorraine. When the days get lonely, I'll think of you. I love you."

And he was gone.

Eyes closed, she heard the car door shut and the engine fade into the nothingness, taking her courage with it. She couldn't bring herself to watch out the window as he left — if she didn't see him leave, maybe he hadn't really gone.

Lorraine sunk to the ground. Roza set the baby in her playpen and held her, rocking and singing a soft song in Polish. Lorraine grasped the necklace Joe had put on her neck, feeling a cross. She held it tight, letting the sharp edges cut into her palm, the pain giving her a place to focus.

"Let it out. Then you need to be strong for your little ones," Roza said.

Regina gurgled and rolled around, the only sound in the quiet house besides her tears. Roza rubbed her back in large circles, making no demands of her, just being there, letting her be weak in a way her own mother never had, not once.

She pulled in a few deep breaths and stood, finally looking at the cross Joe had given her, flipping it over to see the faint lettering, letting the engraved message bolster her. She had shed her tears, and now it was time for life to continue so that when Joe came home to her, they would be as he left them, happy and healthy.

Less than a month to go in this pregnancy. Lorraine's stomach bumped against the sink as she stuffed another paczki in her mouth. Roza had brought over a tray of lemon- and prune-filled ones that morning, but most of them were already gone. She licked the glaze off her fingers then washed her hands. With Regina, she'd controlled her cravings and her figure had bounced right back. With baby number two, she couldn't stop, though it was possible she was trying to fill the void left by her husband with Polish doughnuts.

She waddled into the living room, kicking the basket of still-warm laundry closer to the couch so she could fold it. Once she finished, she'd lie down with Regina, who was napping on their bed. They only had a short time left for just the two of them, so she wanted to savor it while she could. She dumped the basket onto the couch where she could watch the world go by as she matched socks and folded worn towels, setting the neat items back into the basket.

Because their apartment was half underground, the window was level with the yard, where Lorraine could peek out and see Roza's grandkids playing catch on the front lawn. As the kids played, she'd see a ball roll past followed by chubby legs. Their other neighbors were either mowing or watering the grass or sitting in green-and-white-striped lawn chairs watching the action. Once Regina woke up, they'd go outside to join the fun.

With a blue-and-white-striped bath towel in her hand, she folded it in half as a dark car she'd never seen before pulled up in front of the house. The children's chubby legs paused in their play. Two men in uniform emerged from the car. She folded the towel in thirds as they walked around the side to her apartment door. A dark car. Two military men in uniform. Unannounced. Dread filled her like a tiny tin bucket under a waterfall. She dropped the towel as they rang the doorbell. Every military wife in America knew what this visit meant. The men could see her through the screen door, which had been open so she could enjoy the sounds of the summer day outside. She couldn't ignore them, but she didn't want to acknowledge them either.

"Mrs. Sandowski, may we come in?"

She nodded, still standing with the towel heaped on her feet where it had landed. As they entered, Roza scooted in on their heels, as always, five steps ahead of everyone, knowing when she would be needed. As the officers said the words she never wanted to hear, Roza wrapped her arms around Lorraine's shoulders.

It was combat, they said. The body would arrive for burial. He would go in the Wood National Cemetery. An officer would help her plan the service if she wanted. She could only stare blankly at the buttons on their coats, the same kind of shiny buttons Regina had played with before Joe had left. Her legs wobbled, and Roza maneuvered her to the orange-and-white-flowered sofa, shoving the piles of laundry out of the way. One of the officers bent down and picked up the towel she had dropped. He folded it in half. Then he folded it in thirds and set it on the arm of the sofa. Lorraine couldn't take her eyes off it. Loose threads dangled from one edge, so she tucked them under.

Roza took control of the situation, spoke

to the officers, and showed them to the door. Lorraine set her hands on her belly, rubbing it as if it would produce a genie, or turn back time somehow. She was never going to see her beloved Joe again, never hear him call her his lovely Lorraine. Their future crumbled to ash in her tiny living room. She curled into the still-warm towels and pulled them over her stomach and legs, over her arms like a patchwork blanket, the news finally breaking through her shock.

"No. No. No. No. No. No." She shook her head with each word. Roza perched on the edge, ready to be whatever Lorraine needed. Lorraine pulled a towel over her head, one that Joe had used even though it had a hole in it. Why had she ever washed it? Why had she washed anything of his before he returned? Now nothing would smell like him ever again. She had been so sure he'd return, positive they would grow gray together. And now her children would be fatherless.

"Our babies." Her voice cracked as she curled around her belly, trying to protect her baby from the pain outside, her tears wetting the laundry under her head. How would she ever climb out of this darkness? How would she move forward? Regina, who had woken up with the commotion of visitors and Lorraine's crying, toddled over and climbed into the towels and rubbed Lorraine's stomach with her tiny hand, unaware that her mother had no idea what to do.

The next weeks were a blur, marked different only by the clothes she wore. She would get up, drink coffee, go back to bed. Roza practically moved in, feeding, bathing, and caring for both of them.

"Time to get dressed. Your clothes for today are out." Roza pointed to the large black dress on the chair. They had picked it out at JCPenney. Lorraine put it on without thinking. She had cried so many tears that everything had become dull and flat. Roza drove her to the cemetery in the blue Beetle. She sat in the backseat with Regina. There would be no church service, just a ceremony at the cemetery. It was one of those perfect Wisconsin June days, meant to be enjoyed in a hammock as the neighbors mowed the lawn, not dressed in black among the perfect rows of white headstones.

She sat in the front row, an open grave before her. The military had gently suggested a closed casket was the best approach, and she had agreed to it. While she wanted more than anything to see his face again, she wanted to remember him hale and whole. It was a small and simple service, complete with the traditional twenty-one-gun salute, each gunshot reminding her of what she had lost, echoing through the empty shell she had become. He was gone. Her children needed her. She couldn't do it alone.

She had no more tears, not even when the young officer knelt before her and handed her the flag. She clutched it to her chest as their neighbors walked back to their cars, slowly so they didn't seem too eager, but relieved they could now forget the sad business of a young woman burying her spouse. She touched Joe's gravestone, still not engraved, only a piece of paper marking it as his. She wished she could feel his warm skin one last time, but the cold stone would have to do.

"I'm sorry, Joe, that I didn't do this sooner. But I'll make it right." She turned to Roza, who stood an aisle over with a sleeping baby cradled in her arms. "I'll take Regina now." She handed over the flag. "Would you put this in our house, please? I'll be back as soon as I can, but it might be a few days. There's something I need to do."

Lorraine set her suitcase by her feet, straightened Regina's navy-blue dress, and smoothed her own black one over her midsection before ringing the doorbell. The shrubs of her childhood home were perfectly clipped, and the planters overflowed with red geraniums, their earthy scent reminding her of summer. If only Joe's parents were still alive, she wouldn't have to be here. If he'd had brothers or sisters, she wouldn't be here. But her parents were their only family now. She pushed the button until she heard the familiar bing-bong, for the first time from outside of the house. Lorraine had timed her arrival when she knew her father would be working — her mom wouldn't be able to resist a granddaughter.

Her mother opened the door but said nothing, taking in her black dress, her enormous belly, and Regina. After years of being married to Lorraine's controlling father, her mother had mastered the art of hiding emotions. Lorraine waited for some indication as to whether she needed to leave or was able to enter. At last, her mother stepped aside, allowing Lorraine to enter and held out her arms for Regina, neither woman speaking or letting her face betray her thoughts. Lorraine was learning, too.

She'd learned her lesson too well. Lorraine regretted so much about her relationship with Regina — but mostly not opening her arms and heart to Drew. She had been so caught up in pretending she was fine, she ignored anything that reminded her she wasn't. And Drew had been a big reminder of that. Thankfully, she could start making up for it now.

"Hello!" A singsongy voice came from the room's doorway, where Maxine Fuller stood wearing the same brown fur she'd been wearing the past fifteen years. Under her fur she wore slender jeans tucked into knee-high riding boots — even though she didn't ride — and a cream, cable-knit sweater she told everyone she had bought in Ireland, but which Lorraine knew for a fact she had ordered from Lands' End. She'd seen the tag in the club's locker room.

"I heard about your accident and I had to check in on you," Maxine said, looking from Gina to Lorraine.

They all knew she was here to get all the gossip and still maintain her image as the caring and thoughtful friend while she shared all the details about Lorraine's drooping eye and sagging mouth around the club. She hadn't even brought flowers.

"Hi, Mrs. Fuller. It's nice to see you again," Gina said. "And it wasn't an accident. Mom had a stroke."

Lorraine frowned. Regina didn't have to

be so blunt about it. Maxine ruled the club from the center of a web built on collected secrets and carefully laid threats. Lorraine had had to cozy up to her for ten years after Regina's embarrassing outburst in the club. That snake had told Lorraine that anyone who could not control their own daughter wasn't qualified to organize important events.

"Hello. I know you aren't Victoria because she's tall and blond. Always the belle of the ball, that one. So you must be Regina."

Maxine absolutely knew this daughter was Regina when she walked in. She was like a malevolent elephant who didn't forget anything.

"Yes, I'm Gina."

Maxine stepped deeper into the hospital room, scanning for every detail, petting her ugly coat. Someone really needed to tell her it was starting to reek like the dead animal it was — she could smell it from her bed.

"I seem to remember you married the Polish mechanic, right? I was there the night you were celebrating with your parents."

Maxine's lips smirked, thinking she was needling Lorraine about an embarrassing moment, but Lorraine could see the gut-punch on Regina's face and regretted every time she had avoided discussing Regina with the club ladies. She had never mentioned what had happened to Drew.

"The Polish mechanic died almost two years ago."

Maxine gaped and looked quickly at Lorraine, an unreadable expression on her face. Regina picked up her notebook and wrote a quick note while Maxine mentally composed her response to the shocking information.

"I am so sorry. I had not heard anything about that. I lost my father last year, so I can understand the pain you went through." Maxine tilted her head and crinkled her brow in a practiced look of sympathy. Did she really believe anything about her was sincere? "He's in a better place now. I'm sure it's all part of God's plan. How are you doing?"

Lorraine flared her nostrils. How dare this arrogant, superficial flake of a woman act like she had any idea what it was like to lose a spouse, or that she had an ounce of concern for Regina? Lorraine considered herself to have impeccable manners, and she rarely used curse words, but right now all of them boiled to the surface. She settled on the most satisfying.

Fuck off, Maxine.

If only she could actually say it.

Regina, once again showing more strength than Lorraine, merely nodded and casually set her notebook on the side of the bed before standing. Lorraine glanced down.

Can I get rid of her?

Lorraine gave a little nod and set her hand on top of the notebook before Maxine read it.

"Thank you, for saying so," Gina said. "We're doing okay. And I wish you had let us know you were visiting. My mom really does need to rest and doesn't want any visitors except close friends and family. I'm sure you understand. Thank you again for stopping by."

Regina guided Maxine to the door, and closed it behind her.

Well, look at that. Her Regina had some teeth after all.

What Is Your Greatest Heartbreak?

Chapter Nineteen

May spread the napkin on her lap and tried to look like she ate at such nice restaurants all the time. After helping out with her four cousins all afternoon, her aunt had decided to treat her to an extra special meal. Roza came over to watch the little ones and seemed oddly delighted to have a houseful of loud kids to watch. May just hoped they stayed out of her room, which didn't have a lock. Aunt Vicky had declared she wanted real, grown-up food, so here they sat on a very packed Saturday night. May could see the cooks working in an open kitchen, where a short woman with a dark ponytail worked next to another woman with red braids. Flames shot up from the grill, flashing against the white walls.

Aunt Vicky set her phone on the table. "I just texted your mom to let her know we are up to shenanigans." Aunt V sipped her wine. "God, this is amazing. Want some?"

Aunt Vicky held her wineglass out to May, the red liquid sloshing in the glass.

"No." May's stomach churned. She held her hand up as if to block even the scent.

"That's right. You don't like wine. Your mom told me about that."

Of course she had. Her mom always seemed to share her most embarrassing stories with Aunt Vicky.

The blush breaking over her cheeks probably made her look like the flames in the kitchen. "Besides, I'm not old enough, either."

"That never stopped me. It's Wisconsin — you can drink with a parent. I'm close enough. Kidding, kidding." Vicky took a long drink. "You're my DD."

"That might not be your best idea."

Aunt Vicky swatted at the air, but May wasn't worried she was upset with her sarcasm. "You have cars in your blood, you could totally do it. I bet your dad was already teaching you to drive."

May smiled at the thought of her dad, how his eyes sparkled every time he saw her, like seeing her caused them to twinkle or how his hugs made every skinned knee instantly better. And Aunty Vicky was right, he had started teaching her to drive — a couple of times. They'd started by going to a big parking lot and he'd set her on his lap. He'd work the pedals and she would steer around the lot, weaving in and around the lampposts. Not long before he died, he even let her do it all by herself, calmly talking her through the steps, teaching her to push gently on the pedals. Steering was nothing like in the movies, where actors turned the wheel with huge motions. She barely needed to move it and the entire car would turn, and only a little pressure on the gas would shoot it forward — assuming she had pushed the right pedal.

"A few times." May smiled.

Aunt Vicky winked at her. That's one of the things she liked most about Aunt V. She didn't mind breaking the rules a bit — sometimes she encouraged it.

"So tell me about this Connor. Is he cute?" Aunt Vicky grinned at her.

May nodded.

"What does he look like?"

May looked at the ceiling and pictured him in her mind.

"He has dark brown hair, almost black — it's a little longer on the top, but short around his ears and neck. Darker skin than me. His smile is crooked, but kinda cute. And he has one blue eye and one brown eye — that's definitely my favorite."

"Like Bowie."

"I don't know who that is."

"Good God, now I know what to get you for next Christmas. Does he smell nice?"

May scrunched up her nose trying to remember.

"I didn't really smell anything."

"That's a good thing — most teenage boys either wear too much aftershave or not enough deodorant."

"We definitely have those at school."

"Is Connor in a lot of your classes? Is he smart like you?"

May sipped her water.

"Yeah, he's in almost all of them, but he's way smarter than me. He'll probably be a doctor like both of his parents."

May wished she knew what she wanted to be. She used to think she'd be a mechanic like her dad, but now . . . who knows. She picked up her menu.

"Get anything you want. My treat for helping me with the kiddos today."

"I didn't mind. They're fun."

"More fun than hanging out in a hospital room or working in the food truck . . ."

May shrugged at Aunt V's comment. It was true, but she really did like her cousins. It was like having brothers and sisters, but they would eventually leave before they got too annoying.

"I was a teenager once, too. And I know my kids can be a handful when they're off their routine — and Uncle Jeff did not stick to the routine while I was gone. Now it'll take time to get everyone back on schedule."

"Is that why you bought an entire bottle of wine?"

"Precisely."

May looked over the menu. Everything was expensive, not just the wine. Even the appetizers started at fifteen dollars and had weird ingredients like speck and brussels sprouts. She looked around the restaurant and noticed she was the only person her age. The walls were decorated with thick, kelly-green curtains against crisp white paint, and black and white squares checkerboarding the floor. The table next to them was empty except for a small silver frame with a picture of two old people.

She eyed the menu again. It was only one page — and it didn't list the desserts. Everything was fancy. She wished she had worn a dress rather than the jeans and T-shirt Aunt Vicky said was okay. Would the other customers think she was underdressed, too? She sipped the kiddy cocktail she had ordered, pulling a bright red cherry off the plastic sword and popping it into her mouth.

"You know what they use to color those, right?"

May paused chewing to speak. "Bugs. And they are delicious." She returned to chewing. Olivia had told her about the bugs a few years ago over ice cream sundaes. May had decided that plenty of people ate bugs every day, and that cherries were still delicious, so she didn't care.

"That's my girl." Aunty Vicky looked at her menu. "What are you going to get?"

"I don't really know what any of this is . . ." May whispered it. Before Aunt Vicky could make any suggestions, the waiter returned.

"Any questions about the menu, or are you ready to order?" he asked nicely.

"Trust me to order for you?"

May nodded. It was better than having to ask the waiter to explain everything.

"We'll have the cheese plate to start, then I'll have the lamb, medium-rare. The young lady will have your short rib and Parmesan risotto special. And could we get a few more pieces of this incredible bread and butter, please?"

"Of course." The waiter hustled back to the kitchen.

Vicky took the last slice of bread and slathered on the rest of the butter.

"God, this is so good. I don't remember the last time I had real butter."

"You guys eat margarine at your house?"

"Yeah, Jeff likes that olive oil spread. It's supposedly healthy, but it tastes like grease." Aunt Vicky pretended to gag herself.

The extra bread and butter arrived, and May took a piece before Aunt Vicky ate it all again. It was still warm and crusty on the outside. May could probably make a great dessert out of it, maybe a grilled sandwich with Nutella or that spread made from cookies. She chewed in silence.

"How was the food truck with your mom today?"

May shrugged and rolled her eyes. "Meh. It was okay until my friends showed up. One of them kind of made me give them their sandwiches without paying. It was stupid."

"You gave away food? I bet your mom was pissed."

"I lost my phone for another week. But she's such a hypocrite with that lady who complains to get free stuff. And then this guy stopped by." May rolled her eyes, but Aunt Vicky smiled.

"Daniel came back. Nice."

May did not think he was nice at all. He

had no right bringing her mom things or smiling at her. Mom still wore her and Dad's wedding rings. Did he not see that? May chewed her bread slowly, picking another chunk of bread off and eating it.

"You don't think it's nice that a man thinks your mom is hot?"

"Ew. I don't even want to think about that."

"You know, if she were dating, she'd probably give you more freedom."

May imagined her mom going on a date with Daniel and his smile, and the way he watched her move around as she cooked. Creepy. Well, not creepy. But she didn't like it. But she did like the idea of more freedom. Not that she planned to do any more wine drinking, but she would like to go see Olivia or Connor. Definitely not Hannah. Hannah owed her fifteen dollars.

"I guess."

"So how is school? You've obviously got the boy thing down. What's your favorite class these days?"

May looked down at the table.

"It's all right."

Aunt Vicky sipped her wine and studied May's face. She raised an eyebrow.

"Then tell me why it's not great."

"There's a lot more homework. Mrs. Xi

keeps asking me to write about my dad in the journal we have for class. Like I'm going to write about that so she can read it."

"So what do you write in there?"

"I write about my brownie ideas. I'm up to thirty-two different kinds." May twisted the napkin on her lap. "And everyone is so stupid. All they care about is clothes and Instagram and boys."

"Weren't we just talking about Connor?"

"That's different." May smiled a bit. Okay, maybe not so different. "I guess no one cares about their friends. No one really wants to hear when someone is sad, or angry, or if something will get them in trouble."

"You've just described every teenager everywhere — and you're at the worst spot for it because once you get into high school you have more freedom. I hated middle school. I remember crying almost every day."

"What could possibly make you cry?"

"My hair wasn't blond enough, and Grandma Lorraine wouldn't let me bleach it." Aunt Vicky refilled her glass. At this rate, the bottle would be gone before the cheese arrived. "Your mom is doing an A-okay job. She let you do that to your hair." May touched the bleached streak. She had hoped it would be almost white, but it was a dirty yellow-orange. "If one of my kids did that, I would shave their head."

"Your kids are all under eight."

"All the more reason to be angry with them for doing something so silly. At least you didn't pierce anything." Aunt Vicky tilted her head. "You haven't pierced anything, have you?"

May shook her head.

"Tattoo?"

May shook her head again.

"Your dad had great tattoos."

May nodded. He really did. "I liked the one of our names the best."

"I don't think I ever saw that one. What did it look like?"

"When I was little, like really little and could barely write my name, Daddy had me and Mom write our names on his chest with a Sharpie. Then he had the artist tattoo over them so he always had our names right next to his heart. He even had them do my name in bright pink because that was the marker I had used."

When she got older, she was embarrassed by how wobbly the letters were, but her dad insisted that made it more special. She wished he could have done the same to her so she would still have his name in her heart. Maybe she could find a piece of paper with his signature on it. No tattoo parlor would let her get it on her own, but maybe if she had the right kind of help . . .

Aunt Vicky scooped out the last of the butter, closing her eyes to enjoy the flavor as she chewed. May checked the contents of the wine bottle — only half remained.

"Hey, Aunt Vicky, I have a question for you."

Chapter Twenty

Gina sipped her hot decaf coffee as a nurse checked her mom's vitals and ran a few other quick tests to measure her progress. Her head movement had improved, but she was still too wobbly when she tried to stand on her own. Gina stood and looked out the window when her phone buzzed.

I took May to a nice dinner. Roza is watching the kids at your house. How's Mom?

Gina was a little jealous that May liked Aunt Vicky more than she liked her. She knew it was because Vicky didn't have to enforce any rules, but it still stung. She sighed and sent a quick response.

Have fun. Mom's okay. Maxine Fuller stopped by. I'll fill you in later. What a B!

Slipping her phone back in her purse, she pulled out her trusty notebook.

Tomorrow her mom would be moved to the rehab facility. It had already been four days since her stroke. Gina would be glad to be out of the hospital with the perpetual round of doctors. She started a list of things that needed to be done before then.

1. Pack up Mom's toiletries and clothes.
2. Pick up fresh flowers.
3. Breakfast for seven? Eggs? Pancakes?

She put her pen down. The long hours in the hospital were starting to wear at her. Every time she walked through the doors, she had déjà vu of the worst day of her life.

May had been at school, but it was a warm March day, rare in Wisconsin. Spring flowers peeked out of the thawing soil, buds had started to swell on dormant branches, and geese winged their way back north, crossing overhead in large V formations. She had opened all the windows in the house before heading out to work, wanting to clear out the stale winter air.

Both she and Drew had been late that morning, having taken advantage of the empty house after May had left to catch the school bus. She had run her hands down her husband's chest, trailing over his stomach. His firm waist from their twenties had been replaced by a softer layer, though she still enjoyed the way T-shirts tightened around his strong arms. She was no twenty-five-year-old either, with her stretch marks and padded butt, too much time in an office chair and too little time on a treadmill. None of that mattered, though, because they were still googly-eyed in love.

He had cropped his longer locks a few years ago, and now gray mingled with his dark blond. She ran her hand across the tattoos of her and May's names, kissing them.

"Maybe we should both call in sick today," she said, knowing he'd catch her drift.

Drew did catch her drift and chuckled. His laugh rumbled in his chest.

"Should I call myself, then? I think I'll know that I'm full of shit. I can't, babe. I have three people picking up their bikes today. You know this is the busy season, no matter how badly I want to call in sick with you. Everyone wants them as soon as riding weather arrives. The thunder is going to be loud this weekend if the sunshine holds."

"Do you miss it?"

Drew had sold his motorcycle the moment they found out Gina was pregnant, a few months after the night he'd met her parents. Three months after that they married. She didn't tell her parents until the day after May was born. Her mom had arrived at the hospital with an armful of flowers that must have cost a fortune.

"Not one bit. And I get to ride them around the parking lot."

"That's not the same."

"I know. When May is grown, I might get another one, but it's really more fun fixing them up. That was always my favorite part anyway." He pulled his shirt over his head. "Can you stop by later? I want to show you my progress on Grilled G's."

"What's Grilled G's?"

"The name of your food truck." His eyes danced with mischief. "I thought Grilled G's would be a great name, 'cause it sounds like grilled cheese. Get it?"

Gina didn't think it was possible, but she fell in love even more with her husband in that moment. He had found an old square truck and started fixing it for her, salvaging cooking equipment, rebuilding the engine, and replacing rusted sheets of metal. Once he was done, she was going to start visiting farmers' markets and festivals on the weekends. The money would go toward May's college fund and their retirement. And now, on top of all that, he'd come up with the perfect name for it.

"How did I get so lucky?"

"You pretended you couldn't remember any of the information I told you so you could keep setting up redundant meetings with me."

He kissed her, sending heat to every part of her body, even after fifteen years.

"Are you sure you can't call in sick?"

"I wish. But if I ever get there, maybe I can leave early."

"I'll come visit at lunch. Maybe you can close up shop for a while." She winked at him.

He grabbed a piece of paper — his daily note to May — then started down the steps, stretching and rubbing his left arm.

"I'll hold you to that."

Gina went to her underwear drawer and pulled out his favorite pair. She wanted to be very persuasive later.

At noon, Gina parked her car in front of his small shop and turned off the engine. Drew didn't need much room for the bikes. An old gas station with two garage doors and a large storage room for parts was the perfect size. One of the garage bays held the newly christened "Grilled G's." She couldn't wait to see his progress on it.

She stepped through the door, the loud radio Drew liked to listen to while working drowning out the tiny bells hanging on the entrance that announced new customers. She turned down the volume. Two bikes, shiny and polished, waited for their owners to pick them up.

"Drew! Where are you?"

No answer. His car was out back, so he must be around. The bathroom? She looked in the waiting room, but the bathroom door was wide open. The storage room?

"Drew?"

He better not be planning to jump out and startle her. She hated that. He had done it once when they were first married, and she'd punched him in the face. Both of them were surprised to learn she was a fighter, not a flight-er.

Light leaked from the storage room, where shelves were lined up in rows like a library for parts. She looked down each row, getting more and more irritated that he hadn't answered her. After she put on this uncomfortable underwear and everything.

But down the row full of tires, the last one, she finally found him. He lay on the ground, eyes closed and arms at an awkward angle.

"Don't be stupid," she said as she walked

toward him. "Get up. You know scaring me never goes well."

He didn't move, not even a smile or a twitch to let her know he had heard her. He was really committed. She knew how to break him.

"I have your favorite underwear on." She stepped over his body, a foot on either side of his waist. He only needed to crack open an eye and take a peek up her skirt to confirm. But he didn't.

"Drew, knock it off. You're taking the fun out of it." She nudged him with her foot, but it was like trying to move a sandbag. Her mouth went dry as she dropped to her knees, putting her hands on his face. Still warm. His chest rose up and down — not a lot, but he was still alive. Her own breath raced, more than making up for his lack.

"Drew." She slapped his face a little. Nothing. She did it harder, then harder. "Drew!" Nothing. He wasn't playing.

911. She needed to call 911.

A blur of sirens and paramedics, then glaring hospital lights. She couldn't process what was happening. They were supposed to be making love in his office, not roaring into an emergency room. She overheard words like "heart attack" and "nonresponsive." Those weren't words for a forty-three-year-old. He just needed to get up. No one was stronger or healthier than Drew. Why wasn't he getting up? Why weren't his eyes open? His beautiful, laughing blue eyes. Gina moved to get closer to where he lay but was grabbed by someone in scrubs and pushed out of the room. She pushed back, and more people came to deny her. He needed her. Why wouldn't they let her go to him? He would wake up if she was there. She knew it.

"No." Her voice roared above the emergency room din. "Drew! I need to be with him!"

An overstrong nurse in green scrubs pushed her to the waiting room, Gina's feet sliding on the shiny floors as she tried to get around the woman. "Mrs. Zoberski." She held her firm. An NFL linebacker wouldn't get past this woman. "We'll come get you when we're done, but we need you out here so we can work." The doors behind her swung shut, and she could no longer see the room where Drew was. He wouldn't know she was here. How much she needed him.

A low moan of defeat came from her lips. The effort of resisting had been too much and now the adrenaline was gone, leaving limp muscles behind. Instead of holding her back, now the burly nurse had to hold her up.

"Is there someone I can call for you?" She waited for Gina to answer the question.

Gina covered her mouth with her hands. This was serious. Like he might not make it serious. Her mind whirled like a carnival ride as she tried to contemplate a world without Drew's smile and warm feet and warmer heart. Another person in scrubs came to sit next to her, helping her call Vicky. She couldn't speak, so the woman did. She stared at the hospital floor tiles, matte so they didn't reflect the bad lighting.

Time stopped. Her mind detached. Would she be here long? She should get back to the shop so Drew's customers could get their bikes. She should have grabbed his schedule while she was there. She should write this down on a list, but she didn't have any paper or pens with her. Why wasn't she more prepared?

Then her mother arrived. She didn't have flowers. She replaced the faceless person in scrubs. Vicky must have called her. She didn't speak either. Gina could only get one word out from her clenched jaw.

"May?"

"Vicky is picking her up from school right now and bringing her here."

A woman with short red hair in a white coat finally came out from where they'd taken Drew. The red hair stood out against the hospital's bland colors and a bright blue and yellow Tweety Bird bandage was wrapped around her index finger. The edges were peeling back. She wanted to get the woman a new bandage and help her put it on. The red-haired doctor was followed by a person in green scrubs. Gina didn't know if it was the same person who had pulled her away from Drew. They were all concerned brows and folded hands. She hated them.

"Mrs. Zoberski."

Gina shifted her weight to her feet to stand. She didn't want to have to look up at them when they said aloud what their faces had already told her. But the floor seemed to alter, turning to ice, and any strength in her legs fled. She couldn't find her footing and melted to the ground, the cold floor numbing her body. Crumbs of dirt bit into the palms of her hand and a goldfish cracker stared at her from underneath a nearby chair. They should sweep more.

But the doctor still knelt beside Gina.

"Mrs. Zoberski, your husband had a myocardial infarction, what you would call a heart attack. He survived the first one but had another in the hospital. We couldn't save him. I'm so sorry for your loss." She said more words, explanations for why this had happened, but all Gina could understand was the "we couldn't save him" part. They couldn't save him. Drew had never needed saving, not once. He was the saver, the knight in white armor.

A wail poured from her throat as she fought to remain whole, but lost. She wanted to curl into a ball to preserve what she could, but the truth pulled at her, demanding its payment. Her heart tore into two. People talked about a broken heart, a metaphor for sadness. But at that moment, Gina knew it was no metaphor. A ragged cut slowly pulled her apart, like a piece of paper being ripped in two. She would never be whole again. No amount of ointment or bandages would heal it. Arms, not her own, wrapped around her shoulders, doing their best to contain the damage, but it was too late.

"When you're ready, we can take you back to him," a voice said.

She nodded. She'd see him if it meant crawling to him on her hands and knees, but her mom, with strength she drew from somewhere unknown in her modest frame, pulled Gina up and looped her arm around her waist. They followed the doctor together, through heavy doors that closed with a whisper behind them. Past rooms where people waited with small children, past a room where several people surrounded a patient, past a gangly teen boy with his arm in a sling. Machines beeped and people spoke in urgent tones. The hallway went on forever. A part of her wished the hallway would keep going, because she knew what waited for her at the end.

And then there was Drew. A nurse finished coiling a tube and pushing a machine out of the way. He wasn't connected to anything — there was nothing left to track. He looked exactly the same as he had that morning. Same silver-flecked gold hair, same big strong arms, same tattoo trailing down, marking her way home. But everything was different, too. Motionless, he may as well have been wax.

His chest was bare, so she could see her and May's names, still over his heart, still with him. May's childlike writing etched on his skin. Forever. She touched her hand to the spot, begging for a miracle, a flutter, one more second to tell him how much she needed him and loved him and couldn't live a life without him. How May needed him. Her heart stuttered at the thought. She had been so focused on herself and Drew, she had forgotten May. This fresh agony cut even deeper, making it impossible to breathe. What should have doubled her grief instead multiplied it by ten, twenty, a hundred, like some horrific grief calculus. Drew would never see May graduate high school, fall in love, get married. He wouldn't be able to teach her how to drive or move her into her first apartment. The loss pushed down on her like a mountain. She wished she could let it crush her to dust. Anything to make it stop.

How could he be gone? Couldn't they start today over? She swore if she could wake up again, she'd pack him in the car and take him to the hospital to find the problem. Just back it up a few hours.

He was already cool to the touch. She lay her head on his chest, then regretted it instantly. There was no heartbeat, only the husk of the man he had been hours before. She leaned over to kiss his lips, her hand held his stubbly chin for the last time.

"I'd still jump in a river for you."

Her voice cracked.

Her mom took her hand, and they stared together at his body, Gina wondering where the spirit of him had gone. The noise in the hallway continued just like before, and Gina didn't understand. How could life go on without Drew? How could she go on?

"May will be here soon. You need to pull yourself together and move forward. You need to be there for her like I was there for you and Victoria."

Gina yanked her hand away and stepped back.

"No." The anger felt good, giving her a place to funnel all the rawness. "I'm not you, Mom. I'm not going to just get over Drew and get back to my life like you did when Dad died." Lorraine sucked in a breath. "I don't want to move forward. I can still feel his kisses on my lips, smell his aftershave on my shirt. We were supposed to be having lunch at his shop right now. I will not pretend that this isn't destroying me."

Lorraine straightened her spine and pinched her lips.

"You have no idea what you're talking about."

"No, you're the one who has no idea, Mom."

Her mother's lips grew thinner.

"Daddy? Daddy?" May's voice rang down the hall and Gina stepped out to meet her, pulling her into a hug, her body blocking May's view. Vicky followed a few steps behind. Gina didn't want May to see her dad like this, so still and cold. She should remember him vibrant and boisterous. "I want to see Daddy. Is he okay?"

Gina shook her head and looked into Vicky's eyes over her daughter's dark hair. Vicky covered her mouth as her eyes welled.

"No, baby. But you don't need . . ."

Lorraine joined Gina in the hallway, gently setting her hand on Gina's shoulder.

"She does."

"No . . ."

Lorraine's voice grew firmer and she unwrapped Gina's arms from around May, freeing her.

"You can't protect her from this. It's important for her to say her goodbyes herself." Her mom grabbed Gina's hand. "There is a healing in farewells that she is going to need."

May shrieked when she ran into the room, a sound Gina had never heard come from her daughter before. She stopped inside the door and took a step back. Vicky, a step behind her, set her hands on May's shoulders. As she watched May take in the truth, Gina's heart broke in half again for her daughter, leaving her only a quarter to live on. May and Drew had been two peas in a pod. She even knew how to take an engine apart and put it back together, just like her father had taught her. Last year, she'd repaired the stand mixer with his help. Who would help her now?

Lorraine had been right about one thing. She needed to pull herself together for May. She'd keep her mourning private or with Vicky. May needed to be her focus. That one thought, and her quarter of a heart, would get her through the next moment, and then the next, and maybe even the next.

Chapter Twenty-One

Erin, the therapist, pointed at a picture of an apple, asking Lorraine to make the *A* sound. She opened her mouth, and a completely different sound came out. Lorraine tried not to get frustrated, but her mouth refused to make the sounds her brain wanted them to make. Gah! She knew the sound she wanted, but her mouth wouldn't cooperate. She huffed, and Regina looked up from where she still sat on the couch after getting Lorraine's things packed for the move to the rehab facility. Was that girl ever going to go home? What was she avoiding?

"I know. It's frustrating. It will get easier," Erin said. Lorraine liked how she spoke slowly. Over the last few days, it had proven difficult to keep up with quick-moving conversations. This one was young and patient. "Would you like me to freshen your water?"

She waited a moment, and Lorraine nodded.

"Try to say 'yes.' Ya-ya-es." Lorraine scowled, but Erin waited on her chair like she had all the time in the world.

Lorraine thought about how the sound would come out of her mouth.

"Yaa."

"Good. That is good progress. I'll be right back with your water."

Erin left the room with Lorraine's Styrofoam cup, and Regina walked next to her bed.

"You're doing really well, Mom."

Lorraine scowled up at her. She didn't need to be patronized.

"And who says you need words, anyway? You've been communicating with your glares all my life."

Regina smiled at her, her eyes wrinkling at the corners, and Lorraine saw it. Her Regina had Joe's easy smile, and her eyes were the same shade of warm brown as his. She'd never allowed herself to think about it, shoving the thought away at the slightest nudge, but as she looked at her daughter's face, she saw more and more of him. Lorraine gave a crooked smile back.

Lorraine and her dad were there to buy her

a car so she could get to her outings at the club, visit her friends, and get to the local food bank where she volunteered — on her mother's insistence. Every well-bred woman found a way to give back to the community. At twenty-three, she needed her independence, and besides, her mother shouldn't have to be at her beck and call. So there they were at the Houser Used Car Lot on a sunny, Tuesday afternoon in April. The wind still had a bite to it as it fluttered her pastel yellow pleated skirt against her legs. Lorraine crossed her arms as she followed her dad through the maze of cars, trying to hold in body heat through her thin sweater.

"Hi, may I show you something specific, sir?"

Lorraine turned to see a man not much older than she was, with dark hair combed off his face, cropped short around the ears and neck. His big brown eyes and five o'clock shadow caught her attention, tracing his angular jaw and framing full lips that smiled at her. He wore a white collared shirt and a dark blue corduroy jacket over matching pants with a little flair at the ankle. He was dreamy. Lorraine smiled back at him, her teeth chattering from the breeze, then looked at her feet before her dad could notice her attraction.

"We need a car for my daughter. Something manageable and reliable."

The young man held out his hand and shook her father's. "I'm Joe. Joe Sandowski and I'd be happy to help you."

Her father eyed Joe up and down, then nodded.

"You can try."

Lorraine rolled her eyes at her dad's attempt to intimidate poor Joe. Then poor Joe handed Lorraine a thin plaid blanket he'd been holding in his left hand. "It's a bit cold, so I thought this might take the edge off."

She wrapped the blanket around her shoulders. Her father could be so rude with people he thought were beneath him. Joe didn't seem bothered by the attitude. And was it her imagination, or did her eye roll feel like a joke she and Joe shared?

"Tell me more about what you're looking for and the price range."

"It needs to start, even in the winter. She doesn't need some big boat, either. Price isn't a problem."

Her daddy would never admit that cost was a factor, but she also knew he'd nickel-and-dime this salesman so he'd barely get any commission at all.

"Does your daughter have a favorite color?"

Joe looked at her for an answer, but her dad and she spoke at the same time.

"Color doesn't matter," her father said.

"Blue," Lorraine said. She realized he was wearing the color from head to toe and blushed. She really did like blue, but maybe now she liked it a bit more.

"I have one that might be perfect." Joe led them to a powder-blue Volkswagen Beetle. Compared to the long lines and flat edges of the other cars, it seemed to be made from balloons, liable to float away into the clear sky it matched. Lorraine loved it on sight.

"You expect me to buy a foreign car? A German one, no less?"

"I understand your reservations, but let me tell you a bit more about the engineering." He continued talking about safety and cylinders and parts that meant nothing to her, but she hoped he wouldn't ever stop talking because then she would lose her excuse to stare at him. She held the corner of the blanket to her nose, pretending she was brushing some hair away from her face. Then she wrapped it tighter around her shoulders, hoping some of the scent, like campfire and pipe smoke, would rub off onto her sweater.

As he spoke to her father, he maintained eye contact, answered with good humor, and stood with confidence, not intimidated by this man twice his age — and her father loved to intimidate people.

"Would you like to take it for a test drive?"

Joe directed the question at her, but again, her father answered.

"I'll drive it. Lorraine, you can wait in the car."

She nodded and walked back to her father's shiny black Cadillac, glancing once over her shoulder toward Joe, unable to take her eyes off of him. She waited in the car for an hour while her dad drove around with Joe, then they went home. She assumed that was it, but even though her dad never said a word over breakfast, that morning someone from the dealership delivered the car to their house while she and her mom were out running errands. She found the car in their driveway, with the keys waiting in the ignition for her. With a clap of joy and after calling her father at work from the kitchen phone to thank him, Lorraine sat in the car alone and in awe. It was hers. It was freedom.

The seats were a beige leather and creaked when she sat in the driver's seat. She ran her hands over the large black steering wheel, warm from sitting in the sun. She flipped down the visor, and a piece of paper floated onto her lap. It was a note.

You stole my blanket. I'd like it back. Joe

Lorraine held the note to her chest and looked around, worried someone — her mother, a neighbor, anyone who could tell her father — had seen. Joe had guts, she'd have to give him that. Her father could have found the note, and surely Joe had noticed her father's distaste for anyone he viewed as beneath him — which was nearly everyone.

It would be a few hours before her mom emerged from her afternoon nap, where she'd retired after expressing her concern over the Beetle's safety.

Joe's recklessness inspired her. Lorraine snuck quietly to her room and retrieved the blanket he'd loaned her, spraying it liberally with her perfume. Maybe, just maybe, he'd feel about her perfume the way she felt about the campfire and pipe smoke. When she pulled her new car into the dealership lot, he was already standing in front of the building, as though he'd known she'd come to him at the first possible second. A smile lit every angle of his face. She grabbed the blanket and got out.

"I didn't steal it. I merely forgot to return

it," Lorraine said, not bothering with a proper greeting. Damn propriety.

He came to stand in front of her, still all-confidence and charm, and reached out a hand.

"Lorraine. It is Lorraine, isn't it?" She nodded. "Are you sure you didn't intentionally keep it so you could return it to me? Alone."

"Of course not. I'd never do anything so . . . blatant." And yes, while it was true she hadn't intentionally taken the blanket, the perfume was a different matter.

"Too bad."

"What do you mean too bad?"

He reached for the blanket in her hands, making sure his hand brushed hers. She wasn't used to men who flirted. "If you took it, that would mean you had wanted to see me again. And if you wanted to see me again . . ."

He let the words trail off, but his hand was still touching hers where they both held the blanket. She never wanted to let it go.

"And? If I did want to see you again — what would that mean?"

"Then I'd ask you to see a movie with me. Maybe grab a burger at Kopp's. You do like butter burgers, right?"

At last, he reclaimed the blanket completely, leaving her hands empty and restless for something to do. She clasped them in front of her. Her mother always said to keep still and people wouldn't know what you were thinking. But she wanted Joe to know what she was thinking. She wanted to go to a movie and Kopp's with him — maybe share a hot fudge shake and onion rings. She unclasped her hands.

"Then why don't you ask me?"

The way he smiled, she was lost right then. Then he did the one thing she'd hoped he'd do but never expected: he lifted the blanket to his face and inhaled. This was the man she would marry.

"Lorraine, would you do the honor of going to a movie with me this Friday night? I'll pick you up at seven."

She nodded, suddenly shy after all her boldness. He opened her Beetle's door for her and helped her into the driver's seat, shutting the door behind her. He leaned into the window.

"I'll see you then, lovely Lorraine." He started to back out, then paused. "And your perfume is going to keep me up all night."

He had the decency to return to the building, giving her a chance to compose herself and still her shaking hands before driving herself home — though the drive felt more like flying, her head was so high in the clouds.

When she told her parents about her plans that night over dinner, unable to resist sharing her joy, she crashed abruptly back to earth. Her mother began cutting her pork chop into smaller and smaller pieces and pursed her lips so tightly, the wrinkles looked like a cat's bottom. Her father took a more direct approach.

"My only daughter will not be seen with a used-car salesman or a Polack. I forbid it."

"It's just a movie, Dad."

"Do not talk back to me again. Besides, Friday is dinner at the club, you need to be there. The Miller lad said he would be stopping by our table to visit, and you will be there to greet him."

"Benjamin? Are you talking about Benny Miller?" He had tried four separate times last summer to lure her out onto the golf course alone while their parents downed brandy old-fashioneds in the main room. She may be inexperienced, but she knew a cad when she saw one. "I'm not interested in Benny."

"His family does invaluable business with my factory. You'll be there and you will be polite, young lady. Or that car goes back to the lot." He pointed his fork at her as he chewed viciously on a bite.

"I hear the Carrington boy is back from Yale. He should be there, too, Lorraine," her mom said, as though that was a peace offering.

She knew her mom was trying to do a swap. Yesterday Chad Carrington would have been motivation enough to get dolled up for another dull evening avoiding Benny and his friends, but after meeting Joe, Chad held all the allure of a dusty rock. She'd never get permission to go out with Joe — that was clear. But she didn't have to. She'd learned to work around her parents' rules long ago. She had a few tricks yet to try, and if anyone was worth the effort, Joe with the straightforward smile and easy invitation was.

"Oh, it'll be nice to catch up with him." She smiled at her mother and finished her dinner, clearing all the plates when everyone was done, like a good girl should.

On Friday, Lorraine filled a plastic sandwich bag with milk and cooked oatmeal, making sure the twist tie was tight as could be. She slipped it into the pocket of her pink-and-green-checked shift dress, a matching pink cardigan carefully draped to hide the bulge.

"Lorraine, honey, it's time to go." Her mother's voice drifted up from the foyer.

"Down in a minute . . ." She held a heating pad to her face, then stepped carefully down the green-carpeted stairs. Her parents waited under the crystal chandelier, which in her opinion was too fancy for the shag under her feet. Her father checked his watch, and her mom primped in the gilded-frame mirror, tucking a stray strand of honey-brown hair that had escaped from her French twist.

"And I told Maureen about the Millers. I know she was hoping Benjamin would show interest in her Ingrid."

"Mm-hmm," her father responded. He rarely paid attention to her mother's prattling. Instead, he smoothed his navy-blue sport coat over his belly.

As Lorraine reached the last step, she clutched the wrought iron banister, letting her kitten heels catch in the green shag, tripping forward.

"Whoa."

Her mother paused to look at Lorraine. "You okay, dear?"

"I just got a little dizzy, and my head's starting to hurt. But I'll take some aspirin." She smoothed her dress, making sure her sweater still concealed her pocket. "I'm sure

I'll be fine."

Right on cue, her mom touched Lorraine's forehead.

"You do feel hot. Maybe some aspirin will help. I'll get it." Her mother scurried off toward the kitchen.

"Thank you. I wouldn't want to miss seeing Chad."

Her dad watched her with squinted eyes. He was always the harder one to fool. Her mother returned with two aspirin and a glass of water. She swallowed them and drank the water.

"Thanks. That's bett—" Lorraine dropped the glass and covered her mouth, running to the small bathroom off the foyer that her mother insisted on calling a "water closet," even though none of them had been to England. She intentionally left the door cracked so her parents could hear. As she pulled the sandwich bag from her pocket, she made retching sounds, then tore a hole in the bag, letting the contents slop into the toilet. She wrapped the bag in toilet paper and tossed it into the garbage, then flushed the toilet and splashed water on her face. For the final touch, she ruffled her hair in the mirror and rubbed her eyes to look appropriately disheveled.

She left the bathroom, closing the door

meekly behind her. Now for the risky part. Her parents might not believe her.

"I'm so sorry. I'm ready to go now."

Her father had his arms crossed and her mother waited for his cue on how to proceed. He took in her mussed hair, damp cheeks, and slumped shoulders. If this worked, she deserved a daytime Emmy.

"You can't leave the house like this. Get in bed. Mother will bring you some ginger ale and saltines. I'll be in the car."

He exited out the front door, Mom nodded and rushed off to finish her task. In the empty foyer, Lorraine smiled.

Five minutes before seven, she peeked out the front door. She'd reapplied her makeup and straightened her hair, even adding an extra dab of perfume below her ears, hoping Joe would get close enough to smell it. As the grandfather clock in the foyer chimed its seventh bong, he pulled up in a sleek red convertible, way too nice a car for a used-car salesman.

Before he even came to a full stop, she was out the front door, her feet carrying her almost as fast as her heartbeat. He jumped out of the car and hurried around to greet her, stopping in front of her, looking unsure if he should hug her, or kiss her, or shake her hand. Lorraine knew which she would prefer.

"Lovely Lorraine, you're more stunning each time I see you. If this continues, the stars will start to get jealous."

Lorraine blushed. She knew a line when she heard it, but he said it with such sincerity. Could he mean something so nice?

"Flatterer."

"But an honest one." His eyes didn't leave her face, sucking her breath away. If they simply stared at one another for the entire evening, she would consider it a perfect date.

But Joe broke the silence. "Should we go inside to see your parents?"

Lorraine blinked back to reality. He wanted to meet her parents? She hadn't expected that from him — especially since he'd already met her father, who hadn't made the best of impressions. Who would want to spend more time with him?

"They had to leave for the club and couldn't wait. Next time." She didn't like lying to him, but she didn't want to tell him that her parents thought he wasn't good enough, not before she knew him better. "What a fab car!"

He beamed.

"Thank you. My boss lent it to me for the

night. I told him about our date, and he thought it would be less embarrassing than my normal heap." Ah. He opened the passenger door for her, and she slipped onto the long, buttery soft, leather seat. After she wrapped a scarf around her hair to keep it from becoming a mess, they set off into the warm spring night.

Lorraine wiped the tears away from her face.

"I can't believe you took me to *Love Story* on our first date. I must look a mess."

Joe handed her another tissue.

"I think you look even more beautiful. I liked it — they found a way to be happy even though they came from different backgrounds."

"Until she died."

"There are always setbacks." He shrugged. "The point is that they didn't let it stop them from finding whatever joy they could."

Joe pulled into her driveway and stopped the car under the overhanging oak tree as Lorraine tried to discreetly check to make sure her parents weren't home yet. They rarely returned before eleven, and it was only ten, but she didn't want to risk getting caught.

"Don't worry, I'll be gone before they get back."

She could hear the smile in his voice but was more grateful he understood and didn't seem to mind. Lorraine looked at him, and he reached for her hand.

"Lovely Lorraine." He pulled the scarf off her hair and rubbed the soft fabric. "I may not be rich, but I'm smart enough to tell when someone is sneaking around — I did it enough when I was younger. I took the measure of your dad. He thinks a doctor or lawyer — preferably someone from old money — is better suited for his daughter, am I right?"

So this was how this wonderful night — this wonderful experience — would end. He wouldn't want to be with her, knowing her parents didn't approve. She didn't want to answer, knowing that would be the end of the fairy-tale evening. Disappointment pulled at her shoulders until she slumped forward in defeat, her head tilted toward her lap.

"Yes. I'm sorry. I didn't want to hurt your feelings, and I really thought you were great when we met. Honestly, Joe, this was the best date I've ever had."

"Even with the tears?"

She nodded. "Maybe because of the tears."

He reached out for her hand and traced

his finger along the inside of her wrist.

"If this weren't our first date, I'd tell you that 'love means never having to say you're sorry,' but that seems a bit heavy-handed this soon." He laced his fingers with hers so they were holding hands in the dark, in the shiny convertible, alone. Now he was going to ruin this perfect moment by telling her it could never happen again.

Lorraine sucked in a breath. "I don't care what my parents think. My dad has controlled every part of my life until now. All of the boys my parents want me to date are more interested in my dad's business than in me. I've never had a boy ask me out because he liked me. I would very much like to see you again. Please say that you do, too."

He squeezed her hand.

"Brave girl. I don't need anyone's approval to take you on a date except yours. If you're offering that, I'm taking you up on it." They stared at each other in the dark. She didn't want the night to end, but she also knew the clock was ticking.

"I better . . ." She motioned to the house. Joe got out of the car and walked around to open her door. As she stood he spoke.

"Can you meet me for lunch tomorrow?" He was so close to her. His shirt brushed against the front of her dress, lighting her nerves on fire and pulling the air from her lungs.

"I'd love to." She tried to catch her breath, but the words came out as a whisper. "How about noon at the diner on Downer Avenue? They have the best cherry pie."

He looped her arm in his and led her to the front door.

"Until then, lovely Lorraine."

Then he did what she had been waiting for all night, he leaned in to kiss her, soft and sweet. His lips moved gently, letting her match him. She stepped closer so her body aligned with his, and their lips became more urgent until he stepped back, breaking off the kiss.

"If we keep doing that, we'll still be kissing when your parents get home. Probably not the best first step toward them accepting me as your boyfriend."

His crooked smile finished off his confession, as if his lips hooked on the word that caught her attention.

"Boyfriend?"

"I'm not the kind of boy who kisses a girl without meaning it." He winked and smiled. He gave her one more quick kiss and was off before she could open her eyes. "Tomorrow, my lovely." And he was gone. She stood on the stoop, watching his taillights disappear down the street and then headlights take their place. Her parents! She rushed into the house, stripping off her clothes as she ran up the stairs, and making it into her pajamas and under the covers just as her parents turned the key.

All the subterfuge had been worth it. She didn't want a stuffy club boy. She wanted someone who said pretty things to her just to make her smile, and who didn't mind if she cried at movies, who saw how she tried to be brave, who wanted to hear her. She wanted Joe.

Looking back at that night, at how she'd felt so heard, Lorraine realized she had forgotten how to speak way before the stroke. She had stopped saying what was in her heart, stopped valuing her own voice. For so long, and out of fear, she'd parroted the words expected of her by Floyd, by the ladies at the club, by her own misguided belief that ignoring Joe's memory was the best way forward. Not anymore. She would find her voice again.

■ ■ ■ ■

What Is Your Biggest Regret?

■ ■ ■ ■

Chapter Twenty-Two

"May, it's time to go. I let you sleep late because you were with Aunt Vicky last night. We need to get to work."

Her mother's voice came from the hallway outside her door, then her steps retreated back to the kitchen. May could smell pancakes and hear the muffled chaos of her cousins.

May stretched out under her covers. She and Aunt Vicky hadn't gotten home until after midnight. She had been a little worried she really was going to have to drive the two of them home last night, but it all worked out, impromptu plan included.

They had tiptoed into the house, giggly after their adventure. Aunt Vicky had checked on each of her children, then drank a huge bottle of water before going to bed. May had sat at the table, not quite ready for bed yet either. She had found her phone in one of her mom's usual hiding places — the top kitchen shelf behind the spices, like she couldn't reach there. She had a text from Connor.

U alive?

It had arrived three hours ago.

She had wanted to reply. Maybe he was still awake? But she didn't want to get in more trouble. Just knowing he had texted made her smile. She turned off the phone and slid it back into its hiding place. In three days, winter break would be over and she'd be back in school, so she could see him in person. Besides, Aunt Vicky said that if a guy really liked you, he wouldn't stop just because of a little silence.

"May, let's go!"

From her still-flat position, she heard her door scrape open, followed by little feet and soft giggles.

"Coming," she mumbled back, still trying to clear the sleep from her brain.

She pretended she didn't hear the wake-up brigade until they were about to pounce, then while still under the covers she sat up and grabbed them, their squeals waking her better than any alarm.

"You little goobers, what were you trying to do?"

Maggie and Nathan only giggled louder. May kissed the tops of their heads. Greta and Jake must still be eating breakfast.

"Mama said we would go see tigers and monkeys," Maggie said. She couldn't say her *S*s quite right, so her sweet voice held a tiny lisp that was adorable. They settled on top of her blankets, each sitting crisscross.

"Yeah? Are you sure she wasn't calling you tigers and monkeys?"

Nathan scrunched his face up, giving the idea serious consideration.

"I don't think so. Mama said we would see them, not be them."

May stifled her laugh. He had always been the serious one, the scowling baby next to his laughing twin.

"Then we must be going to the zoo!"

"Okay, you two, let May get up. She needs to go before Aunty Gina gets really angry." Aunt Vicky stood in the doorway, holding a cup of coffee. Maggie and Nathan slid off the bed and scampered out. "Sorry, they escaped this morning."

May rolled out of her cozy dark bed, kicked aside some clothes, and stepped into the hallway, still wearing her pajamas — flannel pants and a black tank top.

"I don't mind. They're cute."

"Next time they can't sleep through the

night, you can take them, and then you let me know how cute they are." Aunt Vicky shuffled back down the hallway toward the kitchen, spanking May's mom on the butt as she passed her, who was clearly intending to check on her. Again.

May pulled her hair into a ponytail high on her head so she could wash her face and brush her teeth — the bare minimum necessary for working in the food truck.

"What is that?" Her mom pointed at her chest.

Crap. She had meant to explain first, and then show her.

"It's sort of a tattoo." Peeking down, she saw that the edge of her tank top mostly covered the words, so it probably wasn't clear to her mom what it was.

It took a moment for her mom to register what she'd said, her face crumpling in a growing rage that erupted from nowhere.

"Tattoo? You got a tattoo? Why? How?"

"I said sort of a tattoo." May shrugged, knowing her matter-of-fact tone would irritate her — she couldn't help herself. If her mom wasn't going to pause long enough to really listen, she deserved no help. "Aunt Vicky took me after our dinner last night. We had to try a few places before we found one that would do it."

"Aunt Vicky is not your parent."

"At least she wants to spend time with me."

Aunt Vicky appeared at the end of the hall. "Umm, Gina . . ."

"Nope, you've done enough. We're going to talk later." Aunt Vicky put her hands up and backed into the kitchen at the sight of the anger tornado. "And you, you put ink on your body? That was not your decision to make."

"It's my body, Mom. And it's not even —"

"Not until you're eighteen, it isn't. Until then, it's mine." Her mom stepped closer and pulled May's tank top down a bit so she could see what it was. "What was so important that you needed to have it on your body forever?"

There. May enjoyed watching her mom's face as she realized what the image right next to her heart was. The transition from anger to shock to sadness, and then back to anger. Served her right. It was the note her dad had left on her pillow the day he died. She always kept it with her, either in a pocket or a purse.

Yam. Kick ass today. Smooshes, Daddy

"It's not that big of a deal, and besides Dad would have let me do it, and you know it." May stepped out of her mom's reach, smoothing her shirt back over the words, a little guilt pecking at her edges.

"Your dad isn't here." Gina's voice was a whisper, still taking in what her daughter had done.

"And why is that? Why can't you say it?" Gina's chest rose and fell in deep breaths. Rage filled May that her mom never talked about her dad, never shared memories or feelings. She just plowed on through life, pretending his death didn't bother her, or worse, that he'd never existed. "It's because he's dead, Mom. He's dead. He's worm food. He's gone forever. And you may as well be, too."

Gina's hand cocked back and before May understood what was happening, her mom's hand made contact with her cheek in a blaze of pain, like the side of her face had exploded with fireworks. May covered her cheek, and her mom covered her mouth with her hand. Hot tears sizzled across the stinging handprint.

In the two years since her dad died, her mom had never so much as knocked hard on her door, let alone hit her. In the face. Her mom really did hate her. May turned back into her bedroom and slammed the door, opening it and slamming it again a second time for good measure. If her mom had been worried the tattoo was permanent, she must not know what a slap could do.

Chapter Twenty-Three

Gina's hand stung from where it had made contact with her daughter's face. Shouldn't the police already be in the driveway? Shouldn't sirens be going off? She'd committed the one sin a parent never should — thou must not hit your kid. Where was the rewind button on life? She wanted that moment back, the one where her daughter looked at her with loathing, not fear. How did the moment get so out of hand?

"This is quite the kerfuckle you've created." Vicky stood in the kitchen doorway, mascara smudged under her eyes and a steaming mug of coffee in her hand. Her hair was in a haphazard clip on the top of her head, shooting errant strands from her head like spikes. "It's not even real, Gina. We both tried to tell you, but you wouldn't listen. It's henna. Under eighteens can't get tattoos, it's illegal."

"It's fake?" Gina's voice was quiet. Maybe

if she didn't say it too loudly, she could pretend she hadn't flown off the handle. "Why didn't May say so?"

"She tried. You weren't listening to her. Honestly, you rarely do. At least not where Drew is concerned."

"He was the one with the special connection to her. I was the enforcer." Gina drooped against the wall.

"You've proven that in spades. He's not here anymore and she needs you. That special-connection line is bullshit, and you know it. She's your daughter — there's no connection more special than that." Vicky took a big gulp of coffee and scratched her hip. "I'm going to need at least two more of these." She returned to the kitchen, where her kids were devouring the pancakes Gina had made. Vicky turned back to her and pointed toward May's door. "Fix that. Now."

When had her little sister gotten so smart? Gina ran her fingers over the tingling palm. Every twinge deepened her regret until she was so far underwater she didn't think she could breathe. Was she so old that she didn't remember the painful, impetuous things a teenager could say?

Gina reached for the green beans, scooping

some onto her plate, half covering her mashed potatoes because she was too busy watching her dad for the right time to ask her question. She needed him in a good mood. The annual father-daughter dance for Juniors and Seniors was in two weeks, and this was the first year she could attend. Every girl in her class was going, wearing fancy dresses. Some of the dads even rented tuxedos. Her dad already owned one, so that would be easy. She'd already found the dress she wanted in the *Seventeen* magazine tucked under her seat cushion. It was bright pink and strapless, with two layers of ruffles that made up the knee-length skirt. Sequins in a flower pattern covered the bodice with a large satin pink rosette over the left hip. Just looking at it made her smile. She planned to show her mom after her dad agreed to take her.

Her dad, forehead relaxed, glasses perched on his nose, had a newspaper neatly folded next to his plate so he could read. His hands moved methodically as he cut his chicken breast and lifted the bite to his mouth, his movements unrushed. When he looked up as he sipped his wine, she dropped her eyes back to her plate and nudged the beans around its surface, waiting for her moment.

"How did your test go, Victoria?" her

mom asked.

"Easy. I was the first done." Vicky sat across from her, her hair in a high ponytail with a ribbon trailing down her hair. She wore her blue and white cheerleader uniform because there was a basketball game later that night. She didn't even have to wear it at the table — she only did because she knew Gina hated it. Freshman year, her mother had made Gina try out and she hadn't made the squad. Vicky not only tried out and made it, but was also elected captain of the JV squad. Everything was easier for her.

"We should talk to your teachers about challenging you. Maybe you should be moved up to the next math class. What do you think, Floyd?"

Gina's head swung to watch this rare attempt to draw her father into the conversation. Usually, he just stuck to his paper, unless it was time to report on their quarterly grades. This might be her moment. If he responded well here, she knew she could ask him about the dance.

"Hmm?" His eyes looked up over the top of his glasses with his face still tilted toward the paper.

"Don't you think we should talk to Victoria's teachers about bumping her up in math? It's too easy for her. She needs to be challenged."

"It's always worth a discussion. Set up a meeting, and I'll see if I can make it."

Wait? He was going to go? This was the Brigadoon of fatherly moments. Now was her chance, before he turned back to his paper.

"Dad?" His eyes flicked to her while his head kept the same position. She took a deep breath and pressed on. "The Father-Daughter dance is in a few weeks. Will you go with me?"

Her mom and Vicky stopped eating. She held her breath. She'd never asked him to do something with her before. If they did something as a family, her mom had always orchestrated it.

"When is it?" Her father looked over the top of his glasses at her, an eyebrow raised. She willed herself to keep her brown eyes on his blue ones.

"Um, Saturday. March thirtieth. At seven o'clock."

His eyebrow relaxed.

"I have a work trip that weekend, Regina. I'm sorry."

He didn't sound sorry. He sounded a little relieved, but Gina was emboldened by his response. Maybe he just didn't know how important this was to her.

"Could you change your trip to a different weekend? This is a really big deal, and I think . . ."

"I can't reschedule. Perhaps your mother can take you girls to Chicago. Do some shopping on Michigan Avenue." He smiled as if that solved everything.

"Regina, help me in the kitchen," her mom said. "Now."

Gina looked at her dad, who had returned to eating and reading like it was every other dinner they'd ever had. She had wanted this one special night with him, all the fun of a regular dance without worrying about being asked by a boy who'd probably drink schnapps until he threw up anyway. She bit her lip so the pain could dry up her tears, set the *Seventeen* magazine on the dining room table open to the page with the beautiful pink dress, and followed her mom into the kitchen. The door had barely shut before her mom started angry whispering at her, as if her dad and Vicky didn't know exactly what was happening.

"Since when do you bother your father about school dances? You should have asked me to talk to him and not made a scene at the dinner table out of nowhere."

Gina's mouth dropped. Her mom's face

was pinched and mottled. It was at odds with her smooth brown hair clipped up on one side with bobby pins, sparkling diamond stud earrings, and precisely pressed wool pants. Was it possible that her mom was . . . embarrassed?

"I asked a simple question. How is that a scene? I'm the only one of my friends who won't be going. Can't you talk to him or something?"

"His work comes first. Always. His work is what keeps a roof over all our heads. We don't take that for granted in this house." Her mom slid the cross on her necklace back and forth along the chain while the lines on her forehead deepened.

"I've been waiting since freshman year. There's a dinner, too. And, he wouldn't even need to rent a tux because he already has one. And I promise it'd be fun —"

"Enough." The edge in her mom's voice told her it was time to quit, but she couldn't handle the injustice of it all. He said he would go to a school meeting for Victoria's math, but not take her to the dance. This sucked.

"He never does anything with us. I wish Dad would just disappear!"

She hadn't really meant to shout it, not entirely. Gina's apology was already forming in her mind when her face exploded in pain, sucking the breath from her lungs. She covered her cheek with her hand and looked at her mother, taking a step out of arm's reach. Lorraine straightened, rubbing the hand that had struck Gina with her nonviolent one. Her nostrils flared.

"You will not speak like that. Ever. This conversation is over. Right now, young lady."

Gina swallowed back her tears and ran through the dining room, pausing to pick up the magazine, but it was missing. Her dad didn't even look up, but Vicky watched her every move. Gina ran to her room, slammed her door, and flopped onto her bed. Why couldn't she have a family like everyone else's? A dad who wanted to go to dances. A few days later, the bright pink dress from the missing magazine would appear in her closet, but she would never have anywhere to wear it.

She heard her door creak and turned to see Vicky carrying a bag full of ice.

"I thought you might like this. For your cheek."

Her little sister's face said it all.

Gina took the ice, the cold freezing out the sting but doing nothing for the real hurt.

Her mother could be critical, but she had never hit her before. How could she? When she was a mother, Gina vowed, she'd never, ever hit her kids. She'd always listen to them and take their wants into consideration. She would be a good mother.

Gina opened the fridge, pulling out one of the ice packs she always kept in there. At her age, body parts decided to pop and pull unexpectedly, so having something cold ready to go was a necessity. She massaged it between her hands to make it more malleable and walked down the hall to May's closed door, guilt and dread weighing her down.

When she opened the creaking door, May was sprawled on her bed, shoulders shaking. Gina had vowed to never be like her mother — now was her chance to try and improve. She had to at least try.

"May?"

She flipped over and glared at her mom. "Going to slap the other cheek?"

Ouch. She deserved that. Gina sat on the edge of the bed and held out the cold pack. "This will help. I promise." May took it and pressed it to her cheek. "There is no excuse for hitting someone. I'm sorry and I was very wrong to do it." May nodded, her glare lessening a bit. "And I'm sorry I didn't ask for more information about your 'tattoo' before I got angry."

May nodded. How had they gotten so off course? "Henna, huh?" May nodded again. "That's actually a brilliant idea. When you turn eighteen, you can get the real thing." Gina took a deep breath before continuing. "I know . . ." This was so hard for her to say. Just thinking the words set her tear ducts into motion. Her voice cracked as she spoke. "I know Dad is dead." She had to swallow before continuing. "Of course I know it. I know it with every part of me. The part that still rolls to his side of the bed every day looking for a good-morning kiss, the part that turns to him in the kitchen to share a story about something amazing you did, the part that starts to call him when the truck's engine makes a funny noise. Did you know that I still pay his cell phone bill so I can call it and hear his voice on the recording? Isn't that pathetic? Sometimes I even leave messages telling him about my day, then I go into his phone and delete them." Tears fell from her face, matching the ones on May's. She pulled her daughter into a hug she could only hope conveyed how sorry she was.

"I don't talk about him with you because I can't. I've accepted that he's gone from my life forever, but I can't seem to accept that he's gone from yours, too. That he'll never see you graduate, or intimidate a first boyfriend — he was so looking forward to that — or walk you down the aisle at your wedding. He's going to miss out on watching you become the amazing woman I know you'll be. And that is something I cannot face."

Her arm tightened around May, who still didn't seem to want to speak.

"I'm not enough, May. I can't be both him and me, and you deserve to have him. You deserve to have all those moments, and I'm so fucking angry that you don't get them. I never had them with my dad. You should have had them with Drew. But, instead, you're stuck with me."

Gina lifted May's face and wiped away her tears.

"I need to talk about him, Mom. I'm forgetting things. I don't remember what he smells like anymore. Or his laugh. I don't want to forget him."

Gina understood, because she had the same fears.

"I'll do better. We'll find ways, like your henna, to celebrate our memories — keep him more a part of our days."

May nodded, and Gina smoothed back a few strands that had fallen out of May's ponytail. Her hand kept going until it reached the orange stripe.

"And do we need to talk about this, too? Did you mean to make it this particular shade of orange?"

Even though her face was still red and swollen with tears, May chuckled.

"I wanted it blond."

"I think every brunette tries to go blond at least once." Gina wrapped the hair around her finger, thinking of some options. "We could bleach it again, and try a fun color. How about hot pink? Or green?"

"Blue — dad's favorite."

"Perfect." Gina pulled her into her arms, and May wrapped her own around Gina's waist. Gina kissed the top of May's head. "We're going to be okay."

Chapter Twenty-Four

"So wait, you and our real dad used to live under Roza? I can't imagine you living in that tiny little apartment." Victoria asked.

Lorraine nodded at the question.

Yes.

It was day five poststroke and she could move a little better, but words were still difficult. She could say yes now, but it was so much easier to nod. Erin the Therapist would tell her the practice was good for her, each attempt helping to strengthen the thought-speech connections. That sounded great until every fourth attempt sounded like she'd drunk an entire bottle of chardonnay. She didn't like her daughters seeing her weak. A nod was confident, and there was no confusion about what she was trying to say.

Sitting in the reclining chair next to the window in her new room at the rehab facility, Lorraine could look at everyone at the same time. The entire family was here — Regina, Victoria, May, Roza — and even the littlest members, Jake, Greta, Maggie, and Nathan. The younger ones watched a colorful cartoon on the floor, blessedly quiet for now.

The winter sun warmed her lap. Between the girls, Roza, and her head gestures, they'd worked out a system. If Roza didn't know the full answer to one of the girls' questions, they would ask a Yes or a No question. It wasn't perfect, of course, but they were finally talking. If only she were at home rather than in this godawful facility. At least the food was better than at the hospital, though the decor was still clearly designed by a man, all earth tones and no flair. Would it kill them to use something other than brushed nickel on every light and water fixture?

There was less beeping and rushing here, too. Rehab had more of a hotel atmosphere, with more comfortable chairs and mostly carpeted rooms. People here were meant to get better and go home, which was encouraging to say the least. The therapists came to her room, rather than demanding she be wheeled across the entire hospital, to work with her on speech and movement, trying to reconnect all those neural connections that had been blown to bits during the stroke. She even had someone training her to use an iPad to communicate, but that was more bother than benefit.

Roza's laughing voice brought her back to the conversation.

"Lorraine would have lived in a cave with Joe." Roza sat next to her right side and clasped her hand. "Right?"

Yes.

Well maybe not a cave, she did have some standards. But with Joe, it would have seemed possible.

Regina and May sat on the moss-green love seat. May nestled into her mom's side, and Regina played with the frizzy, bleached chunk of hair — they still hadn't remedied that.

"I don't understand why Grandma would marry someone she didn't love?" May asked. Smart girl.

"May," Regina said, squishing her to her side. Roza laughed, and Lorraine would have too, if she could. Such an impertinent question did not bother her anymore. Instead, she was quite proud of May for asking it. Lorraine nodded at Roza to answer.

"Times were different. Lorraine was raised by a very strict man to marry well, pick a charity to support, learn to host a dinner party, then have children she would teach to do the same. When she fell in love with Joe, she threw all that away. He adored her so much she didn't mind that they didn't have any money. So when he died, she had no useful degrees and no practical skills that would earn her enough to care for a toddler and another baby on the way. She only had a high school education, and her best subject was home ec. She didn't have many choices."

"She could have gotten a job," May said.

"Yes. But doing what? Waitressing two jobs? She didn't have the practicality God gave a goose — I had to teach her how to iron a shirt, for heaven's sake. She needed to give you the best possible future, and she couldn't do that on her own. When Joe died, her entire future had been taken from her, and she was afraid of failing you two girls. Fear and love are powerful motivators. She wanted to give you all the same opportunities she'd had — even the choice to pull away." Roza winked at Regina. "She loved you both so much that the possibility of not succeeding canceled out all her options, save one — and she was lucky that she even had that option. She needed to return to what she did know, and her father wasn't about to let her come home with two babies and no husband in sight. She needed a husband. Floyd wasn't a bad option, all things considered."

Lorraine smacked the blanket covering her lap to get Roza's attention. Wasn't a bad option. There was more to the decision than that.

"Really, you want me to get into that?" Roza raised an eyebrow.

Yes.

"All right, but remember you said this. You remember that Floyd was much older than your mother? And he didn't want a wife in the traditional sense — he wanted someone to help him crack into Milwaukee's social circles. In your mom, he had someone who could introduce him to possible customers. With you girls . . . well, you kept people from asking certain questions. A little bit of smooth lying, which was much easier in the days before the Internet. In return, he provided her with all the security she needed. His only rules were that no one ever knew you weren't his children or that she had been married before, and that she didn't share with anyone that their marriage wasn't . . . intimate."

"But didn't he wonder why you were around all the time?" Victoria asked.

"What do you mean? I was your nanny."

"You took an awful lot of naps for a nanny," Victoria said.

"You had a lot of energy." Roza folded her hands in her lap.

"Wait, what did you mean when you said that thing about marriage?" May asked. Everyone's eyes flashed to Lorraine, and she laughed. That girl was amazing. Why had she never noticed before? She had spunk — not that it came out often, but it was there. It reminded her of Joe, how he always spoke what was in his heart. Lorraine could see twinkles of the bold woman May would become. Her heart glowed with pride.

She nodded for Roza to explain.

"Well . . . Gina?"

"He was gay, honey. Grandma and Grandpa never had sex," Regina said. May's mouth opened to ask a follow-up question, but Regina answered that, too. "Back then, an openly gay businessman would have had a difficult time fitting in in Milwaukee. It wasn't like it is now — and having a wife and kids preemptively answered any questions. So for both of them, it was a win-win. He built his business and met new potential customers, and Grandma didn't have to worry about how she would provide for us."

"They didn't love each other, though. It wasn't real?"

"I don't know." Regina looked toward the ceiling. "I've been thinking a lot about Dad since we found out about Joe." Her eyes found Lorraine's. "He was never a great dad, but he was a great provider. I don't have any of those warm fuzzy daddy-daughter memories, but I do have a lot of good memories of swimming at the club and family dinners. None of those would have been possible without him. He cared for us in the way that he could. If that's not real, I'm not sure what is."

Regina was right. Without Floyd, they wouldn't be here together.

"We went on some great trips together, didn't we?" Roza chimed in. "Remember that time we went snorkeling in the Bahamas, and I kept feeding the stray cats that lived on the resort property. We had so much food at the buffets that I would bring bits of fish and bread back to the room and put it outside the sliding door. By the time we left, our patio looked like a cat hoarder's."

"I remember that," Vicky said. "A few even let us pet them. Dad couldn't figure out why they were outside our room and kept trying to shoo them away so he could read his paper."

Roza chuckled.

"Yes. We never did tell him why they were there. They kept you girls occupied for hours so me and your mom could relax and read. We took care of each other, didn't we Lorraine?" Roza patted her leg.

Yes.

Roza shared her big heart, which was enough for both of them. For far too long, Lorraine had closed off her own heart, afraid it would crumble if she opened it wide. Looking around at her beautiful family, regret rose up in her chest. Why did she wait so long to notice how strong the women she raised were? And now Regina and Victoria were raising their own strong children. She wanted to tell them all how proud she was. How amazed. How she wished she had had Regina's strength or Victoria's frankness. When Lorraine was most honest with herself, which she tried not to do very often, she was ashamed. She had married a beautiful and perfect man, who was honorable and loved her with every inch of himself. Without a second thought, she had shut that all away and taken the easy way out after everything fell apart. She hadn't even tried. It hadn't even occurred to her to stay in that little cozy house. Instead of grieving and growing, she had buried those feelings and pretended those early blissful years never happened.

In all those years married to Floyd, there were even moments when she forgot Regina and Victoria weren't his — and that felt like the biggest betrayal of all. She had caught herself noticing a twitch of the mouth or an awkward hand movement and attributed those quirks to Floyd, ignoring the fact that both of her daughters had Joe's nose with a tiny bump on the bridge and his long, graceful fingers.

All those nights alone in her bed, reaching for Joe — it didn't have to be that way. She had distanced herself from her daughters, believing she was doing the right thing. But had she been? They could have grown up next door to Roza and her grandchildren, learning that happiness and love were gifts not to be tossed aside. She had tossed aside Joe's memory instead of sharing it. Now her memories were distant and fuzzy from disuse, like silver left alone in a drawer for too many years. She wanted to polish each one and share it with her daughters. They deserved to know that Joe would walk Regina all night when she had a fever, then fall asleep with her on his chest. She would wake to find them in the recliner, snoring in tandem. Victoria deserved to know that Joe would sing off-key lullabies to her stomach and she would kick in response.

They deserved those memories and so many more.

"He died in Vietnam, right?" Regina asked.

Yes.

"Then his name would be on the Vietnam Memorial. Did you ever go see it? Did you find his name when we were there in high school?"

No. She'd thought about it many times — especially when she and Floyd had taken the girls to Washington, DC. He'd been there on business, so she had visited the sites with the girls. They walked the entire Mall, from the Capitol to the Lincoln Memorial. The girls were more interested in taking pictures of the Washington Monument in the reflecting pond. She could see the Vietnam Memorial through the trees, a black scar on the green lawn. It had called to her. The girls wouldn't know what she was looking for — she could even say she was looking up a friend from high school who had served. But what would seeing his name do to her? In the end, she had turned her back, as she had so many times.

"We should go as soon as Mom gets better," Victoria said. Victoria was sitting cross-legged on the bed. At least she had taken her shoes off. Greta and Maggie had grown bored with the movie and snuggled at her side while the other two had moved onto a puzzle at the corner table — though Nathan was dropping more on the floor than finding matching pieces. Victoria looked happier than Lorraine could remember seeing her.

Lorraine shook her head and pointed at the girls.

"You think we should go and not wait for you?" Victoria said.

Yes.

"I suppose we could go on spring break, then May could come," Regina said.

No. The system was not perfect.

"She wants you to go now." Thank God for Roza. "I'll watch the children."

Yes.

"We can't leave you with all of them," Victoria said.

Roza rolled her eyes.

"I may be old, but I am not afraid of a few little children. And May will be here to help, right, May?"

May nodded as Maggie crawled onto her lap to play with her bleached hair, trying to braid it.

"That's good enough for me." Victoria had already pulled out her phone. "There are flights leaving early tomorrow morning and coming back late tomorrow night. We could make it a day trip?"

Regina scrunched her nose. She always did that when she thought about something. Lorraine could not remember all the times she had told her to stop or she would get wrinkles. Perhaps it was time to let up. After all, her wrinkles hadn't ruined her life, any mistakes were hers alone.

"Tomorrow's New Year's Day. People like comfort food after a late night."

"Don't be absurd — those people aren't going outside when there are pizza places that deliver. Take the day off."

"I suppose I could . . . But I'll need to update my site."

"Yes!" Victoria said.

"You're sure you can watch them all, Roza? Five kids is a lot for anyone," Regina said.

"Don't be ridiculous. I have been meaning to steal May for a while — the other ones are bonus. May can show me how to get music on my phone, and we'll have a dance party."

"I can show you now," May volunteered.

"I don't have my phone with me."

"If you aren't going to have your phone on you, then why have a phone?"

Good question, May.

"My son gave it to me so we could video talk, but it never works when we try."

"I can show you how to do that, too, Aunt Roza."

Lorraine smiled. That sounded like family.

"Purchased!"

Lorraine savored her family, feeling lighter than she had in years. She had thought sharing the truth would be heavy with sadness and regret, and those feelings were there. She knew they would never fully go away. A person can't keep secrets for so long without them leaving deep scars. But more than anything else, she felt buoyant, optimistic, even.

■ ■ ■ ■

What Is the Best Part of Being My Mom?

■ ■ ■ ■

CHAPTER TWENTY-FIVE

Later that afternoon, May double-checked the order she was putting up in Grilled G's window, making sure it had all the requested condiments and sides. "Number twenty-two," she said. It always seemed a bit odd to shout numbers — she never raised her voice that loudly in class or with her friends, never wanting to draw extra attention to herself, but here it was expected, even necessary.

They were parked outside the hospital complex for the dinner crowd. This was always a busy stop in the food truck rotation, giving the employees and visitors a break from the cafeteria options. Especially for those visiting extra-sick family and friends, their grilled cheeses could be temporary magic. She had learned that lesson early. Everyone always assumed it was her mom who was the grilled cheese aficionado, but it was her dad who had mastered the art first.

"Remember when Dad would make us breakfast grilled cheeses?" May asked.

She and her mom had finally found a rhythm where they could work and talk at the same time.

"I miss those," May said.

Her mom swallowed, then cleared her throat. "I don't know what he did that made them so good. The Nutella and mascarpone was my favorite. I think he browned the butter first — he always did something to make it a little special."

She even managed a tiny smile. May smiled back at her.

"I liked the bacon and egg with marble cheese."

"He grilled that one in bacon grease."

"The house would smell so good."

"Except that one time he got distracted by a crossword and burned the sandwiches. It took all day to get the smell of burned toast smoke out of the house. And you have to admit, not every one of his creations was good."

May scrunched her face, remembering some of the worst. Her mom wiped at her eyes and flipped the sandwiches in front of her.

"Like the pickle and Brie combo. What

was he thinking?"

"That wasn't as bad as the pineapple and blue cheese."

They both smiled at that one. It felt like something inside of May was getting filled up. Sharing stories about her dad with someone who found them as fascinating and comforting as she did was like a grilled cheese for her soul.

"What did you like best about Dad?"

Her mom's face grew distant and her lips eased into a grin.

"That's like asking what I like best about air."

"What a cop-out."

Gina laughed and wiped at her face again. "I suppose it is. I loved his patience. He would spend a day carefully taking apart an engine, laying the pieces in order, then putting them back together, cleaning each part as if it were precious. Or how he spent hours teaching you how to tie your shoes. You knew I would get impatient and do it for you, but he would happily wait a half hour until you did it yourself.

"He could always make me laugh, even when I was raging at him. I don't think he even intended to do it — it was just his instinct to make me happy. This one time, he had left a huge mess in the kitchen after one of his epic experiments and mountains of dirty laundry in the closet, then went out to the garage to spend a day working on an antique bike. I spent an hour scrubbing dried egg and burned cheese off the stove, then stain-treating all the grease stains on his clothes. By the time I was finished, I was tempted to burn it all. I don't know how he knew — he sensed my moods even before I did sometimes — but when he came back in the house, he was holding the T-shirt he had been wearing in one hand and a box of matches in the other. I lit the shirt on fire in the backyard pit as he stood by shirtless and watched. And he was so handsome. Hot, really. Seeing him shirtless never failed to make my knees wobble and brighten my mood."

"Ew. I don't need to hear that."

May served another order.

"You asked."

"I didn't mean for you to talk about that."

"You should be happy. Your dad and I found each other attractive in every way."

"Stop." May covered her ears as her mom chuckled. She wasn't sure how the conversation got so off course. No matter how much she missed her dad, she didn't need to hear this. She didn't want to think about her parents having sex, ever. "What drove you nuts about him?"

"It depended on the day, but it was always little stupid stuff, like his laundry. Sometimes I felt like the bike shop was his mistress, and it was tough to compete with chrome and rumbling engines. That never lasted, though. He always came home to me. What about you?"

May had never thought about what she didn't like about her dad. She was sure there was something. There had to be — no one was perfect. But she always thought about the wonderful parts she missed.

"He would always wake me up by singing the sad songs from the fifties. What was that about? The Mr. Lonely song was the worst. Or he would come into my room and fart, then leave and close the door."

"He did that to me, too. They were the worst, like rotten eggs and skunk roadkill. I have no idea what that man was eating to do that." Gina finished a few more sandwiches, and May delivered them to the waiting customers. "He would snore so loudly some nights, I elbowed him until he woke up. And he never once heard you crying at night. Not even when your bassinet was in our room. Now that I think about it, he was probably just a really good faker."

"And he always tried to kiss me after eating anchovies. He knew I hated them but thought it was so funny to chase me with his anchovy breath." May faked a gag sound.

There, that felt real, because even as he was chasing her with the awful fish breath, or trapping her in her room with his noxious butt fumes, these were things only he did. They made him just as special as the daddy that read her *Where the Wild Things Are* every night until she had it memorized, doing different voices for the monsters and the mom and Max.

"I miss him so much," May said.

"I do, too."

They worked in silence for a few moments.

"Learning about Grandma's life makes me sad for her. And you."

Gina paused what she was doing.

"What do you mean?"

"Well, you're too young to be like her. She never fell in love again. You deserve to have someone, someday." May looked out the window at who was approaching the window. "Speak of the devil." She had spotted him earlier, waiting to approach the food truck, like he was gathering his courage to talk to the girl he had a crush on. Obviously. She couldn't understand how her mom didn't realize this guy was into her — he clearly checked her site to see where she would be working.

"Hey there, G." Daniel paused when he looked at May. He clearly hadn't forgotten their last meeting. "Hi, May."

"Hi, Daniel. Sorry I was rude last time."

He chuckled. He had a nice smile, super straight and white without being like neon. May liked how he always brought things for her mom. His hat was pulled over his ears and a scarf warmed his neck. "Thanks. That's very nice of you to say."

"Hi, Daniel." Gina was looking at May, clearly onto her attitude shift toward Daniel. "What can I make you?"

With a shivering hand, he placed a jar on the counter labeled HOLY SMOKE. Gina picked it up, opened it, and gave it a deep sniff. When she pulled it away, she had a tiny white dab of the dip on her nose. She didn't notice, and May wasn't going to tell her. She wished she still wasn't grounded from her phone so she could live-text Olivia and Connor about this weird scene. And Aunt Vicky would definitely appreciate a play-by-play.

"This is nice." Gina dipped in a spoon to taste it. Daniel opened his mouth to say something about the dip dot, but her mom kept talking. "And why don't you get in here? Your lips are turning blue."

May would swear he blushed at the mention of his lips, but he nodded and walked up the stairs. "Stand by the griddle, that's where it's warmest. How did you get so cold?"

Daniel shrugged his shoulders.

"It took me a while to decide what I wanted." His eyes still focused on the end of her nose.

"The dip, it's . . ." Daniel was pointing at his nose, trying to tell Gina about her own, but she was too busy moving around the small kitchen to notice.

Gina pulled out the potato chips, pausing to look out the window.

"May, why don't you close up the window? It looks like we're done for the day. I'll get Daniel hooked up with something warm . . ."

May tried not to laugh. Did her mom not hear herself? Could she not feel the dip on her nose? Daniel moved into the corner and was joined by her mom in close quarters. He couldn't take his eyes off her face, clearly befuddled. May pulled down the window, shutting out the winter wind. The truck instantly became warmer. May snuck a chip and dipped it into the jar Daniel had brought. It was tasty, smoky and salty with a nice tang, like bacon and mayo had a baby. Her mom finally stopped moving long enough for Daniel to get her attention.

Daniel pointed at her face. "You have a . . ."

"I have a what." This was almost too hard to watch, but May grabbed a handful of chips and did it anyway.

Still dumbstruck, Daniel looked around the small space, taking a napkin from a nearby stack. He carefully wiped the dip away, her mom becoming still, like a deer as a car approached on a country road at night. Any sudden moves and she would bolt.

"There, I got it. It was dip."

"Thanks."

Awkward.

Daniel cleared his throat and tossed the napkin into the garbage can.

"So, do you think you can make something with it?"

Her mom ate another chip.

"If I can stop eating it . . . !" She took one more bite, then got to work.

Her mom assembled a sandwich with chicken, bacon, the dip, and a nice sharp cheddar on thick white slices. While she was doing that, Daniel unwrapped himself from the scarf and hat, his dusty brown hair jutting out in different directions. He clutched the woolen items in his hand, kneading them like bread dough.

"So, G." His eyes shifted to May. She had a feeling about what was coming, but did her mom? "I thought, maybe, sometime you'd like to go out. Somewhere you wouldn't have to cook for me? Or even just a cup of coffee? Maybe?"

He did it. He really asked her out. His cheeks were pink with the effort, and he was sweating in the corner near the griddle. Gina didn't answer right away. She checked the bottom of the sandwich to see if it needed to be flipped. It did. She flipped it, pressing down on the top to make sure the sandwich had optimal contact with the hot surface. The longer she didn't answer, the more Daniel stretched his hat between his hands. What would happen first? Would he tear a hole in it or would her mom answer? Gina checked the bottom of the sandwich, but it wasn't ready yet. She set down her spatula and rubbed her hands on her apron, then tapped her double-stacked wedding rings on her ring finger absentmindedly.

"I didn't expect you to ask me out."

"Really?" Both May and Daniel said it at the same time.

She checked the sandwich again. May

could see it needed a few more minutes, but her mom cut it in half and set it into a paper boat. Normally when her mom cooked, her movements were like a well-rehearsed dance, smooth and confident. Now, they were quick and jittery, like she'd had too much caffeine.

"Here you go." She stepped out of the cozy corner. Daniel stood holding the sandwich. She took a handful of chips and added it to the container, as if that was what he'd been waiting for.

Sometimes grown-ups needed help. May nudged the back of her mom's leg with her toe. Gina turned and May mouthed "answer him." Gina took a slow breath and turned to face him, so May couldn't see her face, but she could see Daniel's. His face went from hopeful to sad, like someone had offered him a puppy then taken it away. He rubbed the back of his neck with his free hand, then picked up a chip from his basket, and let it drop back down.

Her mom crossed her arms.

"Daniel." Her voice was soft, like it was the day she told May her goldfish had died and they would need to flush it down the toilet. "I'm flattered. I really am."

"It's okay. I get it. I shouldn't have asked. I crossed a line." He moved to leave the truck, sandwich in hand, and Gina grabbed his arm to stop him. He looked into her face, his eyes hoping she might give him a yes.

"I lost my husband almost two years ago." Daniel's mouth formed an O. "I haven't started dating yet. Dating again yet." She held up her hand where she still wore both their gold bands. "I'm not sure I'm ready."

Daniel nodded.

"I understand. And I'm so sorry about your husband."

"Thank you. We're all okay." She paused and looked at May. "Actually, that's not entirely true. But we will be." She let go of his arm. "How about this? When I am ready for a coffee, or a dinner, you'll be the first person I call."

Daniel met her eyes and nodded.

"I'd really like that."

"I hope this doesn't mean you'll stop visiting me. I'd really miss your challenges."

Daniel smiled, making a tiny dimple pop at the edge of his scruff.

"I may be shy, but I'm not a fool. I'm not going to miss out on the best grilled cheese in the state."

CHAPTER TWENTY-SIX

Lorraine checked the clock. The girls should have landed in DC by now. She hoped she could someday make the journey in person but wasn't sure that was going to happen. The therapy exhausted her, for such little payoff. She'd already had one session with Erin the Therapist today, and would have another one later today. She was working on a surprise. The physical therapy was even more exhausting. Just standing and shuffling a few feet forward sapped her energy. At this rate, she couldn't imagine ever living on her own again.

In the corner of the room, May colored with the kids, working on WELCOME HOME signs for their moms. They had brought a carton of glue sticks, glitter, and scissors to go with the paper. The ground would sparkle for weeks, holding on to the memory long after she had been released to go home. They'd even managed to get a few sparkles on her hands, which she hadn't expected to like so much.

"When do I get to say 'I told you so'?" Roza entered the room and flopped into the chair near the window. Lorraine tried to scowl, but couldn't tell if she had succeeded. Lorraine envied Roza's mobility. Of course, she had envied so much of Roza's life. She loved her husband for forty-eight years before he died, and they had four strong boys and an entire bushel of grandchildren to spoil and cuddle. She had never known Roza to be unhappy — sure, there were frustrations, like not having enough money to replace their rusted-out Bonneville or her husband not listening to the doctor's orders to cut his salt intake. But Roza had the life Lorraine had chosen once and been too scared to choose again. "I'm not gonna lie, I kind of like this no-talking thing." Roza chuckled.

And to answer her question, no, she didn't need to say "I told you so." Roza had been right.

"Why did one man need so many different navy-blue suits? They all look the same."

After Floyd had died, the two women boxed up his room, dumping armfuls of clothes into cardboard boxes to take to

Goodwill. Floyd had always been a dapper dresser — his closet full of custom suits proved that. The navy were just the beginning. He also had black, pinstriped, tan, and even a few summer suits for the occasional summer wedding or lawn bowling party. He had a suit for every occasion, even his own funeral. Floyd would be buried in a dark green Italian suit he'd bought on his last business trip. She dumped another armful into the box.

"Who knows. He didn't like to wear a suit more than a few times a year."

Lorraine looked around Floyd's room, her eyes searching for some evidence that he had been married to her. He had always kept his room spartan — only his bed, nightstand, and lamp for furniture, and art she'd chosen on the wall. Other than his closet, this could have been anyone's room — his office had been where he'd made himself at home.

"Now that he's gone, you can tell the girls the truth. Won't that be a relief?" Roza sat on the edge of the bed to rest. They'd both begun to do that more these days. "I still have the box."

Lorraine looked over her shoulder before she could stop herself. Old habits died slowly.

"Absolutely not. There's no reason to dredge up the past now. What good would it do?"

Roza stood, retrieved an armload of white shirts, and dumped them into an empty box, not even bothering to remove the sturdy wood hangers.

"They deserve to know the truth. They should know Joe was their father, not Floyd."

"They've both grown up just fine, married and with their own babies now."

Lorraine knew these were excuses, so she did what she always did when she felt uncomfortable feelings, she ignored them and focused on something else, something practical. She stopped to rest and stretch her arms, which had started to ache from packing. Floyd's room, the house's master bedroom, was a touch bigger than hers. Maybe she could turn this into a guest room for when Victoria and Jeff came to visit — then their kids could bunk in Victoria's and Regina's old rooms and the whole family wouldn't be crowded. She'd take this one herself, but her room did get better natural light.

"Are you listening to yourself? Someday it's going to be too late, Lorraine. Gina and Vicky should know that Joe loved them, and that you loved him, and that you were happy once."

That caught Lorraine's attention.

"I am happy," Lorraine said.

Roza snorted.

"I have been. How could I not be happy with my girls?"

"You know that's not what I meant. It's time to let them in, after hiding for thirty years. Don't you want them to know you?"

Lorraine thought about it. Thought about telling her daughters her biggest secret. Would they understand? Would they forgive her? They were both so capable — could they grasp why she'd made the choices she'd made? No. It was too big of a risk.

"No. The past is the past, and there is nothing to be gained from airing dirty laundry at this late date. That's the end of it."

"Fine. But when you die, I'm telling them." Roza closed the lid on a box, folding the flaps so it would stay shut.

"You're assuming you'll outlive me, but you have almost twenty years on me."

"It's more like fifteen, and you never let me forget it."

Had Lorraine taken Roza's advice that day, she would have been able to make the journey to DC with her girls instead of waiting for them to return, worrying about their flight, and wondering what they were thinking. She'd been reflecting a lot on the mistakes she had made in her life — almost always, it seemed now, the choices she'd made had been based on what was easier. She chose marrying for convenience, really, over hard work. She chose keeping Joe a secret over facing the anger of her daughters. She chose artifice over authenticity every time. Since the stroke, she'd begun to wonder if easier was not always the answer.

But she had to believe it was never too late to change. She wanted to be the woman who'd fallen in love with the flirtatious used-car salesman, the one who only needed love to be happy.

Lorraine smoothed the sheet on her lap, admiring the way the glitter picked up the sunshine streaming in the window. Roza had fallen asleep in the chair, a soft snore rumbling with each breath, almost like a cat purring. They both nodded off a bit more these days. Nathan crawled onto her bed, his hands covered in glue and more glitter, leaving a trail of specks on the white bedding.

Nathan's large brown eyes were exactly the same shape as Joe's, down to the long, thick lashes. His sticky fingers clasped her cheeks as he gazed at her intently and seriously. Lorraine sucked in a breath, overwhelmed. It felt like she was seeing him for the first time.

Sure, she had always spent time with her grandchildren, Christmas and Easter, when rooms were crowded, parents were stressed, and kids were exhausted from being on their best behavior for too many hours in a row. Before the stroke, she was too busy finding fault in their behavior, or their parents' parenting decisions to really see them. Or for them to see her.

As frustrating as not being able to speak was, maybe there were some benefits to it. Room to breathe. Room to see.

May had watched the exchange and retrieved a damp washcloth from the bathroom to clean off the glitter coating her face. Lorraine waved her off, squeezing her hand so she'd feel her gratitude. She was sure that she looked ridiculous, but she had no intention of removing the physical evidence of Nathan's affection anytime soon. She'd leave it there until the day she died, if she could.

Chapter Twenty-Seven

"It's ridiculous there are no nonstop flights from Milwaukee to DC," Victoria said. She and Gina had been up since 4:00 a.m. to finally arrive via Atlanta. Not the most efficient, but at least they were here. They had three and a half hours before they needed to be back at the airport.

"At least we don't have any luggage to drag around," Gina said.

"Always the fucking optimist. Can't you just be grumpy like the rest of us?"

Gina nearly snorted her cold coffee — not cold because it was iced, but because it had been warm three hours ago when she bought it at the Atlanta airport during their layover and was now cold.

"Be thankful I put on a happy face. Grumpy-Gina wouldn't function well in society."

"Just saying it's okay to not always be happy. Life might be like a box of chocolates, but sometimes all the chocolates are filled with that crappy orange cream filling."

They joined the taxi line. Gina pulled out her hat and gloves. She had hoped the weather would be a bit warmer, since they were farther south, but no such luck. Winter had come. They shivered next to each other as the line shuffled forward.

"The orange filling is okay," Gina said.

"You've just proven my point. Life is too short to put up with the fake orange-flavored goo. Toss it and move on to the dark chocolate–covered coconut."

"I'm confused. Is this an analogy? Is being a widow accepting the orange goo? And what's the coconut? And what if I really want the toffee, but not the ones with nuts?"

Victoria stuck her tongue out at Gina. They reached the head of the line and scooted into the waiting taxi.

"The Vietnam Veterans Memorial, please," Gina told the driver as they pulled away from the curb.

"Jeff is the crappy orange filling. I want the coconut," Vicky said. Gina hugged her with one arm. She really did understand. "Hearing about Mom and her marriages — I'm still taking in that our mom had multiple marriages — I don't want to be stuck unhappy forever. She was happy once.

Really, true-love happy. You were, too. I want that, even if it means I'm alone with four kids. The only reason Jeff hasn't left me already is because he doesn't want to deal with alimony."

"Do you want to talk about it?"

Vicky looked at her, chewed her lip.

"I'm pretty sure all those late nights at the office weren't at the office. The worst part — I don't care. The kids and I do our thing, and he does his, but that's not enough anymore. I want the happy ending. I deserve the happy ending." She looked at Gina's face. "Even if it doesn't last forever. I want it."

"You deserve it all."

"Do you know what he did when I told him about our dads?" Gina shook her head. "Nothing. He mumbled he had to get off the phone and hung up. He hasn't heard a word I've said in five years." She leaned her head on Gina's shoulder. "It's probably wrong that I'm looking forward to this, isn't it?"

"I can't even imagine what you're feeling — but I'm here for whatever you need."

"I know you are. That's what makes you the best sister." Vicky sat up straight and looked at Gina, a smile spreading on her face. "Whatever I need, huh? Care to test that theory?"

Gina rolled her eyes. "Sure."

"What if I call you every day to complain about Jeff?"

"No problem. You always took my calls."

"What if I require extra cash to make ends meet before payments start?"

"Of course. That's what family is here for."

"What if I need to move into your house?"

"Too far. You're on your own." Gina nudged her sister with her shoulder. "You dork. Whatever you need means whatever you need."

"Okay, big talker. I need you to go on a date with Daniel."

"Did May tell you?"

"She may have mentioned an adorable moment when he wiped dip off of your nose."

Gina sighed.

"He's sweet and cute . . ."

"And patient."

"Yes. But I have to believe when I'm ready, I'll know it. And I'm not there — especially with all of this about Mom and Joe and May. It's only pulled Drew closer to the surface. It wouldn't be fair to Daniel or me if we tried to date right now."

The drive to the Washington Mall was short. Vicky and Gina hopped out on the north side of the Lincoln Memorial, the white square building bright against the blue winter sky, where the snow on the ground was still fresh with only a few footprints crisscrossing the grass, while the sidewalks were clear. Gina hadn't been back to Washington, DC, since that trip with her mom when they were teens. For a cold day, tourists littered the steps, eating their lunches and admiring the view of the distant Washington Monument, World War II Memorial, and frozen reflecting pool. A few brave souls slid around on the slippery surface near the edge.

"Are you ready for this?" Gina asked.

"Bring it."

They followed the signs leading to the Vietnam Veterans Memorial, tucked into trees that shielded it from the more festive activity around the reflecting pool and the hustle of the nearby boulevard on the other side. Against the fresh snow, the gleaming black walls slashed a harsh line in the surrounding white. It was quieter here, more solemn. The laughter and chatter of the Lincoln Memorial steps was gone and replaced with somber reflection. Gina had always found the long wall difficult to absorb, preferring to not think about the tens of thousands of names — names of men and women who never came home. Today, that was not an option.

"How do we find him?" Gina asked.

The long straight lines of the wall were daunting. So many names. Along the bottom, red roses and American flags added color to the stark black and white. Between the sky, snow, and flowers, it was all red, white, and blue — an appropriate setting.

"Funny enough, there's an app for that. I downloaded it last night. Here's the information." Victoria held out her phone.

There he was, in an old service photo in which he wore his uniform, not much different from the only other picture she had seen. His short dark hair was barely visible under his hat with not a scrap of hair on his face, lips hinting a smile. She saw their nose and arched eyebrows echoed. Her own chin lacked the same barely-there indent that was on Vicky's. He was young, too. Not teenager young, but with a full life ahead of him that he would never get to enjoy. A young family he would never see again. Below the photo was his information.

Wall Name: JOSEPH M. SANDOWSKI
Date of Birth: 12/2/1947
Date of Casualty: 5/13/1975
Home of Record: MILWAUKEE

County of Record: MILWAUKEE COUNTY
State: WI
Branch of Service: AIR FORCE
Rank: SGT
Panel/Row: 1W, 120
Casualty Province: QUANG TRI
Associated Items Left at The Wall: Color photo of two carved wooden elephants. Inscription on the back, "Hand-carved by Sgt. Joe Sandowski. April 1975."

Underneath were pages of faceless people thanking him for his service. A fresh wave of anger sloshed over Gina. She and Vicky should have been visiting this place. Or more importantly, his grave. They had never once put a flag on it, or a wreath at Christmas, or a stuffed animal when his grandchildren were born. They had never expressed their sorrow at not knowing him. She didn't even know where his grave was.

"We haven't visited his grave yet, Vicky. We have to go as soon as we get home."

Vicky had been studying the panels.

"We'll go."

"In the morning, after we see Mom. We've never been to his grave. We came here, but not his grave. We're idiots."

"Agreed. But I'm glad we're here." She

looked around and pointed to their right. "His panel is toward the center."

As they walked, Vicky kept flicking through the comments in the app. Gina led them to where the east and west walls collided and counted down the lines from the top. They traced their fingers along the row and . . . there it was.

JOSEPH M. SANDOWSKI

She expected it to be bigger, or a spotlight would appear, or at the very least a sunbeam. Something to differentiate it from the names surrounding it. But it was in the same sans serif font, the same one-inch in height. Nothing that told the world this was their father.

Gina and Vicky touched his name. Gina traced the J in JOSEPH while Vicky's fingers brushed over the SKI at the end. The edge where the carved black granite met the polished surface was crisp and even. Here was proof the entire, nearly unbelievable story was all real. She traced it over and over again down the line and up the hook of the J then back again, wanting to remember every detail, wanting it to make up for a lifetime of lost moments.

Other visitors held pieces of paper up to

the wall to trace a name they had come to see. Gina opened her purse, digging for her pen and notebook. A few years ago, she would have always carried a few crayons to keep May occupied in an emergency — she panicked that they had come all this way and she didn't have the proper supplies. They should have paper for something this important.

A man in a yellow jacket approached them, a volunteer.

"Did you know him?"

"He was our dad," Vicky said, matter-of-factly, like this was something they'd known their entire lives. Vicky set her hand on Gina's arm that was still up to her elbow in her purse. "We forgot to bring something to do a rubbing. Do you have anything?"

He pulled a few pieces of paper from his pockets and some pencils. Vicky was always better in these situations, knowing how to ask for help and making it seem so easy.

"It works best to start out light, then go darker. Try to use the side, not the point. I'll be over there if you need anything else."

"Thank you" they both echoed as he walked away without another word.

Gina looked down at the pencil — a naked stick of shiny and hard graphite, the size of a child's crayon, the thicker kind that was easier for tiny hands to hold. One end came to a point, and the body had six flat sides like a pencil. She rubbed her finger on it, and a dark gray streak appeared in its path. Somehow this tiny stick of fake lead needed to create a connection to a man she had never known, who was only letters on a stone monument. That was a lot of pressure for a writing utensil.

They took turns making their own rubbings. With each swipe of the pencil, Joe's name became clearer, more real. When they finished, they had three rubbings to bring home on the special sheets of paper the volunteer had given them. Gina slipped the papers into the pages of the book she'd tried to read on the plane. She wanted to make sure they didn't get wrinkled, then she and Vicky stood there, staring at his name silently, each lost in her own thoughts.

"Hey, look." Vicky held out her phone

It was one of the comments, or Remembrances, as the app called them.

"Joe was my friend," it read. "I left a photo I took of two wooden elephants he was carving during downtime. He made them for his daughter and the second baby. I've tried to find them on the Internet, with no luck. If his children or wife ever see this, please contact me. I have the elephants. You should have them." It was posted on October 7, 2004, by Gilbert Novak — gilnovak449@aol.com.

"Do you think that e-mail still works? We have to try."

"Already on it."

Vicky's thumbs tapped out an e-mail to Gilbert and sent it, fingers crossed. They stared at his name again.

Gilbert might even have more stories to share, another part of their dad they could cherish.

"We have to leave something. Should I run and get some flowers? Mom would want us to leave flowers," Gina said.

"Hang on. I have a better idea."

From her wallet, she pulled out a picture of the two of them and Mom from last year's Mother's Day and flipped it over. On the back she wrote:

Dear Dad,

Sorry it took so long to visit. We just found out about you. We don't remember you, but now we'll never forget. We love you.

Gina and Vicky (your favorite)

Gina looked over Vicky's shoulder as she wrote the note.

"How could you be his favorite? He never even met you. You were a bump. He didn't even know you were a girl."

"The youngest is always the favorite."

Vicky slipped the picture into an envelope she had brought with her, wrote JOSEPH SANDOWSKI on the outside, and left it at the wall below his name. Both women let the moment sink into their hearts; something had changed and they wanted to remember every second to share with their mother.

What Do You Need Me to Know?

Chapter Twenty-Eight

Lorraine was antsy and exhausted. Her muscles ached, her head hurt, and even her cheek muscles twitched from trying to form words. The girls were due to arrive soon, and she wanted to be ready for them. Her occupational therapist had helped her brush her hair so it was smooth and straight, and even dabbed a bit of lipstick on her mouth to brighten up her face. She'd walked to the bathroom by herself and wasn't even embarrassed when the nurse cheered.

As she shuffled from the bed to the chair near the window, she could hear voices in the hall. So she moved a little quicker and plopped onto the fake leather recliner — not a bad fake, not like vinyl. It was soft and smooth, a light tan. The morning winter sun had warmed the spot before she sat down. She liked that. Ever since the stroke, she hadn't felt warm enough for even one moment, intentionally wearing black to absorb the heat as she sat in the sunbeam like a cat.

"Mom, we're back." Victoria set a vase of fresh flowers on the windowsill where Lorraine could see them.

Regina kissed her cheek and pulled over a small chair so she could sit next to her. Victoria did the same on the other side. Her girls.

"You look good, Mom," Regina said. She looked tired, they both did. But they also looked relaxed. "The trip was smooth."

"As smooth as an overlong layover in Atlanta can be," Victoria added. "Even Gina thought it was awful, though she'll never admit it." Victoria winked at her sister, and Regina smiled back.

"Vic and I were talking. We're going to go find Joe's — Dad's — grave after we leave here. Is he in Wood Cemetery?"

Yes.

"Did you ever visit after you married Floyd?"

No.

Lorraine had thought about it, every time she drove on I-94 past the cemetery where the stark white headstones lined up like alligator teeth. For years, her car had always wanted to get off at the exit, but she worried it would open all the old pain.

Gina pulled her notebook and book from her purse. She set the notebook on her lap, ready to add to the current list, then opened the book to where a piece of paper lay perfectly unwrinkled. Gina set it on Lorraine's lap.

They had found Joe.

Along the top of the sheet was a black bar that said VIETNAM VETERANS MEMORIAL. So official. His name was formed where the pencil missed the paper, just like their family had been made by the lack of him. He still made his mark, even in his absence.

With one hand, she touched his name, and with the other, she held the gold cross she normally wore on her neck. The nurse had helped her take it off earlier. Her neck felt naked without it. Holding the smooth gold always gave her comfort, like he was watching over her.

"It was so special, Mom. We left a photo of the three of us and a note," Victoria said, her voice sparkling with excitement. Regina leaned forward, still studying the sheet on Lorraine's lap. "And we connected with someone who knew him, while he was overseas. We can FaceTime later. He wants to meet you. He said Joe never shut up about his lovely Lorraine."

Hearing Joe's nickname for her after all

these years gave her tingles — she could feel them going up her right arm.

This was the moment she'd been practicing for all day. She licked her lips and opened her mouth to speak.

"You . . ." She took a deep breath. Regina and Victoria leaned in. "You . . ." Regina rubbed her arm.

"Take your time, Mom. We aren't going anywhere."

She reached for each of their hands, slipping the necklace into Gina's open palm, then taking in both of their faces. She felt whole and warm for the first time since she'd had her stroke. It had taken her too many years to be content and happy again, so she planned to savor it. She didn't want to lose this feeling.

Between her girls, Joe appeared, and Lorraine's lips curved as they always did when she saw his face, an instinct more natural than breathing. The morning light broke around him, blurring the edges of his body. He grinned at her with the jaunty smile he'd always saved for her. Now the moment was perfect.

"It's time, my lovely Lorraine," he said.

If only Victoria and Regina could see him, too. Just once.

She looked at her girls, their beautiful

faces. They had become so much more than she had ever hoped they might be. Bright and strong and wonderful mothers, both of them. Regina had Floyd's business sense, Joe's relentless optimism, and her stubborn determination was all Lorraine. Victoria had Joe's humor, Floyd's pragmatism, and Lorraine's impeccable style. They would both be fine.

With another deep breath, Lorraine relaxed enough so she could say the words she had practiced just for them.

"You're . . . best parts of . . . all of us."

She squeezed their hands and leaned her heavy head against the back of the chair. Joe nodded and the sunbeams around him pulsed.

The room blurred.

Lorraine closed her eyes, savoring the warmth and company of her family.

"Mom?" Regina's voice whispered, then got louder. "Mom?"

Behind her eyelids, the sun grew brighter and brighter, until the glow was nothing at all.

CHAPTER TWENTY-NINE

Her mouth wouldn't stay closed. Each time Gina tried to shut it, it would pop back open. *Why hasn't modern medicine figured out a way to keep the mouth closed?* She didn't like seeing her mom sitting there with her mouth gaping open, like a flytrap. As a woman who had strived most of her life to be elegant, Gina knew in her heart her mom would be mortified by this undignified turn of events.

She pushed Lorraine's mouth closed and held her hand there. A nurse walked in and out of the room, pausing briefly to observe Gina's actions. Vicky returned with water cups for them both.

"What are you doing?"

"Her mouth was open. I'm trying to keep it closed."

"You can't do that all day."

"Yes, I can."

Victoria gently pulled her hand back from

their mother's face.

"Let it go."

But what she was really saying was to let *her* go, and Gina couldn't do that. They had finally begun to understand each other, and now she was gone. Just like that. She wasn't ready to let Lorraine go yet. For the first time that she could remember, her mom had said something nice. She wanted to hear more.

Lorraine had only been dead for a short time, but her skin was dull and mottled, lacking the vital blood pumping through every cell. This was how she had failed when Drew died — she had never really let go. She'd never accepted that he had gone on. But looking at her mother, mouth wide, hands and feet tinged purple, it was so obvious. Lorraine was gone. Her spirit had moved on, hopefully to be with Joe, finally having the time together they'd been robbed of once.

Gina looked at the necklace again. Her mom had worn it every day, yet Gina had never seen it up close. There were small scratches and dents from years of daily wear, and on the back was a faint inscription she'd never seen.

On my mind, over my lips, in my heart. J

All these years, Lorraine had carried a part of Gina and Vicky's dad with her.

Her mom and she had been making the same mistake. They both had tried to navigate life by keeping one foot in the same spot. Instead of getting anywhere, they merely traced the same, one-footed circle over and over. There was no room for anything else — or anyone else — on that path.

It seemed cruel to discover they had so much in common at the end. Gina had never wanted to let go, worried the pain was all she had left. But she needed to free herself to blaze a new path, one with room for May — and maybe someone else.

Gina latched the cross around her neck, a reminder to break the circle and move forward.

Gina sat at the kitchen table, a large shadow box frame open in front of her. Vicky had taken her brood home for a few days before the funeral. She had things she needed to settle. After wiping her nieces' and nephews' fingerprints and peanut butter smears off the table, Gina laid out Drew's old T-shirt in the frame. She carefully pinned it flat, smoothing out the wrinkles.

"What are you doing?"

May slid onto the chair next to her, her brow confused.

"I've had it tucked into a Ziploc in my closet. I thought we could frame it. Maybe add in a few other mementos of your dad. What do you think?"

Gina set her hand on May's back and rubbed it. This past week had been a roller coaster for them, but she finally — finally — felt closer to her daughter.

"I love it." May chewed her lip. "Can I add something?"

"Of course. Go get it."

She couldn't wait to see what it was. May skipped out of the kitchen and was back with a small piece of paper. It was one of the notes from Drew.

"This is perfect." She handed some pins to May. "Put it where you think it works best."

May studied the frame and laid the paper in a few different spots before settling on slightly off center of the shirt — almost exactly where Drew's heart would have been.

Gina reached over and plucked the red and white wianki off the wall. "Did I ever tell you about this?"

"No, you barely even let me touch it."

"That's because it's very precious to me,

and you were little. Your dad gave this to me on the day I knew I would marry him."

"On the day he proposed?"

"Ha! No, this happened way before then. You'll discover, eventually, that boys sometimes need more time to learn what we already know." Gina winked at May and told her the story about how Drew won her heart forever.

"Are you always going to love him?"

"No question." She answered quickly, but then took a few moments to think about what that would mean. "I will always, always love him. If he popped into this room right now or ten years from now or fifty years from now, I would love him. I know that will never go away. But I think, maybe one day, my heart might expand so I can love someone else, too."

"Like Daniel."

"Let's not get ahead of ourselves. I'd have to go out with the guy first." Gina nudged her shoulder. "But something like that, maybe, someday."

Gina set the flower wreath on May's head.

"When your father did that to me, he said that now I was Polish, too. Little did we know I was already halfway there." She kissed May's nose. "Now, should we put it in the frame?"

May nodded enthusiastically and took it off her head. She studied the frame, and set it over the piece of paper, so it created a frame within the frame. They secured it with pins and closed the glass lid, keeping the treasured memories visible and safe forever, but making room in their lives for new ones.

A week after Lorraine's death, their small family gathered around Lorraine to say their final goodbyes before the rest of her friends and acquaintances and fellow club members arrived to pay their respects for Lorraine Sandowski Price. They had included her full name on the "In Memoriam." Gina, Vicky, May, and Roza gathered around the pale wood casket, Lorraine properly attired in her favorite cream-with-black-trim Chanel dress, the one she wore for only the most special occasions. Gina supposed this qualified as a special occasion.

"She looks like . . ." Gina began to speak.

"If you say she looks like she's sleeping, I will slap you," Vicky said. She had returned last night, happier than Gina had seen her in years. And with a lot of luggage.

"I was going to say she looks happy for once."

"She ought to be. Look at all these flowers. There must be three florist shops' worth of blooms in here."

Roza sniffed and pointed to an arrangement near the end.

"She would have been disgusted that the Millers sent carnations. Honestly, who does that?"

"I think Mom has finally rubbed off on you, Roza," Gina said. Her eyes kept wandering back to her mom. It was hard not to look, knowing she'd never see her face again. But she could practically hear her mother say, "It's rude to stare, Regina."

Vicky's phone honked from her pocket.

"Why do you even have your phone with you?"

Vicky ignored her and looked at her phone with a frown, then smiled.

"The papers are officially filed."

"Papers?" Roza asked, walking over to stand by Gina and Vicky.

"Divorce papers," Vicky said.

Roza made the sign of the cross then hugged Vicky. "My tenants just moved out, so the bottom flat is open. I'll give you the first month free if you need it."

"Tempting, but I don't think we'd all fit. There's a house down the block from Gina for sale. Then May can babysit after school. I put an offer in on it yesterday."

Vicky took a deep breath, then turned off

her phone. Gina studied the flowers, reading some of the cards. Most were from friends at the club. One was from the Patels. When Gina turned around, she saw Vicky slip a piece of paper into the coffin.

"What was that?"

"Nothing."

Gina pulled it out. It was a printout of the e-mail their mom had sent them regarding their poor Christmas gifts.

"You can't put this in there."

"Why not? I said I would."

Gina smiled. A week ago, she would have pulled the paper from the coffin. Now, she went to her purse and pulled out her own addition — a jar of coconut oil. She slid it next to the printed e-mail. After all she'd learned, her mom would have appreciated that this humor was part of their grieving, that there wasn't a right or a wrong way to handle their loss. Gina kissed her mom's forehead one more time. With one last glance, she took her place in the receiving line, finally ready to let go.

The service was lovely. Lorraine would have been thrilled with the turnout, and even about the confused whispers as to why she was being buried at the Wood National Cemetery. For the burial, the mourners gathered around the closed casket poised above Joe's grave as the priest said the final words.

The small, marble headstone was etched with his date of birth, date of death, and rank on the front side, with an inscription below that Lorraine must have authorized so many years ago.

LOVING HUSBAND AND FATHER

In a few weeks, the back of the headstone would read out their mother's name, date of birth, date of death, and an engraving:

WIFE OF SGT JOSEPH SANDOWSKI
MY LOVELY LORRAINE

Now they would have eternity together.

After the burial, most of the mourners walked solemnly away, having already said their condolences during the wake. Gina and Vicky stood near the headstone while Roza and May rounded up the cousins to get in the car.

Maxine Fuller appeared in front of them wearing black from head to toe. She even wore a black wool cloche and dark sunglasses — not that she had any tears to hide.

"Girls, I am so very sorry about your

mother." She gave them each an air kiss on the cheek. "She was such a dear friend."

Vicky elbowed Gina in the ribs, only semi-subtlely.

"Thank you. I'm so sorry, but your name seems to be escaping me," Vicky said. She was always better at the sneaky insults.

"I'm Maxine Fuller, dear. I must say, I — and many of the ladies — were surprised to find Lorraine was being buried here. Who is Joseph Sandowski? I've never heard that name at the club."

"He's our dad," Gina said. This woman wouldn't leave them alone until she had the dirt she was looking for. Gina had had enough of being polite. Maxine already had her mouth open for another question, but Gina kept talking. "Mrs. Fuller, Vic and I would like a few private moments with our mother."

She pulled Vicky around so they were both facing the casket, leaving Maxine no choice but to rudely intrude again or slump off. She took the hint, and they heard her feet crunching through the snow.

"Wow. That was almost rude. I know Drew would be proud," Vicky said.

She was right. He would be. And something told Gina he would have liked this crazy adventure she and Vicky had taken, with all of its secrets and drama. She hoped that if there was a heaven, Drew and Joe were up there talking about their girls and swapping stories.

"What are you smiling at?"

"My new happy thought."

"You and your happy thoughts." Vicky rolled her eyes. "Our lives could have been so different if only Mom had told us the truth a long time ago."

"There have been some pretty awful spots, but I like where our lives are headed."

Gina hugged her sister tight, and Vicky wrapped her arms around Gina's waist. They stood in the icy snow, their mother's daughters.

CHAPTER THIRTY

The sun shone where the food trucks lined up along the west side of the park, allowing customers to take advantage of the trees for shade. Several families already had blankets spread out as they plotted their next move at Tosa's first annual Food Truck Feast. A few better-prepared families had even brought tables and chairs. A live band played on a constructed stage, covering songs from eighties hair bands — or at least that's what May's mom had called them.

Inside Grilled G's, her mom did all the cooking, easily keeping up with the steady stream of orders. She took the orders and delivered them, along with a new addition, the Lorraine Bars — vegan brownies made with coconut oil and toasted coconut. May had created the recipe to honor her grandma, and today was their debut. She felt a little smug each time a customer ordered one, actually. When Connor and his family stopped by, he ordered two. Dork.

"Hi May, hi Gina." Their down-the-street neighbor Patty stood in the window, her chubby-faced baby gnawing on the edge of her baby carrier, making a huge wet spot. Gina nodded in greeting, holding up a spatula.

"Hi, Patty. How are you doing?"

She gave her order to May, then answered Gina's question.

"Good. I've finished the sign-up sheet for the Memorial Day block party."

"I can't believe that's in a few weeks. Where did the winter go?"

"I know. I can barely carry this drool monster anymore. I've already got you signed up for brownies, May. You make the best, so you're trapped by your own excellence."

May handed her the order with a smile, wondering if the Lorraine Bars would be a big enough crowd pleaser for the block party or if she should do something with peanut butter.

"Can't wait," Gina said. "If it's okay, I'll swing by tomorrow and sign up."

"Perfect."

May used the brief lull in customers to wipe down the surfaces, starting on the shelf next to the counter where she normally took orders. The one spot that wasn't used for food truck supplies, this shelf held special items — each with a story. May's favorite were the two wooden elephants, only a few inches tall. They'd arrived a few months ago. The warm honey-colored wood had rough knife marks, clearly still works in progress. Their curved trunks could loop together, and May was convinced they each wore a small smile. The day they had arrived, her mom and Aunt Vicky opened the box slowly, carefully digging into the abundant packing peanuts to find the wooden animals until they each held one cupped in their hands like a delicate treasure.

Next to the pachyderms were framed photos, one of Grandpa Joe and Grandma, and another of Grandpa Floyd with an old dollar bill folded around the edge. She swiped at the dust and set those back, careful not to knock over the nearby picture of her dad.

May looked out to see if any new customers were coming just as Charlotte approached, her scraggly pale red hair tied back in a scarf. Now that she wasn't buried under layers of winter clothes, her wiry frame scuttled from food truck to food truck, still carrying a worn plastic bag.

"Three grilled cheeses, Mom. Charlotte's

on her way."

May picked up her mom's phone and sent a text to Monica.

Incoming: Charlotte.

By the time she set the phone back down, Charlotte peeked into the window.

"Hi, Charlotte. How are you?" May smiled at her. "Mom's already got your sandwich going."

Charlotte slid her money across, and Gina set the paper boat with the slightly burned sandwich on the counter.

"Here you go, Charlotte." She stepped back into the warm sunshine and ate her sandwich, then headed back toward the window.

May handed down the sandwiches before she could say another word.

"So sorry for the trouble. And here are our new Lorraine Bars as an extra apology." She set two of the brownies alongside the sandwiches.

Charlotte looked up and gave her a tiny smile, tucking the brownies and sandwiches into her bag.

"I think she likes you more than me. I've never gotten a smile from her," Gina said. She was scraping the griddle, getting a head start on cleaning.

"Obviously. I gave her dessert."

May looked out the window again, to the picnic blanket she'd been keeping an eye on for the last half hour. On it sat her boyfriend — still the cutest boy in school — and her best friend, Connor and Olivia. She was going to meet up with them after her lunch shift. Breaking into her line of sight was a bearded man heading toward Grilled G's.

"Hey Mom, look who's coming."

Her mom peeked out.

"Eeep! He's early," her mom said. She picked up a notebook, then looked out the window again. After running her fingers down the spine, she handed it to May. "Can you start the list for tomorrow?"

May nodded and opened the notebook to a fresh page. She'd been in charge of the lists more often lately, and seriously believed it was a good sign that her mom wasn't living her life one to-do item at a time anymore.

Her mom smoothed the stray strands of hair around her face with her ring-free left hand. "How do I look?"

"Great," May said. Her mom acting nervous reminded her of the way she and Connor used to be. After her grandma's funeral, they finished watching Buffy with 100 percent less kissing. Not that May didn't want to — she just wasn't ready yet. Well, they still kissed a little bit, just with all their clothes. Her mom found all sorts of reasons to come down into the basement while they were watching TV.

"Now ask how you smell," May said. " 'Cause you smell like a grilled cheese."

"You say that like it's a bad thing. The man is my best customer." She looked at May. "You okay to finish cleaning up?"

"I've got this."

"You sure? Vicky will drive it home later, but make sure to lock all the doors."

"Go, Mom!"

Gina leaned out the window and waved. "Daniel!"

In khakis and a button-down shirt with sleeves rolled up to the elbows, he carried a six-pack of something in one hand and waved with the other. His head was hatless, revealing sandy-brown hair already highlighted from the spring sun.

Her mom took off her apron and went out to meet him.

"Hi, you look great, G," Daniel said. He looked at her like he couldn't believe his good luck. Gross, but nice.

Gina blushed.

"Thanks, you too."

"I brought some cider I picked up when I was in Door County last week." The bottles clinked when he held them up for her to see, each with a bold color on the label.

Her mom didn't say anything, just smiled.

"Say something," May whispered.

Her mom turned. "I can hear you. I'd like to see you on a first date with your daughter watching."

Daniel finally realized they had a witness and waved at her.

"Hi, May."

"Then maybe you should go where I'm not," May said to her mom. May handed her two Lorraine Bars and shooed them away.

Daniel pointed to an open picnic table in the shade. They sat next to each other in the dappled light, eating bars and drinking cider. She hadn't seen her mom smile like that since Dad.

May finished cleaning the truck and locked the doors, giving it a little pat before heading toward Connor and Olivia, more brownies in her hand for each of them.

Her mom had turned to face Daniel, leaning in and nodding as he spoke, throwing her head back in laughter at something he said. She looked really, truly happy. It was a little weird seeing her like this — okay, more than a little weird — but she deserved it. Her mom wasn't just her mom, anyway, she had a past and a future. She had dreams and disappointments and regrets. It was complicated.

When May jumped over a puddle to meet up with her friends, she remembered her dad, as they sat in the mud, saying that everyone should get messy — even her mom.

May looked up in time to see Daniel reach over to wipe something off her mom's face — probably brownie crumbs — and smile.

No matter how messy things got, they had people who loved them, who watched out for them, who would help them clean those messes up.

They would all be okay.

ACKNOWLEDGMENTS

When you get in this business, it's easy to be intimidated and overwhelmed — writers are artists first, after all. Thankfully, I have Rachel Ekstrom, my fabulous and formidable agent. Part adviser, negotiator, therapist, cheerleader, and friend, I'm so proud to have her by my side.

I could write an entire book about how grateful I am for Kate Dresser, my talented and brilliant editor and friend. After four books together, it's possible our brains have melded and I couldn't be happier about it. I send her haphazard, incomplete drafts and, miraculously, she sees the potential through the muck, offering the exact right feedback that finds the heart in what I'm trying to accomplish. Thank you to my rockstar publicists, Theresa Dooley at Gallery and Kristin Dwyer of Leo PR.

I love being part of the Gallery family! Thank you to Jennifer Bergstrom, Molly

Gregory, Gina Borgia, Monica Oluwek, Chelsea Cohen, Liz Psaltis, Diana Velasquez, Mackenzie Hickey, Sade Oyalowo, Jaime Putorti, and my fantastic copy editor, Shelly Perron.

Dziękuję to Baror International for their foreign rights work.

I borrow freely from conversations I have with my friends (sorry, not sorry); thank you to Peggy Armstrong and the rest of the Town Bank gals, Mary and Jason Ells for sharing a spectacular story with me that was the first inspiration for this book, Bob and Val Wisniewski for their Polish-Milwaukee expertise and letting me steal their last name for Roza. A huge thank-you to Caitlin Croegaert for helping me with the stroke and speech portions of the book. Any errors are my own.

To my writer friends, Sarah Cannon, Gail Werner, Carla Cullen, Nina Bocci, Colleen Oakley, and all my Tall Poppies! A special thank-you to Melissa Marino and Karma Brown, who give me invaluable feedback and share all my writer highs and lows.

To all my family, thank you for putting up with my flakiness when I'm under deadline (and when I'm not), especially Mom, Pam, and Sandy.

My little loves, Ainsley and Sam, who

aren't so little anymore. Ainsley, while you are nothing like May, you inspired her nonetheless — and thank you for making sure my teenager sounded like a teenager. I love that we share a love of writing.

To my handsome husband, John, this book explores one of my greatest fears, having to navigate life without you by my side. Twenty years in and I'm still stupid in love with you.

Lastly, a thank-you to all those who serve in the Armed Forces and the families who support and miss them. You are not forgotten.

ABOUT THE AUTHOR

Amy E. Reichert, author of *The Coincidence of Coconut Cake, Luck, Love & Lemon Pie, The Simplicity of Cider,* and *The Optimist's Guide to Letting Go,* loves to write stories that end well with characters you'd invite to dinner. A wife, mom, amateur chef, Fix-It Mistress, and cider enthusiast, she earned her MA in English Literature and serves on her local library's board of directors.

The employees of Thorndike Press hope you have enjoyed this Large Print book. All our Thorndike, Wheeler, and Kennebec Large Print titles are designed for easy reading, and all our books are made to last. Other Thorndike Press Large Print books are available at your library, through selected bookstores, or directly from us.

For information about titles, please call:
(800) 223-1244

or visit our website at:
gale.com/thorndike

To share your comments, please write:

Publisher
Thorndike Press
10 Water St., Suite 310
Waterville, ME 04901